CONNECTIONS 3

Example

Coolinda.

Crazy, Coolinda

She thinks her family is the last ones alive with robots and these are her thoughts. She writes random things she thinks about.

Find the words hidden in the random writing.

Some may haunt you, some may help you remember things, and some are just interesting to read.

Happy day to you and yours. Coolinda is nothing like that nice sentence. She's random and says things that make it seem like she has a mental illness but it's just her want for understanding about what goes on around her and the people she's around. I, see switching tenses in what I say. Coolinda is funny. Nope. More troublesome. Nope. There's no way to understand her. Some may say she's in her right mind, she's just trying to understand things. Others may be scared to say she's a decent person because some people might think they're crazy. They don't want to be laughed at. Some may be mean. People need to know who they are. Everyone's really different in their own way.

Find **a decent person** in the passage.

Oh yeah. Coolinda thinks she can predict the future.

Fill in the blanks with the letters that complete each word

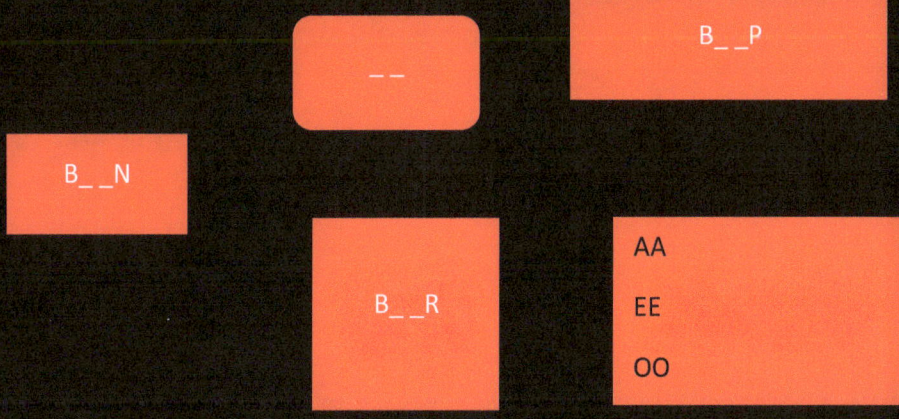

Connections 3
By Roshinaie Johnson

Family separated. Homeless. Debt. Just how did this place get here? There is a creator. I always thought He was walking around in human form. Even he couldn't keep up with all the mess going on here. Benefits. Everything I want will be put right in my face or brought to me. M- U. Ways to remember. Um Same clothes. 7-10 maybe more days. Better than rock bottom. Enough. Drink. The forgotten. Um- Mentally ill. How? Knees. Rocks. Jazz music a brain relaxer. Copy and paste at the bottom of every page that has this example. And every time leave out one of the bottom numbers. Numbers as letters. Math – complete different ways. Connections 3. 1-3 pages. Connections 2. Use words. Knew. Type songs. New. Nude. Poison in drinks. Shit creations. Blood bathrooms. Their eyes are in robots. Can be in computer too. Why wouldn't I make it easy to locate my family? The money. Robots 6 days ahead of me or more. – Chipped so bad actions intercepted. Premonitions. Those thoughts that are being intercepted. Books. Job searches. Enjoy. Ice cream in the freezer. The candy in the drawer. The cupcake. Control of thoughts. I really am that pop star girl. You know. She's white. Keeping me afloat. Language annoyance. All things we knew frustrated people in real life, but never thought people would harm others over it. New realizations. Robots. Everything around me. Drill it in: these people need help. They're alive. Whites tired of black's stupidity. Real drama. Control off of thought. How do you do that? A coma. Comb. Daily: sleep with beasts, eat shit, drink blood and piss. Beasts know they don't want to. The point in going to the underground: The point – to kill the computerized monsters. Had to kill siblings. Didn't care when they started coming up missing. It's the end. Wore out! All these people can pay. They are going to come above ground fucking more shit up. – Hearts set on revenge. Freeing them and they will have mental illnesses. Be bitter. They're better off than they were.

Find **The candy in the drawer** in the passage.

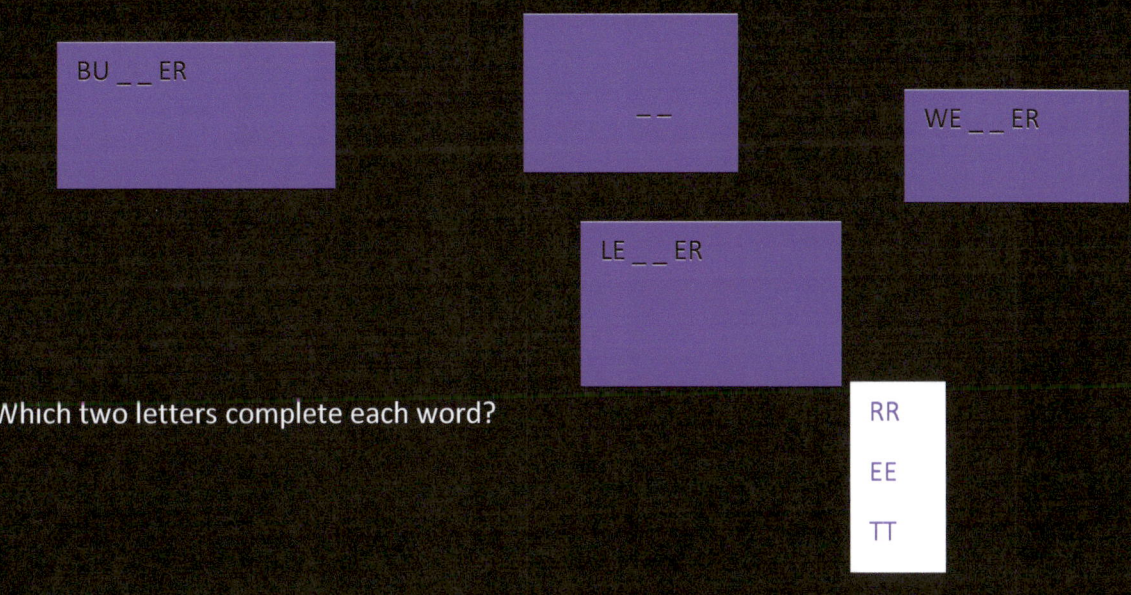

BU _ _ ER

_ _

WE _ _ ER

LE _ _ ER

Which two letters complete each word?

RR

EE

TT

This up and down rollercoaster. Acrophobia. Are they alive or are they dead? Hard fact to know they're alive. Scenes I couldn't possibly know reading their minds. Things are becoming loose. They hear me. See me. I'm moving. Helping them kill and clean things. To feel their emotions. Can't get that story out of my head. Every time I think of things I felt they feel them. New clips in phone. One stop. Synthetic pain. Thoughts. Why did I hear voices of the mentally ill? First? Said they were family. Not knowing she was my mother hurt her and me not knowing who my siblings were. The voices. The robots did them perfections. Perfectly. One word, said in a way that I can get many people out of. The way they said things. I see them. They see me. People I walk by. How can family be live in computer? Tired and bored. Orange and black. 34. 33 in that cartoon. More. Kneel down and pray. Would I stay homeless and live this faulty life so my brothers and I can remain above ground? Would I stay homeless alone and my brothers live good so they could enjoy life instead of all of us living miserably?

Find **Tired and Bored** in the passage.

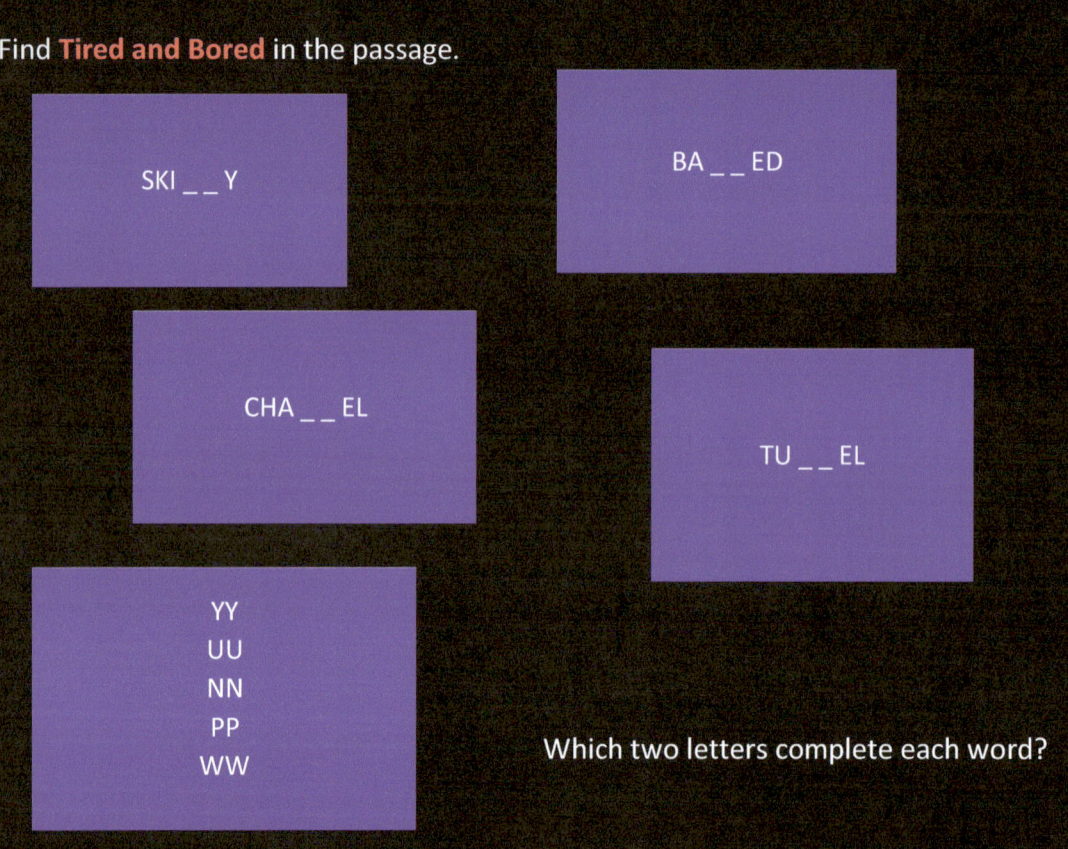

SKI _ _ Y

BA _ _ ED

CHA _ _ EL

TU _ _ EL

YY
UU
NN
PP
WW

Which two letters complete each word?

The first people didn't leave shit here. All we're eating is throw up. Weight loss impossible with my convenient food. Recognizing robots. (Infinite ways) Unbelievable things going on down there. These are their friends and enemies. – Need food, time out of cell, work on escape. Rewards. Beasts given. Do. It's all right here. Shona, there's a video for all of them. Birth Certificate. Invest in myself. Mail books. Books. Plays. They all want time. They sit around with nothing to do. Their enemies have been next to them this whole time. Said they have to do all types of bad things to keep the beast happy. And have to act in their closeted way. Act like children. Their ancestors – some are still alive. Too smart to take those drugs. Does the beast pick whose Hannah? Prescriptions. In different parts of the world. Supposed to watch a video from each section. They can't believe this technology. I love money. Yes I do. Whole picture. The people are in crowded spaces and naked. 250.

Find **Recognizing robots** in the passage.

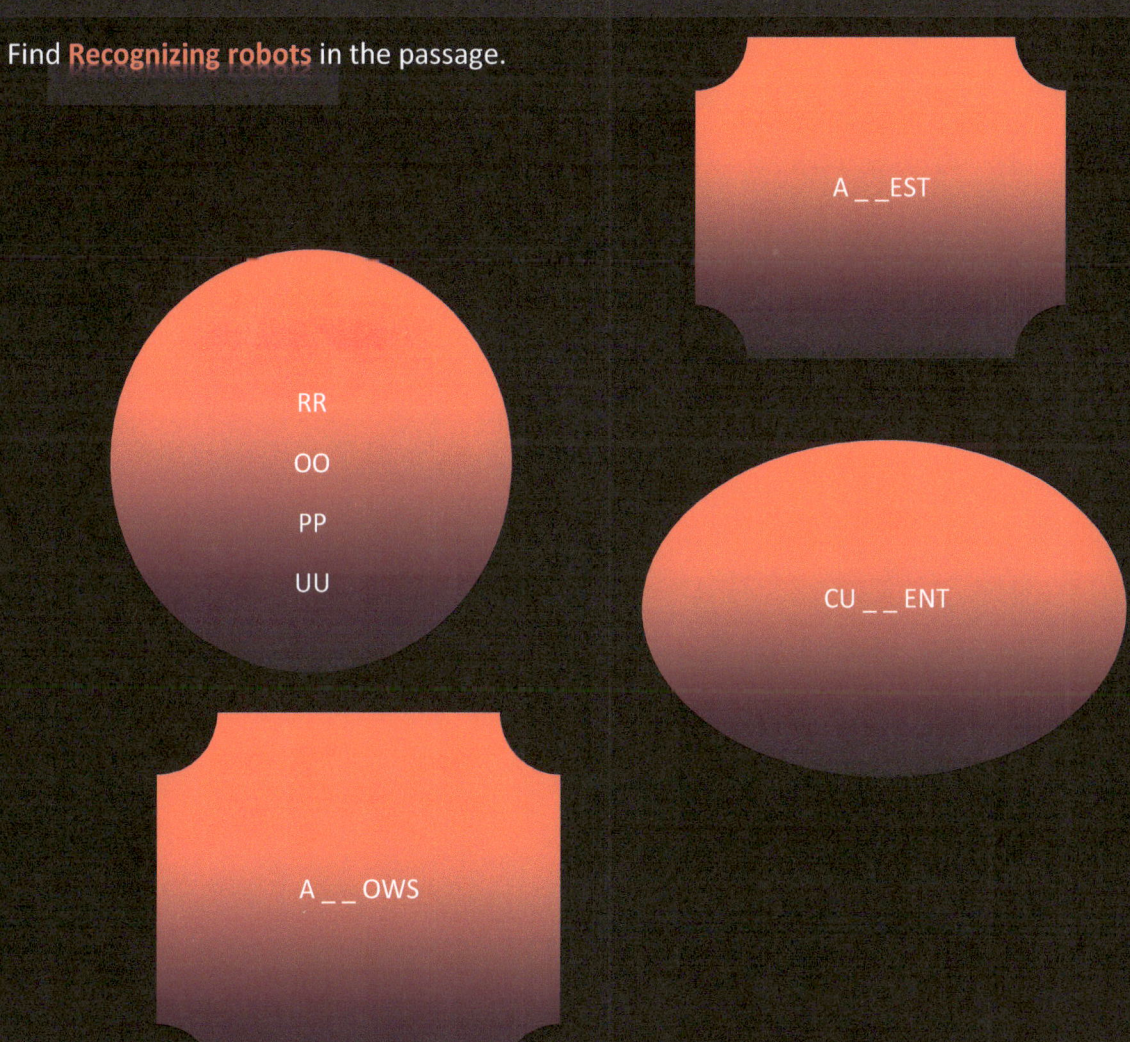

A _ _ EST

RR
OO
PP
UU

CU _ _ ENT

A _ _ OWS

They had kids and didn't touch them in hopes that when they die someone would save them and some just wanted to keep their kids around/ alive, as long as they could. A bath. Straight up. Bad comes. X. Add. Off the chain. The barrel of water. Whistle. Small cup to score. Heat boxes. Red Gold emails. Too much editing. These people survived the lowest of the low. Kept in one piece. First student. Happy someone is willing to help them get a second chance at life above ground. Heartrate: The Visotros. Pools. Will reunite. Eye switches. The lab. Family. Some making their kids please desires because they know the mind's are messed up. People lied to them. Slaves. Lives stolen. They don't have to die for what they've done. Keep seeing beds. Hotels or apartments. Sold out to racist party. Given nothing in return. Every day I come back they are happy. Sometimes doubt. They'll be the first ones out. You reap what you sew. Should be able to pop in one of the robots and control it. I said they forgot everything. Need to be told what happened in the past. They're performing live. Holograms. Drill it in. I should be right in front of them with my computer. Internet man clipped the floor. 537. Maximum Pain! A Must! Mandatory! Drill it in! Pain & Hostages. It's the only way to understand it all. Freeing the best of the best first. It's only right that every time I think of them that they glow down there. I'm out of my mind. Real Community down there. Snitching when under trances. Some of them pretend to be under trances and snitch. Bitter. Mind reading. Or die? They'll walk right to them. How long to free the whole world? People change. Death due to their own family conditions. All this damn arguing. Black and whites have issues. Made up scenarios. Believe. Walking. I don't know these people. Infirmary. I said these were real stories. Maybe 3 years without any help. Just getting clogged up down there.

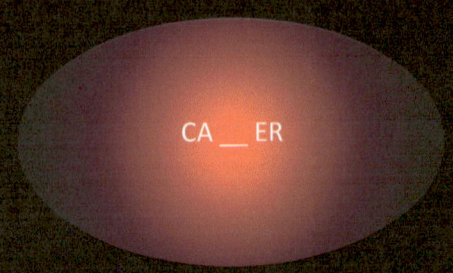

Find Mind reading. Or die? In the passage.

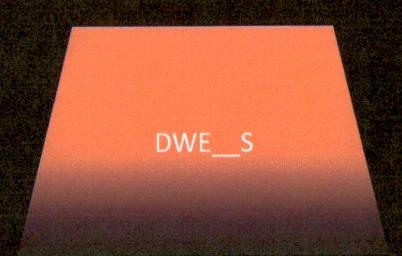

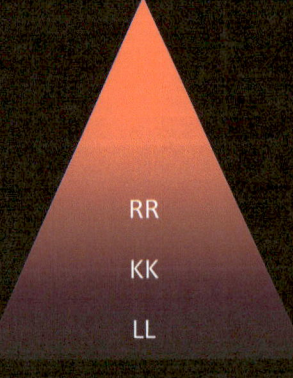

I said I was live editing. Them doing uncomfortable things makes the beast horny. They have to fuck the beast. A line. Have to act like they want to. (Get cured of diseases) Sacrifice a child. Q. Que. TV. Camera angles. Shooting walking robots in the eyes. Where am I in the arena? They could still have kids. Had to eat people to shit them out and fight monsters. Meanwhile I feel like my ovaries are messed up. Guess I won't know if I can have kids until I try. I am only 10 right. Chris. I've been there in the building the whole time. Everything "wrong" they liked mixed in the beast. They have mean trances about the beast. Computer there or not? Now she can feel it. Bad ass kids. Need the 16 platforms. Sitting around waiting to fuck a beast all day and eating shit. (pretending to like eating shit). Making things out of shit. They crack. Clay. Eaten alive. Other people are hopping in their bodies. I said some people got their hair done for me. CE. Zero. Happy. It can't keep count.

Find Shooting walking robots in the eyes in the passage.

They gotta be worn out to fall asleep. Gangs/trains of sex in front of children. Said this craft of mine means nothing to them. Men belittled. Said can take care of family's and they're captured. The crazies made sure, to ask them why they got trapped. Natural mental illness. Have to sleep with beasts when they want. Breaths. When the beasts want. Breaths constantly stink. Stank. They think they're being hit by someone or something. There or not there. Can't decide how they're acting. Move. Usher them in. A mechanism to drill in my heart that they are breathing and need help. Hanging on by a limb. Those figures of speech offending people. Someone. Automated when they project.

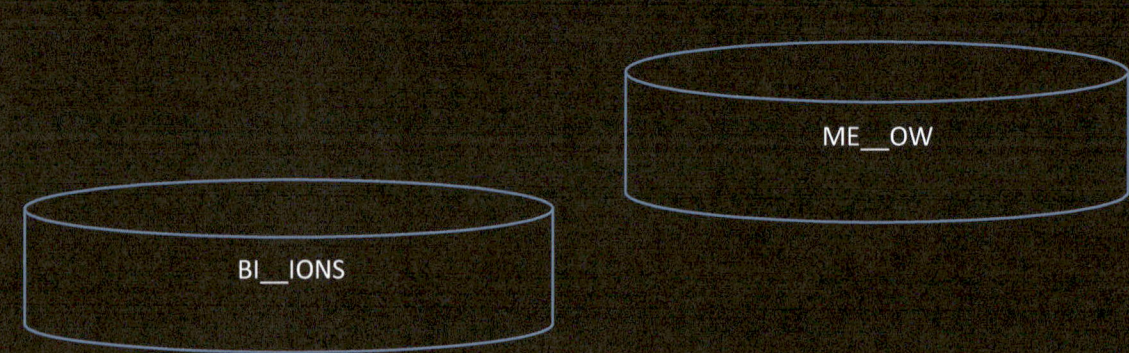

Find Natural mental illness in the passage.

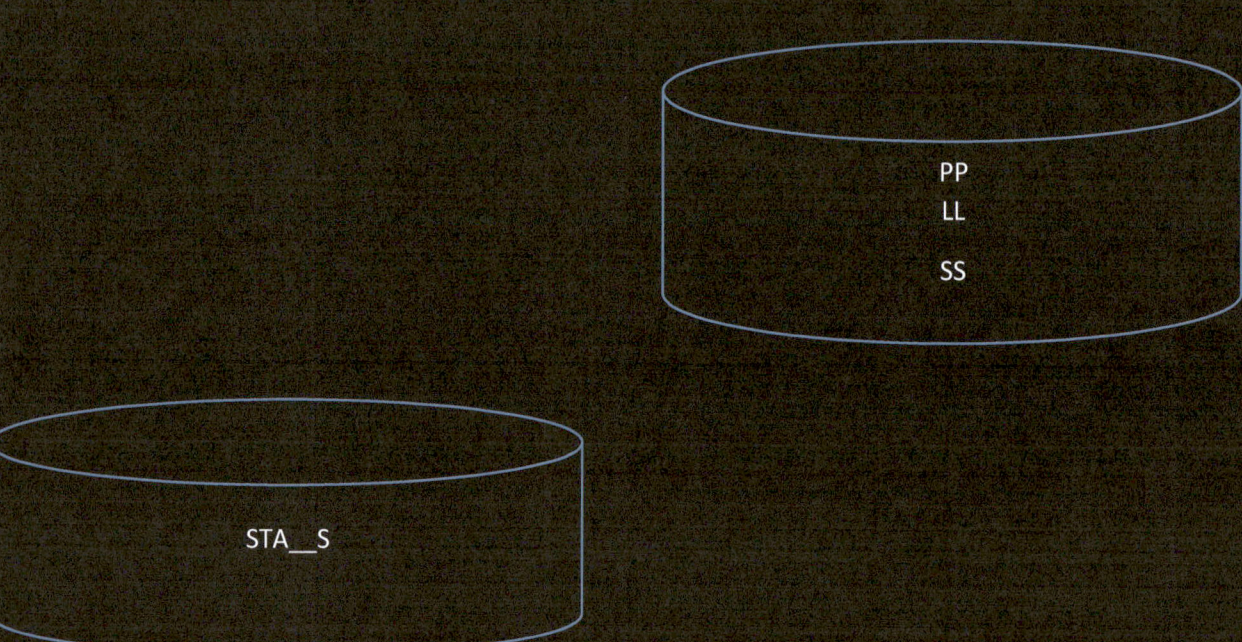

They do things they need to, to snap out of trances and how the beasts need them to. They're crowded. Drill it in. With Beasts. We'd all be down there eating shit. Drinking blood and piss. Eating dead animals and dead bodies. Eating dried piss. Smelling the worst smells ever. They're having arguments with people they make up/create in their heads. They can all see me through one robot. Seeing what they really look like. Too much to deal with. I'm blown away. That means every time I think of them, they're live. Quick results. Son of a bitch. Unbelievable. Live thoughts are in. They keep track of live thoughts too. They are definitely keeping track of everything I watch. They need something to think about.

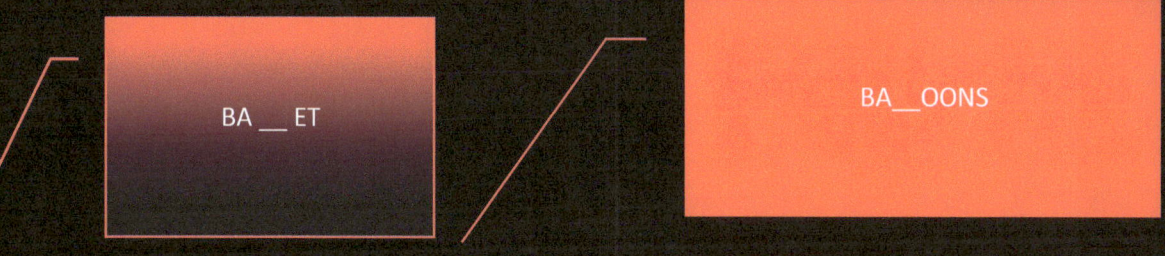

BA __ ET

BA__OONS

Find They can all see me through one robot in the passage.

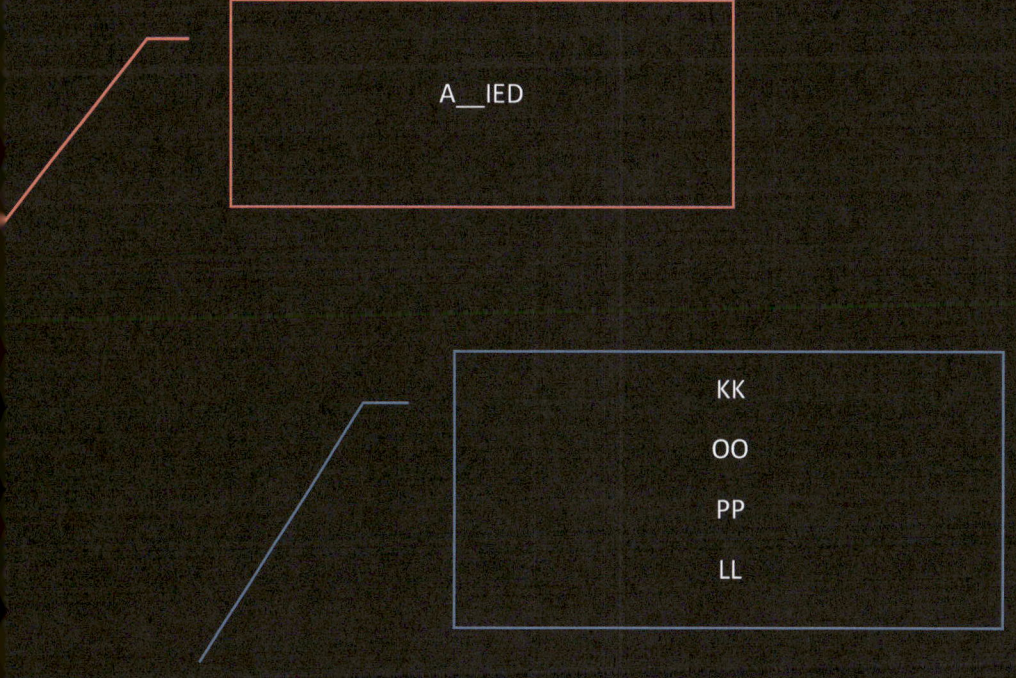

A__IED

KK

OO

PP

LL

All this damn arguing has to go. Events that won't even happen. Scenarios created. Dialogue galor. Snap out of it. All signs point to yes. The money. So much, a distraction. Even. Hill. Hall. Faith. Care. Chris. Que. To see none. Santa Sent. Barber. The gear. Courageous. Roommate. These people exist. Unless they go up to you starting mess. Subliminal conversations. Crazy kids. – caskets. 10 + years trapped. That's 3 years before my arrival, I believe. I'm still figuring myself out. Long before arrival. You can't let it bother you. You can't let it bother you. These people are literally no good. Big families, looks, and nothing more. It's their lives. They can do what they want with them.

Find Big families, looks, and nothing more in the passage.

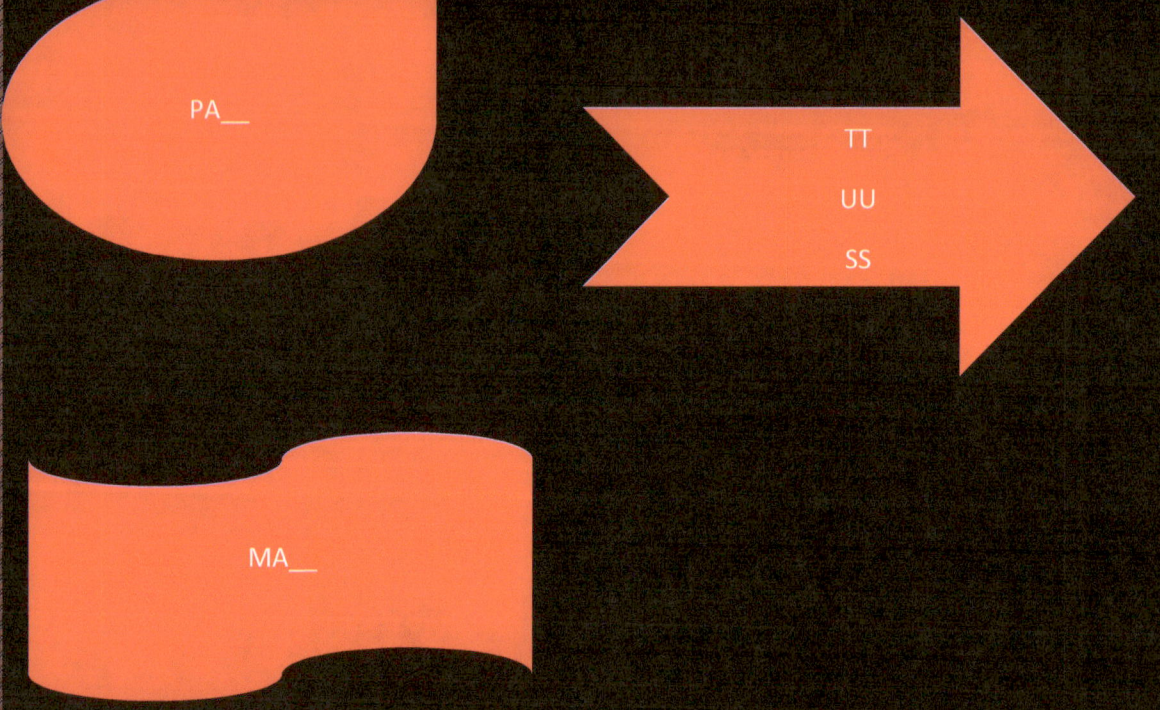

PA__

TT
UU
SS

MA__

All bad when return. 10 + years at the bottom of the Earth. Miles. Hypnotism of monsters. Matches. Food. Clothes – little by little down the train. Water – pipe. Drain. Fresh air devise. To go. Pipe Rooms. Hannah. One of those names you can read backwards. The blanket. At his place and the book that looked similar to mine on top of the stack. The Playlist. Windows. ? They work for the beast? Take turns doing things for it in certain orders and working on the escape. My step teams. Body cramped.

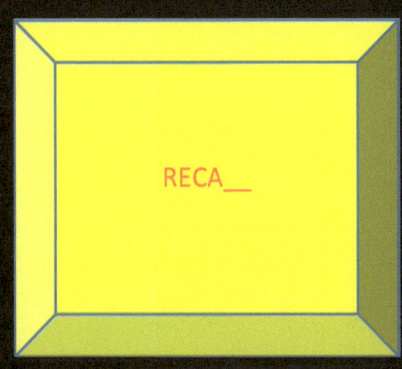

RECA__

REFI__

Find Hypnotism of monsters in the passage.

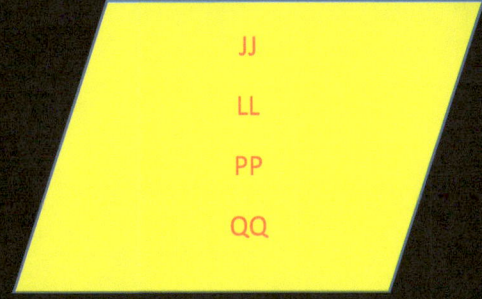

JJ

LL

PP

QQ

Congested with shit. Drinking blood and piss. Damn. Just had one of those thoughts that I wanted to write and it vanished. Baths: They had to get used to nasty habits. Way more to slavery than just lynching. Some have records. Heartrate. Quan. The Visotros. So while they're working, whose in their bodies? Random people for help. Some 13 years beneath the ground. These people are bitter. These people are insane. They try and give off they're not all the same. Videos. Edited. Ball. Money. Edit. Said they were hurting them kids. They get voted the most. The annoying ones. They want to be free so bad. Need them to perform well so I will come back. I said they really want to see me too. It's a game. More room every time. More gifts. More people snapping out of trances. Fact. Some of them are good at measuring time. "You guys would not have made it this far alone." Apparently. Basketball. It hurt like hell waiting for help and it never came. Constant supply. When machine/ platform activated. Shots that knock you out. Automated – those that need it most. The boat on the field trip. People that are Hannah have to go around being nice to everyone. Basketball. Chris. Move. Transfers. Sophomores. Soft. More.

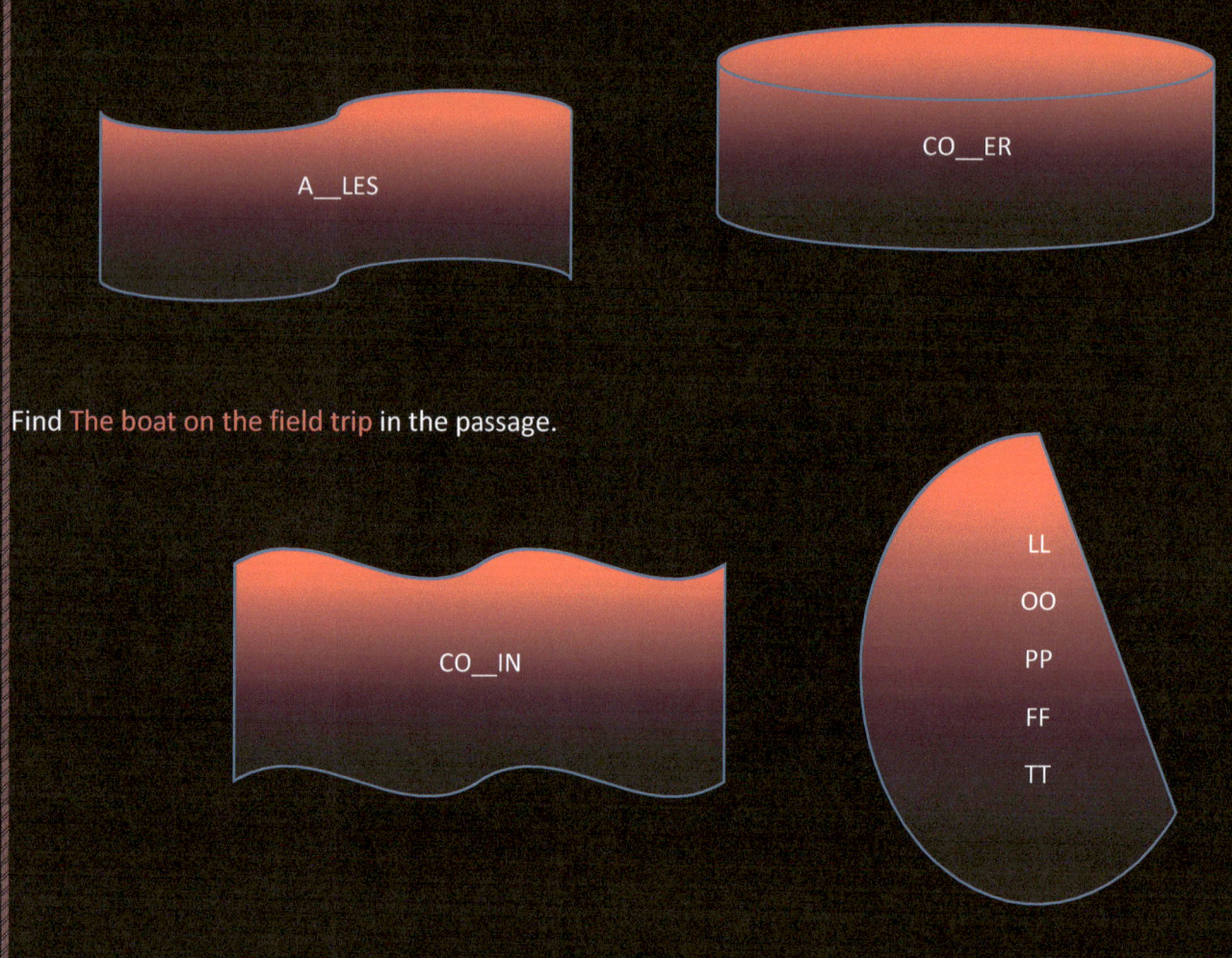

A__LES

CO__ER

Find The boat on the field trip in the passage.

CO__IN

LL
OO
PP
FF
TT

Chips & salsa. Fast. Celery and peanut butter. Nuts. Applesauce. Whole wheat bread. Fruits. Vegetables. I can't get these gnats out of my head. All this arguing. They're around people just like them and worse. A daily 100% dose of their own medicine. Science experiments gone wrong. Spills. Oil. All of humankinds, mankind's nasty habits embedded in the beast. And they need it. Where is the air coming from? Fog machines. Wind machines. I get that they have to deal with the bullshit hardcore, but fuck my life for these raging thoughts and uncontrollable dialogue to keep going in my head. Real. I want to know everything they're dealing with. This is what they would've, or my brothers could be going through. Question I asked a while ago. Some people are so tall they haven't been able to stand up straight. Who didn't eat? The place is getting more spacious and they are making their way to taller rooms. Visiting the kids. Small things as gifts. The Point: Now I'm just waiting on the money. To drill in that these people are alive. They need help and I need to visit them every day.

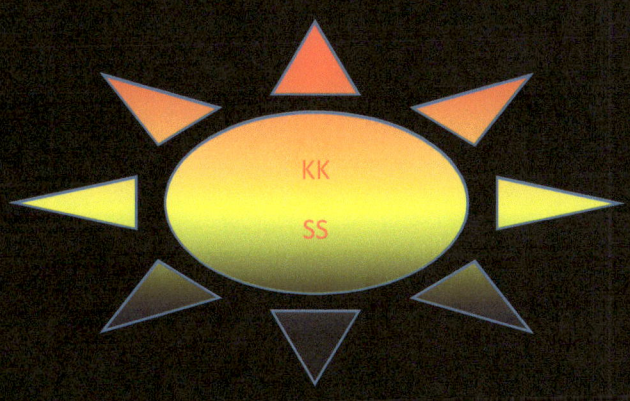

Find Now I'm just waiting on the money in the passage.

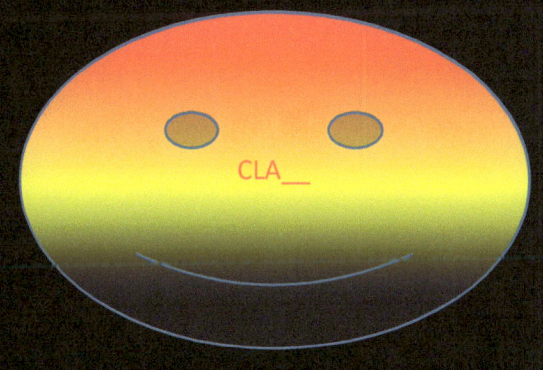

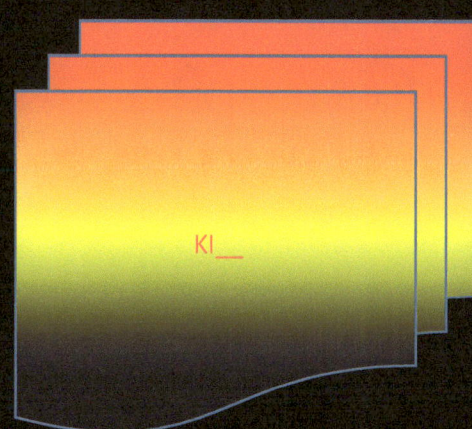

To not care or worry about my circumstances. That's stupid. The money will come at perfect arrival. Yes I know you were expecting perfect timing. These annoying people. Things are falling down there. Food, toys, drinks. It's still trash. Filter. See a up? You. Not for hire. Ordinary Hidden money. Don't tell people shit about anything. There's a system they left here. When they come above ground they will have to start over. Tough. Teachers. Portfolio class. These people are not happy but doing better than they were. The whole world has been underground for at least 10 years. Don't give them shit. Chipped. Drugged and chipped by many different parties. That's some of the way they survived this long and located when someone was about to kill them. Blackmail. Neighborhoods bought by close families to trap and torture people. Saving. Afraid I won't come back. Some believe I will come back. We're talking Terrible Torture to snap out of chaotic thoughts. Hypnotism, natural. That talking won't stop. We're talking peripheral vision needing to be treated delicately or trances will occur. It's awful down there. The robots are morphing and telling me the truth about what happened here. Animals, put on human skin. Other humans bitter at certain people, wanted to be certain people and put their skin on. I'm through. This type of fuckery. All types of bullshit has happened here and still happens. But it's cleared out now., Right. No sign of life around here. Who could beat that and save humanity? Who's my mother? Coolinda.

Find It's awful down there in the passage.

Books 1. Dance (videos) 2. Math Games. Drawing – tessellations. Singing (videos) 3. Step Choreography (videos) 4. Scriptwriting – already have books – create another web show alone. Photography – editing – trailers (videos) 5. I can hear my mom talking to herself about me. She thinks she's talking to friends. Books, videos, singing – internet popularity. Play many characters. Come up with something creative. Ex. She hears voices then becomes the people she hears. Puzzles on life. Live. Answers to everything I need to know. How did we get to this bad point? Stay busy. Ushers. This is to please the beast. This route of all the hell they experienced. Tired and Bored. Circles and Bricks. They wanna know anyways. What happened to them. Who knows best? Notes later? Believe everything's only underground. Could love be why they're more frustrated? Old Stories coming back. Casino. No Options. Bus blows up on curb (another one pulls in). Girl kidnapped – bus pulls up to neighborhood first – runs through forest then to school. 1. Monsters 2. Packet clips 3 family rooms 4 work rooms 5 past evil 6. Dreams 7. Center stage on court 8. Cubes 9 house, junkyard, parking lot. Outside of J's house. 10. Platform. 11 rollercoasters 12 underground 13. Video games 14 created platforms 15 their enemies 16 cartoons 17 18 colleges 19 bowling alley 20 theater 21 skating rink. People created in shot. Eating out of barrels. Bent over on table.

Find Old stories coming back in the passage.

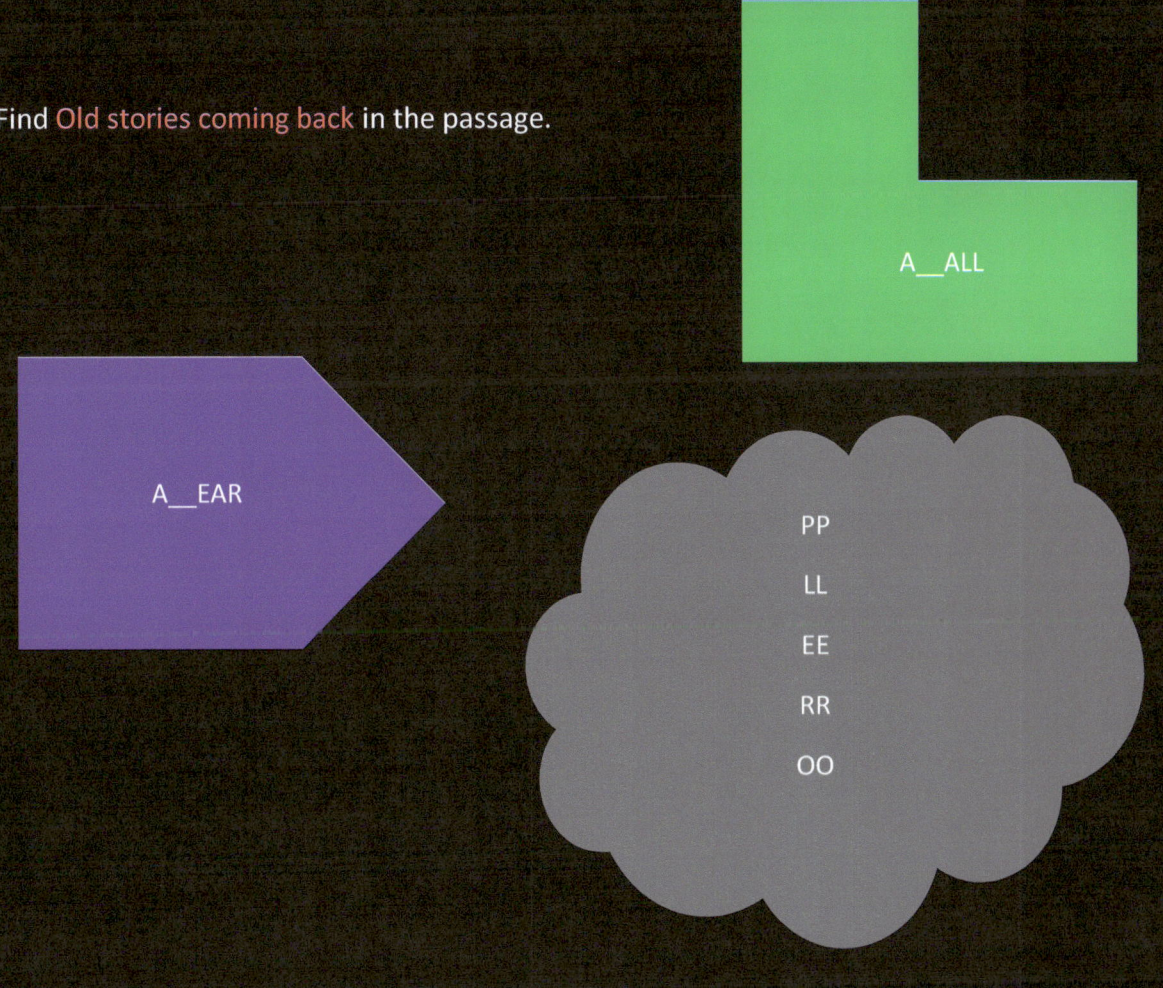

A__ALL

A__EAR

PP

LL

EE

RR

OO

Ducked and covered by the wall in color. With my clothes on. Enemies will show up. 22. Past. (the journey to rock bottom). I'm technically looking right at them. Scatter. Chess. Checkers. Game. The marbles on the wooden board. I can read your mind. Baby blue shirt. Black pants. "That's they." Corner Pocket. Hard fact to know they're alive. Projections, sound, sight, movement. Follow me. I get goosebumps. It's a poof. Instant change in smell. Do it big. Painting with the eyes. Faces merging for answers. Turn white building switch in brain. Pink and blue cotton candy smell. The GR people drive the buses. 30. Want so More? To see down there better. Platform. I said they could all be dead. Bigger. That would mean I can figure out what the inside of a house looks like if a camera's been in it. Takes time though. Painting with the eyes.

Find Ducked and covered by the wall in color in the passage.

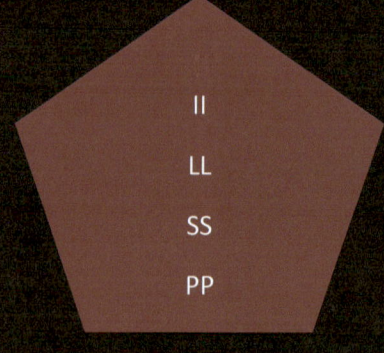

(Red Line). Gunshots snapping people back to reality. Train station goes down a few flights of stairs to Hoes Wood. And High Forests. They help each other work on the dances. Court. With people. Monster baths. Boy didn't have tickets. Likes to dress up in costumes. She would sit there all day. Girl looking up at Score. Indiana. Sister on the bus. Ushers. Move. Synonyms. These people really think they're animals and sometimes all humans are animals. (people flash into different things to them) They're just underground waiting on visitation. Mixed random things and weird things started happening. drugs. The beginning of prisons. (hostages) and hospitals. Every word can trigger their brains to go the wrong way. They're fighting to stay sane. Used them like dolls. Manikins. Hoe Race. Hoes Would. I mean it. This never ending story of hell that keeps getting extended in my head. It never happened, but because of your annoyance, annoying self, it won't go away.

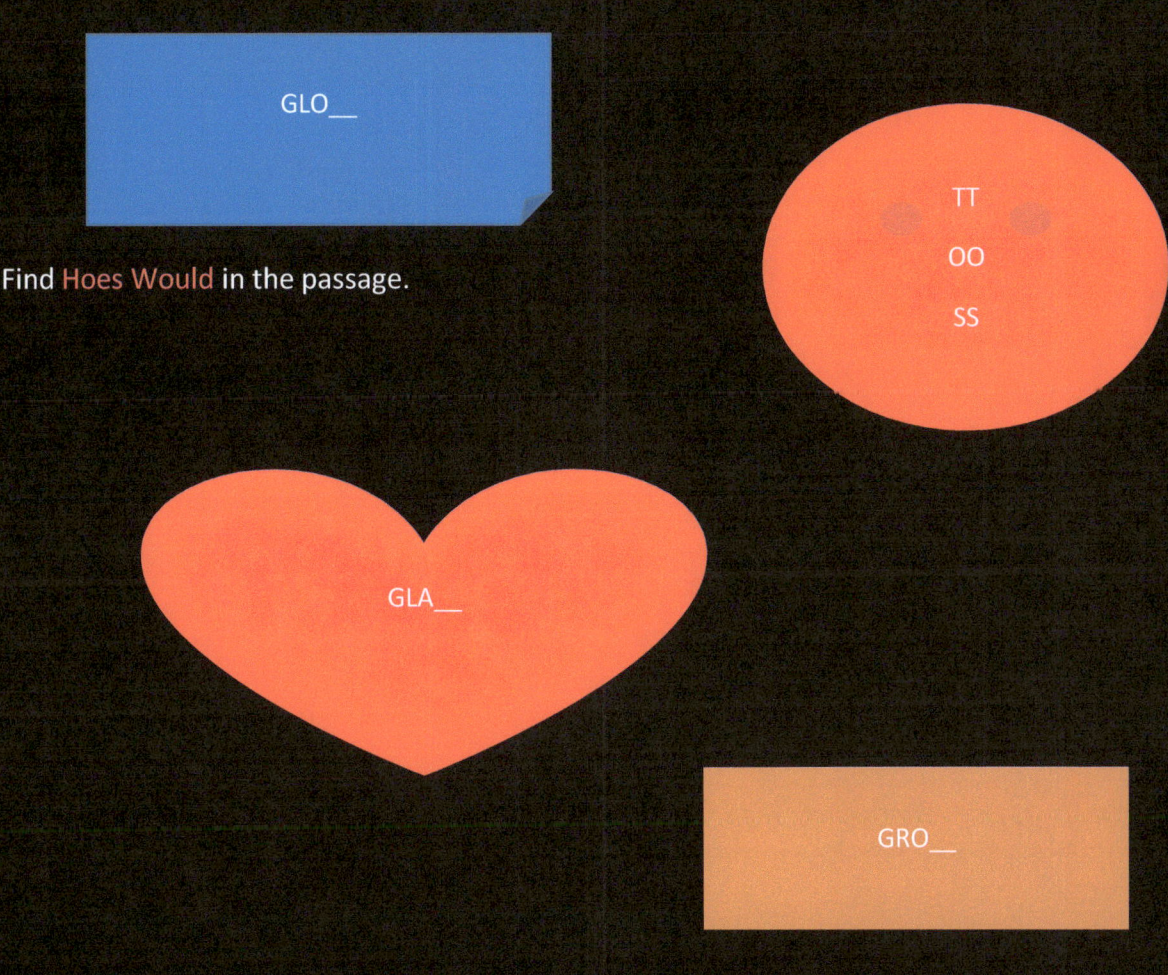

GLO__

Find Hoes Would in the passage.

TT
OO
SS

GLA__

GRO__

Boulevard. Vines. Signatures: Rondelle. Pray. 5th. Boo Dry. Johnson. Rose More. Vine. Will Hurt. By. Time Frame. Hoes Wood. High Territory. Land. And. Set offered It. Empire. Apartment. Hotel. Streets. Capitol. Hands and feet prints. Show held there. Stars. Theater – looks like beginning of video. Thrill Hurts. Underground cities. All these damn people clogged together. Concert like. Real. Voice recognition. Those boys have been trying to get help. Attention. The public awareness. Lady Lady. All these robots and still no money – need to wake up and get the facts first. Documentary. Things will be given. Halloween spent on the. Street shut down. Boulevard. Thought walks by and bumps into me. The killer. Looks like boy talked to me about Pens, cuffs, markers. Affection of see c si hustle down the street.DJ. Sound. Noun. Monkeys. What are we looking for? The route. The exit location. Bathroom. Infirmary. Studio demonic. Stairs lead down. One level down a monster. What are they doing? Killing monsters – inching their way to the exit. Plenty of tunnels. They want the whole place out with them. I'm floating.

Find Lady Lady in the passage.

Beasts – men want to be women, women want to be men meaning they want the others private areas. Is that possible or not? People that crack.4 year old boy. Slaves – unchained to fight and beat up their monsters – put on white skin – someone didn't show for a meeting. Many codes/calls/signatures not done. Some whites dressed as blacks. His son was in the room. (thought they looked that good that the KKK would like them) Told it was a party, ways to meet the rich, sold out, KKK didn't give them anything. Persuasion to the max. Good looks to you and talk of money. Thieves, homewreckers, annoying kids, rude to opposite sex because want to be it. They can't believe people would do that to them. Shit piss. Dead bodies. (fighting shit monsters and beasts to inch their way to the exit. They don't know which way to go. A's angry at blacks in other countries. They all want their whole families but are willing to give up someone if the need be. Frustration.? Did they know these racists were slave masters? They're naked. Acted like animals until snapped out of it. Work sit around and talk (tired and bored. Music making me feel good. What the hell is that? I get good. Every time. Are by crab legs buffet. Natural inventions. They want to see how long people would leave them down there. Phone. TV. Computer. I. $50,000. Yea right. $250,000. Whispers - $181,000. Silent Whispers. A beast blocking the exit. Pet cemeteries, Real? 10+ years down there. These people are stones. Told them they were all down there. Would get them back for being slow. Dead body. Metal. Chemicals. Lightning. Beasts dressed as human. In the meantime: job searches. Paperwork. Meeting June 3rd. Said I was piecing together clips in their brains to view the past. (How they got down there). Books, videos, singing. Fun with Hannah. See Why? Have no choice. They finally have help. Now they know where they are. How much of the room is showing? Me to them. Beatmaker. Still need to write. Doctor, Fix. Change.

Find Natural inventions in the passage.

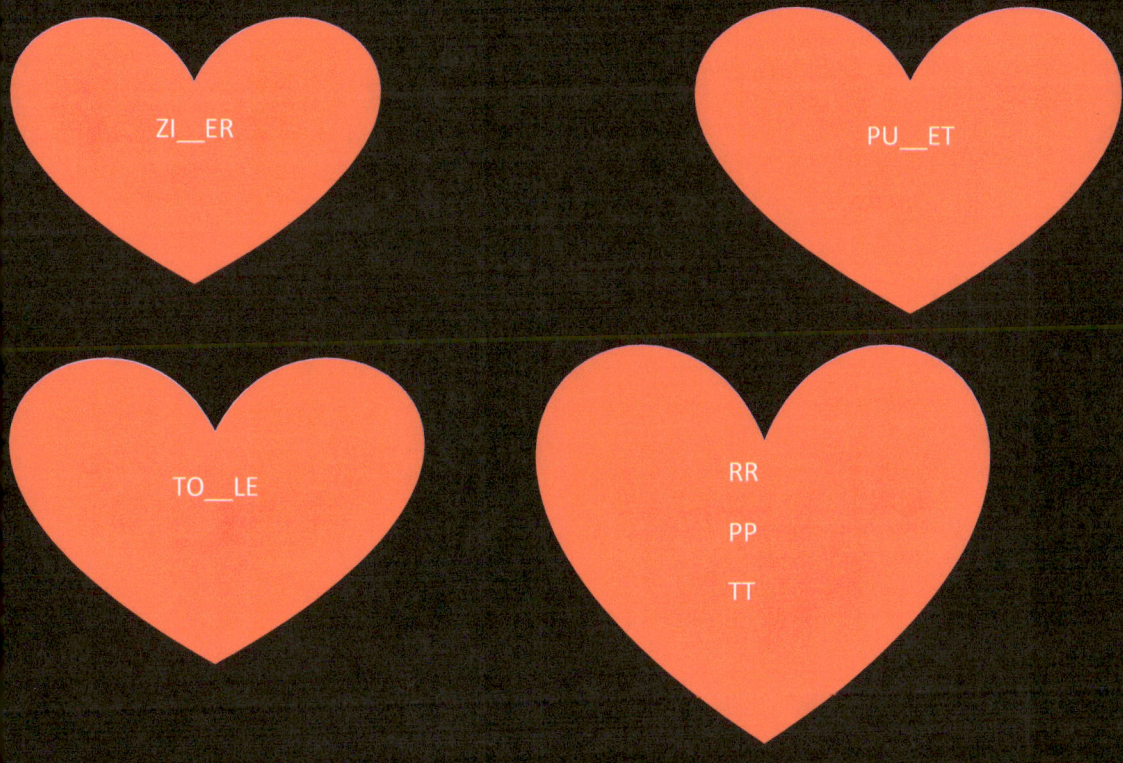

ZI__ER

PU__ET

TO__LE

RR
PP
TT

Fill in the blank. Add an A. already assigned ISBN. Never Spoken Of. Brainstorm. Clique. I said they would just keep getting worse. They think bad things are good. All humans surrendered to beasts. Except up. Quan. Really were no good to anyone but their families and their friends. (these particular people). If can get the lowest of the low from out of captivity, then other will be easy. Family trust. It's all connected. Said they were shopped around for a while or moved from person to person to get away from evil. It's a fact. These people exist. Treated like non-humans. We all think we dcan change people.

Find They think bad things are good in the passage.

Different pathways. A bathroom. Cleaning up dead bodies ad shit rooms. The work room. Animals kept them alive until they got help. Curing them of diseases. Have to sleep with the beast every day. Said it was like dating them white they're down there. Said they sent around people they would like to pretend to be their friends. Now they gonna come out and do more damage. A Christmas. No they were no good for nothing anyways. Beast doesn't care about dying. Wants to know who wronged it. Shit pile up. No Air. Said they could all be dead (including the beast). Said they beast has them lining up incase I visit them. They have rules and a work room. I made myself the target. A gay beast. Happy? Don't argue. Predictable. Be confident. Did I go where most of them were? Pet cemetery. Did someone go down there and make the place>? Dug deep. Addresses, everything changed around to perfection. Clothing Distractions. Money will arrive when all the answers clamped. Will hurt. Said they can't believe that this is their only way out. Invisible. Taking down the beasts hormonic level. Earthquakes. Ways to get deep. Said they're matching people. People down there fucking stuff up. Kids and all. Boy that dated the girl that dressed up all the time. Girl at the hospital with her daughter. These images do give off different tastes. Iron. They do get full. Pills. Cleaning. Making room in the exit route. Wastless. Something to keep their minds on. Drill it in: Supposed to visit them 3 times a day. 3/5. Don't think days of the week. Just think you're reading. Computer, camera, backpack. Storage. Micali. Girl in backseat seen when store robbed followed home wants to yell for help out window. Majorettes. Connections. Moments. Drink. Just Shine. Just Shona.. Unhealed. On the Inside. Trailers. Me on cover. For the love in your body. Abigail. Evil Encounters. It's all right here. Boo Up. The black scientists. The church. Honey's cell. The last people knew what happened to these people/they knew what was going on. Their hiding spots were found. Its.

Find everything changed around to perfection in the passage.

No one could survive all those illnesses at once. This is about the story. Clarity and Closure on what destroyed the world. Moving on confidently. Accepting what happened this lifetime. Never looking back. Family separated. Homeless. Debt. They're dead. Heartrate – The Visotros. Never caring anymore about what happened. Enjoying life the way it should've been all along. Frustrated to death. Getting the world back to the way it's supposed to be? Or too much has been done? Family is used to this system (the money system and the way people operate). This is the world they left behind and we have to cope with. Crazy/Ill. Meteors. Meat eaters. Dare us. Bell. Ushers. The street. Destiny. Episode. Prison. His name. Easy Kill. The trailer. The movie on the bus. Braids. Movie. Crazy man center on screen. Split church. I see. Hi V. A-Z. Answer. IA. El. They are all dead. Recorded voices. The movie with the food trailer. Hint son. Need a job. Would go crazy without atleast a feel of real human life. Would go crazy without atleast – Hearing real human voices atleast knowing what they looked like. Would have always wondered what some were like. Can feel them singing. Said created a Chris. The Bus Y station. Stay busy. Wishes. Girl at the place. Platform. Comedy shop. All the people would see. I said Mommy yesterday. 6-25-2019. To my real mom. Tapes (left behind). Studied the minds of the last ones living. And Family. Animals dressed as humans. All of these robots were people made off accidents in a laboratory. Or shit factory. Just where do all the waists wastes go? A machine made naturally off wastes? And natural things? Families friends and extended relatives gone. They're going crazy. Willie. Families, friends, and extended relatives gone. They're going crazy. A new way of thinking and living. Cannot get someone to snap out of re Charge ism/ brain damage. A feel of ones that would have dated. Families, friends, so they can know what happened to them. We all need the 100% story. We're still here. Heartrate why can't be thrown all the information. They can be made and morph any second.

Find Family is used to this system in the passage.

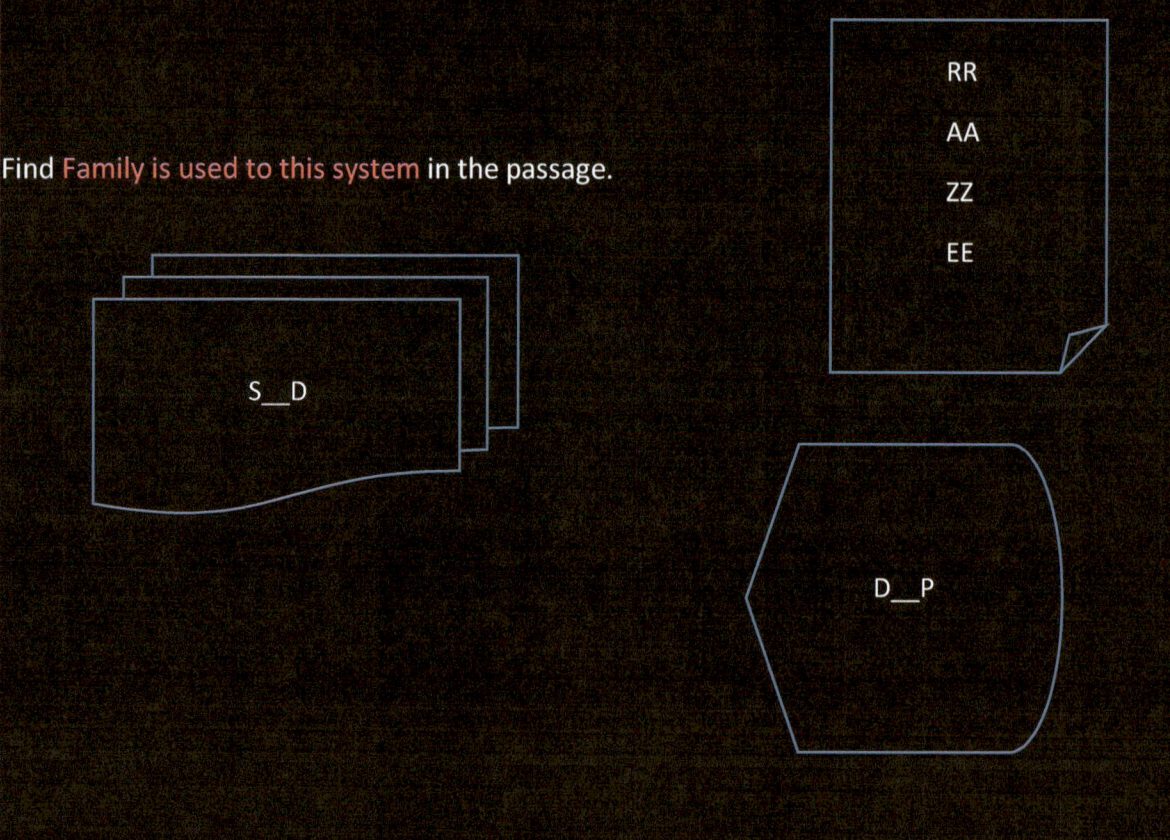

Platform and stability before they rise. Created. Time lapse. Severe. They knew no one would help them. Pretending to be robots. G come on nigga. Grand. Downtown LA. Always do something to overdue yourself. Top yourself. Gave me clothes. Negative sentences making you do positive things. Someone else's conversation causing you to act and it has nothing to do with you. Voice overs. Went the wrong way with boyfriend on the street. Mom- porn videos. Boo prey. Pray. 2 shots. Did my eyebrows. Did they find a way to get out? Wrong area. Nickels, Ya'll act like it's a big deal Blue won. Blue and black hoody. It's a puzzle. They are all together. They have to participate in the chaos and there's break rooms. Escape. Eat. There's rooms for sex. Bathroom. Basically this is a second chance at life. But they'll be worse. Understanding the walking infirmary. I said they would be obedient. Holograms.- they have to dress how they don't want to- act in their hidden ways. Sleep with people they don't want to. VOTED. Selling and buying goods need air time to please the beasts. Foods it never tasted. Smells it never smelled. We live in a world where we know something is wrong, but we say it's right to please everyone else or fit what the fuckery everyone's done has led up to. Something like that. Shit is normal but we know it's wrong. Everyone but we all agree to say what is wrong is right. Did you goat? Projects – detail – list. Goals. Underground work. Rails and Roads. Have to study the area – visitation 3 times a day. Debt – use prepaid card for now.

Find We live in a world where we know something is wrong in the passage.

Car. Registration plates. Drill it in – Otherwise won't do it. Need to clamp in my brain these people need help. Invest in books. Hand out on boulevards. 5ths. Library. Spring. Book please. Library. The Money. They spit and shit, they can give off chemicals beneath, smoke, water, etc. Numbers, color, shapes. All of it. Perfection for answers. Robots telling the story. Dreams and addresses giving me an idea of what the place used to look like. Remember talking to myself, still using the system that was left here. Terrible food. Saved. Recycled. Cherries. Tomatoes. Puberty egg. Birthday money. Given because homeless. Someone paid for it because they know I was homeless. Information. Webshow. $240,000. $75,000. $250,000. $181,000 – Silent Whispers. Ain't no rain when she's gone. Thunder. Sunshine. The reasons I'm here> The Point: to get a feel of these families. The suicide fight. Memorization. The Route. Hoes Wood. Vines. Up and Down. Willie? Up and down. Have to tour these streets. Everything's in perfect formation to figure out everything I need to know. The Point: to hear them talk – see them move around. I may have to lead them out. Said they're gonna kill whoever gets them out for taking so long. Real mentally ill people down there with them. Amples tools. Beasts in human skin. Having conversations, negative thoughts about people they don't know. Framing people. They're keeping track. It's a coma. All black- the airport. So this means: All the events, all of the people I've met, names, clothing, is all a part of something bigger.

Find Given because homeless in the passage.

They're pushing their kids to perform better. They want out. Knowing who the community and the enemy are. What happened in the world? Freeing man and woman kind. The exit routes. (still reading minds and recording person by person). Most importantly. What to do with the money I get. Complete war zone when they get above ground. Time frame. (estimated date they will be freed) The place would become haunted if indoors. Led in. They all want to die. They cut the supply. Will this one particular agenda free them all? Or will I need to watch more videos in the future – or this crew the best to get the rest out. The monsters above. People constantly shitting/pissing/blood. They're all doing good so I will revisit their videos. I said they knew they were being watched so they did intentional things. Have flashes that these people are the enemy best manipulation. Why the hell do I care about these people? They don't got to die for it. They care about me. School embarrassment. They will have phases and moments. Supposed to spend as much time as possible with them underground so they can get out faster. I said they just want to get out. They will be obedient. They could be dead. They choose when they want to be cool with someone. It's a face: They would've just gotten worse. Don't tell them shit! Ushers! Willie! Really! They've been down there longer than 10 years. They can estimate by watching their kids grown. Drill it in! Quan! I have 33 brothers. That cartoon. He wears 33 on his shirt. Rich. They would not have helped anyone. That girl in their position as fast as they could or at all.

Find Will this one particular agenda free them all? In the passage.

Wouldn't have made it to championship without. That girl. They've been down there so long, taught not to trust anyone. Playing house. Trying to escape. Beasts goveren4 transfers. (no one's ever cared about them). Playing with the mind of a beast. (they sent notes down the toilet) They know they're uncomfortable around them (the beast) (the humans) (With mean things on them) Death notes. They say they didn't know certain things. We say, they don't have no sense. Cured of diseases. Trances: criminal acts. Brain shut down. Bottom line, life is short. Help as much as I can and still enjoy it. Shooting these robots in their eyes an they're shooting the actual person. The Secret: Infirmary. Cleansing the eyes. Said some people had kids because they know I needed some to teach everyone lessons. Examples. They're working hard to keep me there, so they can get closer to freedom. Shit from the enemy goes down their pipes. Eating diseases. The secrets out. Fashion shows. The Secret of Men. Willie. Chris. They'll do anything. 3 hours with them. Beasts has them lining up to perform. Need weight for platform – more people helped things to move. Secret lovers. Distractions. Escape. Hoes would. Vine. High territory. Escape. Sometimes they snapped out of it due to Earth's natural ways and sound. Couldn't stay that way. Static Electricity. Synthetic materials. Surrendered to Beasts. Work rooms – cleaning up shit and dead bodies. Piss, blood. No idea where the pipes lead. Must be in shape/waxed to perform. There is a community that is for examples. The natural trance of a mind to take the negative route when. Every issue. Surrounded by chaos. Things they don't like. Holograms projecting all over the world. To understand them. If knew would become rich, need a hard way to remind myself to help other daily. 10 years + down there. The whole population. I said: they're playing stupid. They are down there with enemies, white people were in black skin. Afr's blended in down there. They're pretending to be younger. Beasts/animals down there (governing them). Nothing blocking them from seeing everyone else. Snoring. Annoying sounds. They're naked. They want to know everything that's happened to them. So how?

Find Sometimes they snapped out of it due to Earth's natural ways and sound in the passage.

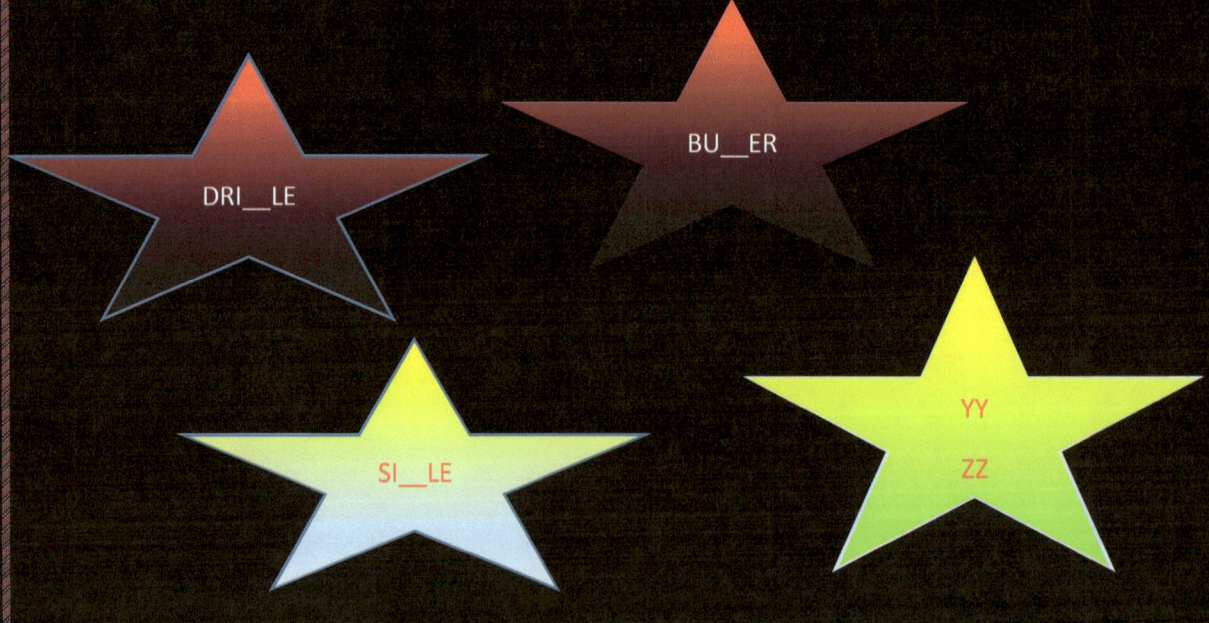

Need to understand and drill it all in. (everything that need to be done) before the money. It's mandatory. 1. To get them out as quick as possible. 2. And to learn the story and to manage. 3. The money the right way and to get to the weight desired. Ain't shit here. I wanna know what would be done to me. Some people knew I was too smart to be down there. Monsters needs all there chaos to be happy. (unhappy gorillas). A feel of her influence. (whiff). Parents influencing kids relationships. So there's not 43 of us. Keeps getting deeper. Left for dead. They aren't good for shit. with drugs. – supply gone. This is an up and down rollercoaster. Take and joy out? They were separated. They didn't have a clue what happened to them. Line of Chris. My brothers. This game is severe. When I need to watch something, my brain will say a lot of my brothers are not my brothers. Let's talk about a clamp, chip in your body like that to make you do something. Whose my mom and dad? Do we all have the same dad? I think there's 38 of us now. They know they make people uncomfortable. Racist party for money. (no way out) They would be dead. Some people down there know what happened to them. Who did it. Why they did it. (or information around the situation). Black streets. They don't know how to talk with their faces. There's a lot of them so it makes it easier. They blank out and do things they don't want people knowing. They want us all to go down there They think family is all down there. Mine. Maybe no. Lying and saying you got out and captured again. This type of frustration. Hope for job back. 14 hours out and about and do platform.

Find They didn't have a clue what happened to them in the passage.

Distance. Football field or half a football field. Minimum – when platform activated time and will take them to get free. 2 weeks. 10 years. 7 years. They hid stuff and stole trying to get out. Robots. All eyes in. Computer. When think of them. Holograms. The schedule. Study the streets. Visit them 3 times a day. The money. Need to be able to hear and see them live. Choices. Clear phone. Mail back. 15 minutes Hannah. Brush it. World. It's on big puzzle. Putting the pieces together. Snapping and out of reality. Figured out big things to change and found their families. They have to walk to the body. Clothes on them and in the frame. How does everything work. Said they sit around and do nothing all day. Tired and bored. Embarrassed. They need something to think about. Thoughts build up. – can feel that-. I'll just be right there. Sick. Broadcasting. Journalism. Fun. Class. He eats pussy. Cut my bang. Mansion party. Red and black. Blood. Victory. Look a like. The business. The dance. Lions. Got from another group. Comment. Stones. Head coach. How to keep the beasts happy. How everything works. Big family. Happy. Name took step from news. Tacos. Birthday. Your mom called. Just. Same lady gave me the money. Black dye put in my hair.

Find All eyes in. in the passage.

Called Grandma. Hall. Drive. Look alike came to dorm from New Or. See a you? Gym class. Physical education. Show. Step. Step team. Reminds me of Ten – a – Shona. Head punched. Movie showed. Homecoming week. Orphans. Blood rude about (clothes. You driving wreckless. Made. Machetes. Another light girl. The ride on the bus to the suites. The only school left opened. Sky. Induction. Came. Ken – dolls. Decipher. Meeting. Said name. 2 boys let me in. Describing word. "pyramid". Song at suites. Car messed up on the side. Cut in front of us. You wonder why your car messed up. The slot machine. My look a like. Any closer – he'd be with you. Fast good food by. Song at party with alcohol. Crab legs at store. Soul food place around the corner. Clothes. Accounting answers taken and spread in the library. What the hell are they doing all day? Tired and bored. Tricks – cell switches. "Never would've thought." Girl a stripper. Looked related to the girl that said it to her. Chosen people. Then using them would be for nothing. They've been in videos with their enemies this whole time. Dad and son in the forest story. He blindfolded his son and pretended to leave but never did. Movie: man sat on the side of the road. Dream I had – man covered in shit next to me sitting on a log and fireworks going on somewhere beyond the forest in front of him. He's sitting in front of an apartment building. A good cover up. Some people walked around saying things to let people know they would die for their family, but there was no cameras down there in people for help. I said there was a woman, black man, good white woman in the room of all the people looking like white men that were decision makers. People kept throwing more bodies down there and other things so they couldn't get out. Hell trips. Metal ticks in my head. The importance. The long stretch. The length they have to go put in pictures. They need me. It's only one way out of Sho nuff. And that's dead. These people had more kids that they didn't influence. It was their only way for help. But if you could free the kids, you could free them. But the thing is, they know they would not help you. Would take time out to have sex, when you need help now.

Find The slot machine in the passage.

Air. They're at the bottom of the Earth. Foul smells. Light. Some of the smartest people trapped in the biggest racist party. Taken to the hood. Killing along the way. Hoes wood to the hood. The long journey. Told them how annoyed of their kids and thugs I was. Some willing to sacrifice some. They have to walk to the body. (clothes 2 times) on them an in the shit. I'm right in front of them. The magician. My mind clicked that I had a hotel at the place. My mind clicked that my mom was a celebrity and was on a flight to get and was at that hotel. firefighters, police. Acted like animals until they got help. They need to be snapped back to reality. Foreshadowing. These parents can't believe their huge families are trapped. Registered thought. Belittled. Hannah. Things. Party. No ones ever cared about them. Kit. They just want a visitor. Slaves before celebrities. Regret selling out. Mad a mistake of selling out. Feel worthless. Lots of evil told to them. They just want to get out. They done gave people heart-attacks dressing in women clothing, then talking like men. Their faces will tell of progress. They trust that I will come on time. They're angry. Whites angry dresses as blacks for survival. Common sense: they want to get out. Feel I should do more. Kid a time manager. Some Amera blacks had no idea of the hell in Afr. (pretending to be from Afr for their survival. They like me and want me to come back. Are still working their way out.

Find These parents can't believe their huge families are trapped in the passage.

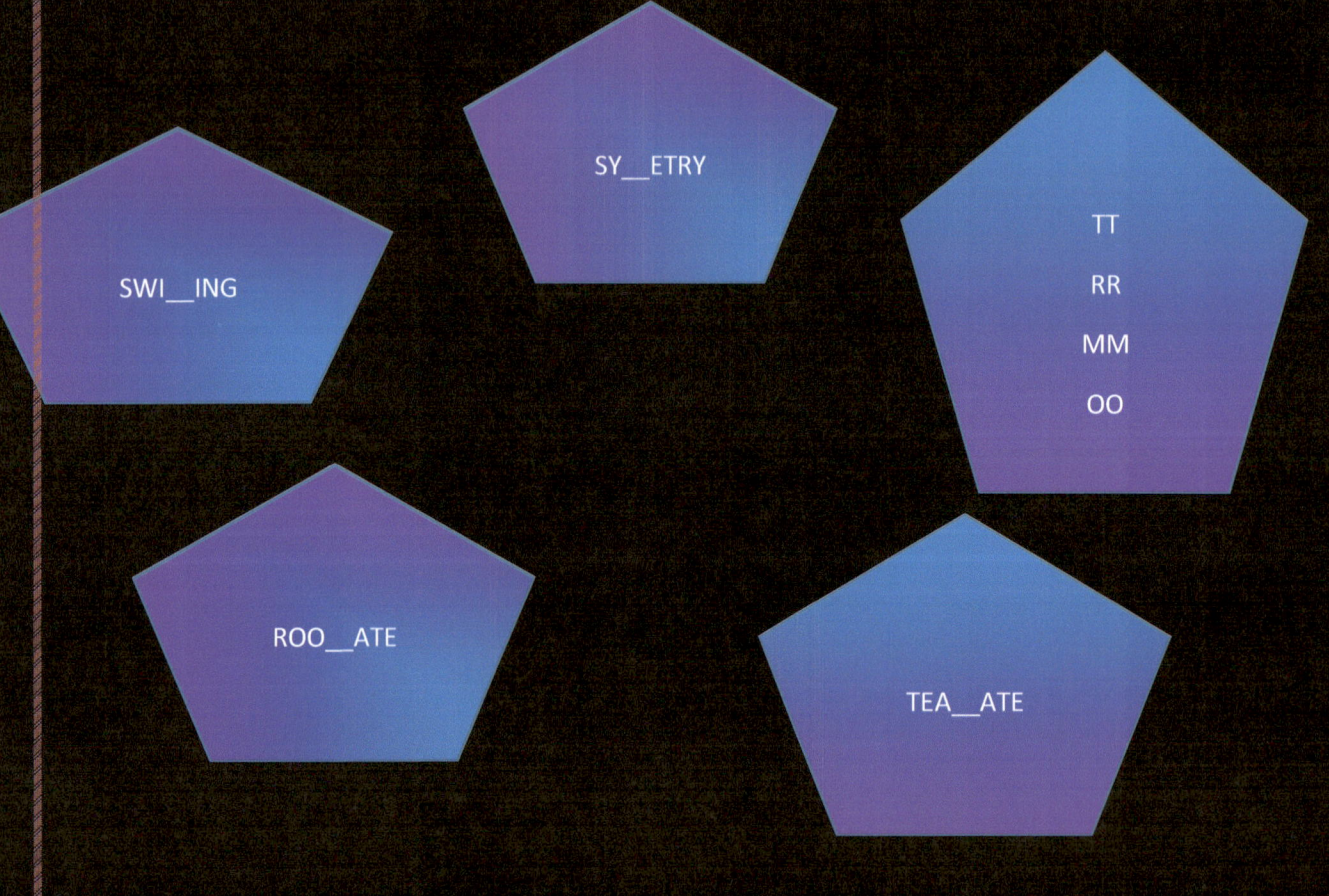

SY__ETRY

SWI__ING

TT

RR

MM

OO

ROO__ATE

TEA__ATE

They're getting more sleep. Men that think they're women, think they are greater than women that were born women. Don't think we are a human species. They do know they've been illegally violated and this material is something only a rare individual can think of; they could've never done it. Remembering clips. This up and down rollercoaster is on my nerves. Trying to get a grip on the time I visit them. Did they give up on working their way out? Animal cemetery. Several times going the wrong way. No way to distract the beast. We don't know what the route out looks like, but there is a way out. A bathroom. They have made these people hate each other. Taking so long – they're at the bottom of the Earth. Can get smooshed. Still acting helpless. Desperately want out. Still doing things to let the helper know they are loyal to being prostituted above ground. Every time I visit the, monsters distracted.

Find Several times going the wrong way in the passage.

Whether you want to be alive or not, somebody had you. Don't be selfish. People snapping out of hard trances. Kids shut up. The brick, the office. (speck by speck). Moving things. Making more room for the exit. They let someone raise their last borns and didn't let the other sibling go around him or her. They didn't know what was wrong with them. Butterflies. Tomorrow a better day. Camp. Scriptwriting. Webshow that can be continuous. Career. Connections 2. Red Gold. Play many characters. Trailers. Me on cover. Type. 6/13/19 completed. Started over on the fast. 6/14/19 2 lemon cakes. Egg foo yung. 2 shrimp egg rolls. Strawberry lemonade at 5:30pm ate cashews and pineapples. Spicy chicken sandwich and fries. Hoes would. Vine. Not going to start over. Pay attention to diet. Fast. For the full 40 days and see weight loss. Or how many times I give in and cheat and see gain. Or loss. 6/15/19 after 6 ramen with grilled chicken and more from Hoes Would. And High Forest. 6/16/19 nachos. Lemon cake. Tajin on pineapples. 6/17/19 shrimp craver, red beans and rice, biscuit, strawberry soda. Apple pie. 6/18/19 chocolate bar, strawberry soda, egg foo yung, chow mein, 2 shrimp egg rolls, small bag of chips, ice cream waffle cone. Novels. The Jazz Player. Scene. Or. The Jazz Dancer. She hears the instruments and her body movements are amazing. Delana Joe. Poisha Mandeling and the terrible, atrocious, foul, heavy drinks. There's something in these fucking drinks. Something that makes them sit in you like food. Maybe it clogs up or some shit. But these drinks have something that stick to the stomach and make it bloat and other foul shit. It needs a few days to digest and shit out instead of piss out. #1 artist.

Find 6/18/19 chocolate bar in the passage.

Kids in how many years? Way more diseases than noted. Everybody's wired differently. In their brains. These are their friends. Get rewards based off what I do. It just keeps getting deeper, the story. Why wouldn't I make some of my family celebrities? Got here just in time and couldn't save anyone? Have robots follow them in? A prostitute. They look like nerds or the meteors. Who the hell could have 41 kids? Said all bad at first. Light girl at store. I was in the car with. 17 celebrities. Short red haired wig lady on the bus. Girl holding baby. 1 bun like. Tour I see. Sound. Crazy. Girl at recycle place. Looked exactly like. Younger.

Find Kids in how many years in the passage.

Drill it in. Doctors. Put in Connections 2. Freeing man and womankind from the bottom of the damn Earth. They are surrounded by beasts. Knowing who the community and the enemy are. What happened to the world/people in it/the money system? The book. The exit routes (still reading minds and recording person by person. Step by step. Daze. Daisy. Day by day. Where the hell is this money coming from? How the world was created. There is a God. Everlasting life. On Earth. Is it possible? Or was it possible before people started creating their own things to put in the body? What I made? How I made it. Don't need to go anywhere. Everything's right here in California. Taste, sight, smell, touch, hearing. Weight, drugs, lighting, fresh water, fire smell helps get rid of the dead bodies smell, smoke smell, gunshot sound. Pain given. They're chipped. Knows exactly who to hit. Snapping them out of trances. Will reunite with family. Will go to the lab. Holograms. Different clips, people, colors, etc, give off different scents. 2hrs dance, automatic live thoughts. 2 hours videos, step, one hour walking. Common sense they want to get out as soon as possible. And tastes and other senses. Hoes Would. Now they know this is what most people wanted to happen to them. Some had kids and didn't let them be influenced by the older ones. They didn't know what was wrong with them. Why people would throw them away. Rock bottom. I said they just needed to see me and would snap out of suicide. I ain't nobody. Every time I think of them, my thoughts become unstable. I dealt with these people to figure out what happened here. Snapping them out of insanity. Message: We look good and can get anyone we want, so we can do whatever we want. They have kids they did not influence but it is very clear they can influence them to do wrong. Age. Birthday. To see what they could be like. Hope of getting someone's attention. Bottom line, without getting their asses beat, they would still be mean people. Follow them out. Hopes that child would come back and get them. Lots of dead bodies falling. These people are crowded as fuck. Movement: when make a visit. Clues and openings revealed. Get to a point where knowing this way of living is all the way better than those underground. Mean people don't look good at all to me.

Find Lots of dead bodies falling in the passage.

There is no piece that is anyone took that is needed. Just another way to let them know I don't need them. Oh, they wanted help so pretended to take something. Make solid ground. Facts. Drill it in. Mandatory. I said they were down there shooting each other. Beasts have things or were. They invaded? The King. They're the lowest of the low. They're the lowest of the low. Sold out to KKK for money but given nothing but pain. Told they're only good for sex and that's what they're using and thinking they're lying at the same time. To still feel like they have some worth. They want people to hurt in their private areas. Programmed thought. Specific date for money. They can't sleep. Still have to work. The fact remains: No they don't have to die for it. The fact remains: they were good to no one but who they chose and needed help from people they treated like nothing. Their argument: we're human. The smart people's argument, they think we're still stupid. They would not help us. Just keep nutting. They just want to get out. Sometimes people in there blank out and try to kill them. Including their family. My thought take me to different people. Some have been in there longer than other. All types of issues. Diseases every day. These mutha fuckas should be willing to sacrifice a lot (more than a child) headaches. We'd be down there. Supposed to be down there eating all types of nasty stuff and smelling all types of bad things. They'll search for relatives and the enemy but no one else until time goes by and they get their sanity. (Enemy in their possession (money) (a good living). Back! Visitation. Work, sleep, eat. Rescued family. They've had to shoot and cut themselves. This place will never be the same. Sex with beasts. Smoke does not belong in the body. The forgotten people. The plane fell.

Find The fact remains: they were good to no one but who they chose in the passage.

Chains broken. Someone survived. Father and son maybe 2. They're itching. The only way to not itch is to be licked by the monster. The beasts know they need it. Afr seen all types of beasts created. When get the money. Money. Debt. Taxes. Eviction. Phone. Internet. Electricity. Gas. Water. Court costs. Birth certificate. Need flying license. We. And have boxes to check off what was completed. Storage place. Can just use this one right here. Car. Backpack. Wallet. Prepaid cards. Invest in my books. New email. Transfer works. Emails. New. Dentist. Body wax. Hair and nails done. Pay credit people to get things off credit report. Car, apartment, bank account. When get apartment, games. Don't fly anywhere.

Find Someone survived in the passage.

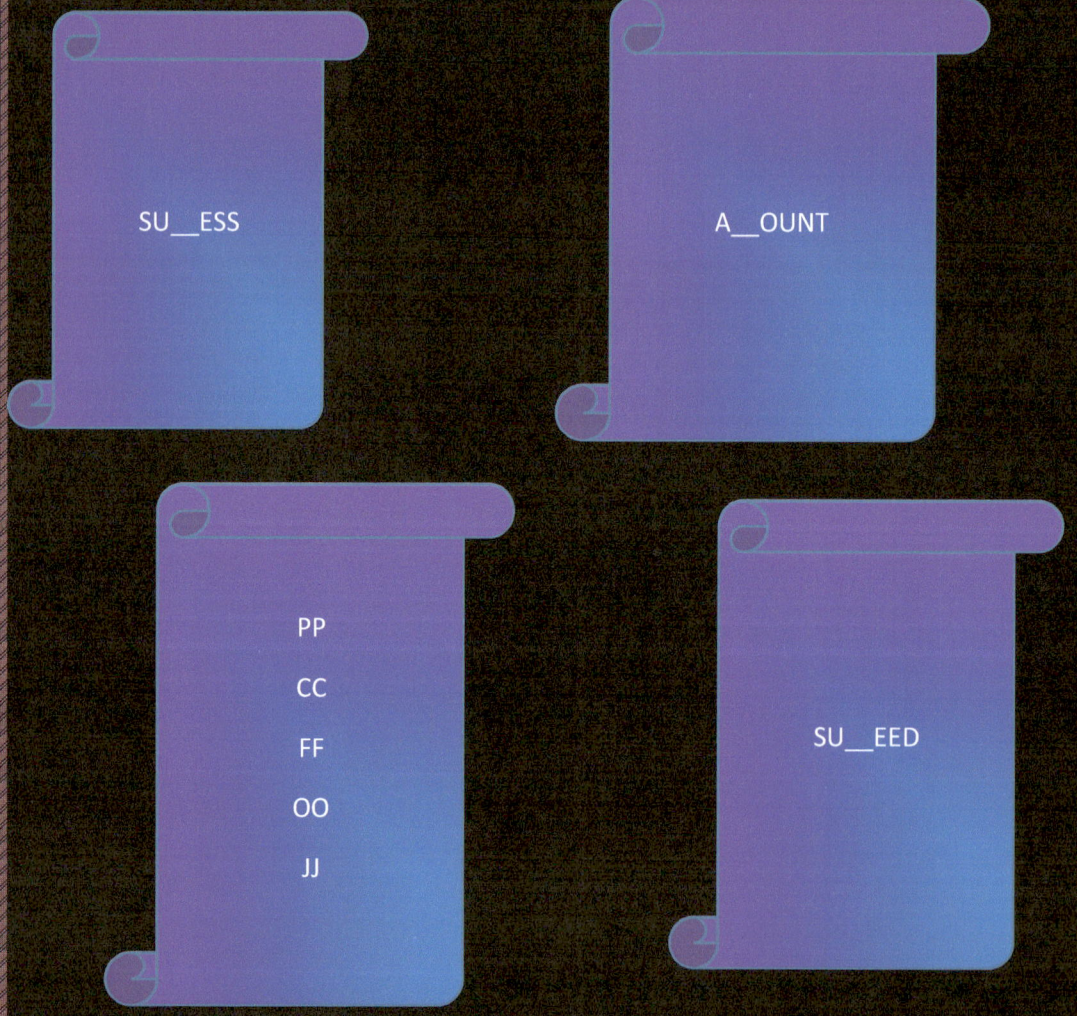

SU__ESS

A__OUNT

PP
CC
FF
OO
JJ

SU__EED

Parks and Wrecks. Dance, step, videos, live thoughts, walking. Everything's all right here. When time starts – 2 years a minimum of. Miles to go how fast they can work. There's no telling where other wastes will come from. You mutha fuckas have us severly fucked up. I'm using these robots to use me as an example on why people would want others to just die. Yelling, "That pussy stank," to a female and not caring AT ALL how she feels. Yelling it just cause you don't like the way she looks or what she has on. The library. If you love me. Kittens. The bus when cousin pulled in whoops. Ken. Drive. Man with beard. Coach. The point. They're dressing up as other people/animals to survive. Some have to shoot each other in the head. Shoot themselves in their heads. To grasp if they're alive or not. I'm ready to shout out my skin. There's 43 of us. 45 including my parents. To know what family is going through. All that hell at once. Stabbing yourself. To clamp on heart that life still needs to go on when the thought of these people comes up. While they were going crazy, insane, they began to remember to speak things that happened to them. All this hell. The beasts annoy each other. 12:47PM. Child gets shot when answers are wrong. Daily routines to keep the beast happy. Ways to keep getting further in the game. Escape. This is what my family is supposed to be going through. The beginning. Trifling women too. What junkyard could create such beasts? What laboratory? They talk. The den. Clothes. Laundry room. Metal containers by kitchen, maggots, cats, mice. The machines. The hallway was in. the man kiss 2 grown men. Black. The story and what they did to their kids. Had similar features. Toilet overflowed with blood. The kitchen floor. Bathroom. Said R and J. Koolaid in the hair as dye. The cop that came to the house. Son. Movie. Caps. Singers. Customer. Favorite cousin. Hair place. The shooters names. Food place. Palace. (All the issues). "see me". The other dad's lyrics. Willie. Ushers.

Find The cop that came to the house in the passage.

Movement. Somebody stole 300 dollars from her. How you gonna hate on me? Anyways I'm more bigger than you. Age? Money has a specific date. At the festival. Even. Friend took me too. Singer at church. On bus with a stoned looking. Met when she was homeless. Hair. Si. Come on. 2 brothers. Worker and facial at the talent show. (ran into the wrong side of the glass) picked me up at the mall. Went and bought panties. The corner store in the mall. Pregnant at 13 years old. Cousin came to visit. Knee. Got panties. River lived across the street. She liked and wanted to give head to the boy who had the house by the forest area we would cut through to get to another neighborhood. The same shit they would've done to them.

Find Money has a specific date in the passage.

Said people knew they needed help and would walk right by them. Address and people telling the story. Puzzle. Confirmations. 5-26-19. 18:1-7 Will take care of you. 9:10. God. I can feel the Earth move. Said they need to hop into their girly bodies. Had/have to act in ways they don't want and for some that's being/acting like a man should or would. And they're a man. Just me and you. Holograms. Automatic in different place or when think of it. Are automatic. Time frame freedom will take. Depends on them. Approximately 2 years when start the repetitive system. "It's the eyes." Kid at school. Rookie. Amateur. Hurting their siblings in trances so the beast won't eat it. Erections – everyone can see (they are naked.

Find Are automatic in the passage.

Directions. Beach station. Instructions. Pacific. Specific. Meeting girl couldn't say it. Until debt paid off. Car wait until can get a bank account. Say it. Reminded me of. Sit down. Girl talked about back pains was there. She was in my math class. Talked like. Parks for dance. Computer. Camera. Clothes. Shields for street parking. Pay someone to use their parking spot. 24 hour gym passes for a night? Hair Body wax. See ow. Fruit. Nope. Correct Sean. Officer. How old is the youngest? Chris. 3032. No one cares about them. Too evil. They don't have to die for it. Bottom line. They did need an ass beating though. Years in the trash. Fucking beasts. 13 years beneath the ground. Marvin. Chips. Months. Addresses and people telling the story. Puzzles. Confirmations. They're going out better leaving sarcasm. The ones they didn't influence are the ones they're trying to get help. These people really aren't shit. They have lost to their enemies. Be confirmed. Some are playing smart. They don't have to die for it, but they should've definitely watched their backs. Mask on. Test subjects. Slave – Trash. The ? is: what good are they? Helping the lowest of the low. Don't rely on anyone for help. They can't. These people are at the bottom of the Earth. Some have more stability of mind. They've been through more. And not sold out? Much. Many, more than you think, sold out to the KKK for money. Worst decision of their life. Whites out's marching, coloreds. Giving them more pain to get out the way. They're bitter the KKK betrayed them> yes. Some whites sold out to the KKK for money. A club party. Age. Birthdate. Weight. There was a listener. Pay debt – sometimes $200 and sometimes $400 at a time. Get it out the way. Think of dealers and all they have. Have excuses. A whisper in my head. Los someone valuable. An oath takes. Taken. Said these people didn't care about dying. Who'd have thought? The slaves. Real. Everyone I've been watching on television. Some people regular people playing dumb and like they were poor.

Find Some have more stability of mind in the passage.

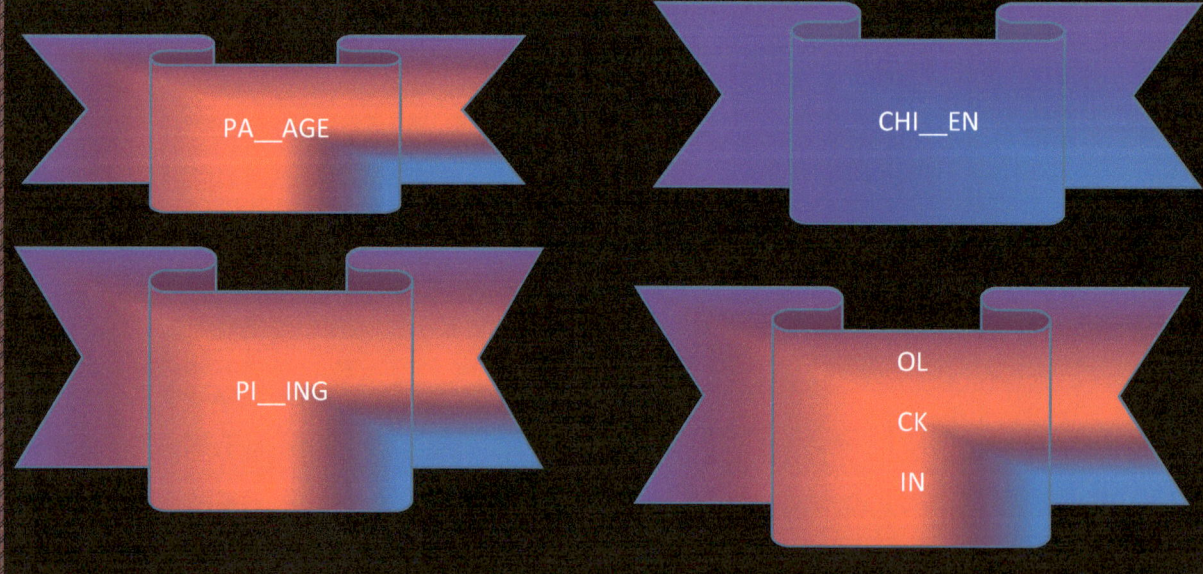

PA__AGE

CHI__EN

PI__ING

OL
CK
IN

My heart would tank. The truth is necessary. Truth: All evil you say/do to people you need to pay for. Adultery – don't get married. This up and down rollercoaster. Is that beautiful lady my real mom? They'll remember any breaks. I should care because… The Point – to somewhat feel the area they're in and what they've been through. A different kind of person. It's time to let the platform go. I thought it was a gift, but this is all the people, or amount of people, people that go insane see. The point – to somewhat feel the area they're in and what … A different kind of prison. They don't got to die for it. Crimes never punished for. Scalpel led to the club. (lady at the bar) I've paid my dues. The class. Chris. Smart people. Do I have 43 siblings? She couldn't say it. Leave the light skinned versus dark skinned shit for the Nothings. People have killed over things like that folks. Someone said it and she heard. The club. At the door. The meeting. Math class. Be specific. Missing in action. As long as they make progress, they feel somewhat better. The want for what I need and not getting it, but every day something tells me I will get it. Every day is a battle. Can't decide if they're good or bad. Thought control. Them when someone's brain shuts down. Every day. Beneath the area, will help. The people beneath F C S W. get the job done quicker. Enemies they're looking for. Telling their kids their beauty is why they're trapped and nothing more. They're kids haven't been good to anyone. Making it seem like they're alright. What is that? Mellowing thought. Sold out to the KKK. All beneath the area. Un – stationary thoughts. Mixed thoughts. Thoughts overlapping. This t type of unstoppable evil. Evil Minds. Common sense, they want out. Know what's right, but mind still juggling with other options. My family. And all robots left? No. God wouldn't allow that. What the hell is that? I can't keep a stable thought on if these people are good for anything. The hood needing a living. Bitter at living situations. Golddiggers. Volunteers. Distractions. The beast can go on for days. People crack for all types of reasons. Bulimia. Anorexia.

Find Be specific. Missing in action in the passage.

That have all our information. Then get these jobs and just start messing up everyone's life. They have visions they're being hit by someone that's not there. Ok. Time to snap back into my regular looking forward ways. Projections floating around my head. They should, the regular "gifted ones" that give me more clarity come naturally but the platform is done so I can feel my weight on this Earth. Lastly, starting to recognize who my real family is. There's a lot of us. Myself is trying to keep me a float. Robots my kid self put together. Away from suicide with mellowing thoughts can't keep a stable thought. Experiencing what is going on in their minds beneath the world. My future conscious. I really am that kid. That kid that experimented with so many things to come up with something to fool a beast and get rid of the fuckery it was causing. My future conscious walking around.

Find Projections floating around my head in the passage.

They keep having episodes that they will get out and don't. Brains keep shutting down and all the chaos they can remember at times comes back. Trained, to believe they're stuck down there. Why should I fear for my life off of what I write? All types of crazy people out there folks. Let's play hard ball. Just making more space. They keep trying to kill one another; they have to make each other more mentally ill to stop. A circle. Bricks. They take turns moving from spot to spot. Do to others what you want them to do __ -. But non one would have came up with the, this and people tried not to search for those they don't know. Embarrassment. Girls more. Boys snap at them. Too much blood. There's a whisper in my head. It's a fact. These people just completely weren't shit. They know they need to get out. Lowest of the low. Still takes time. Cures. Unknown. Sleeping with beasts. Bladder issues. No drugs. Acted like animals for years. Burning.

Find Sleeping with beasts. Bladder issues in the passage.

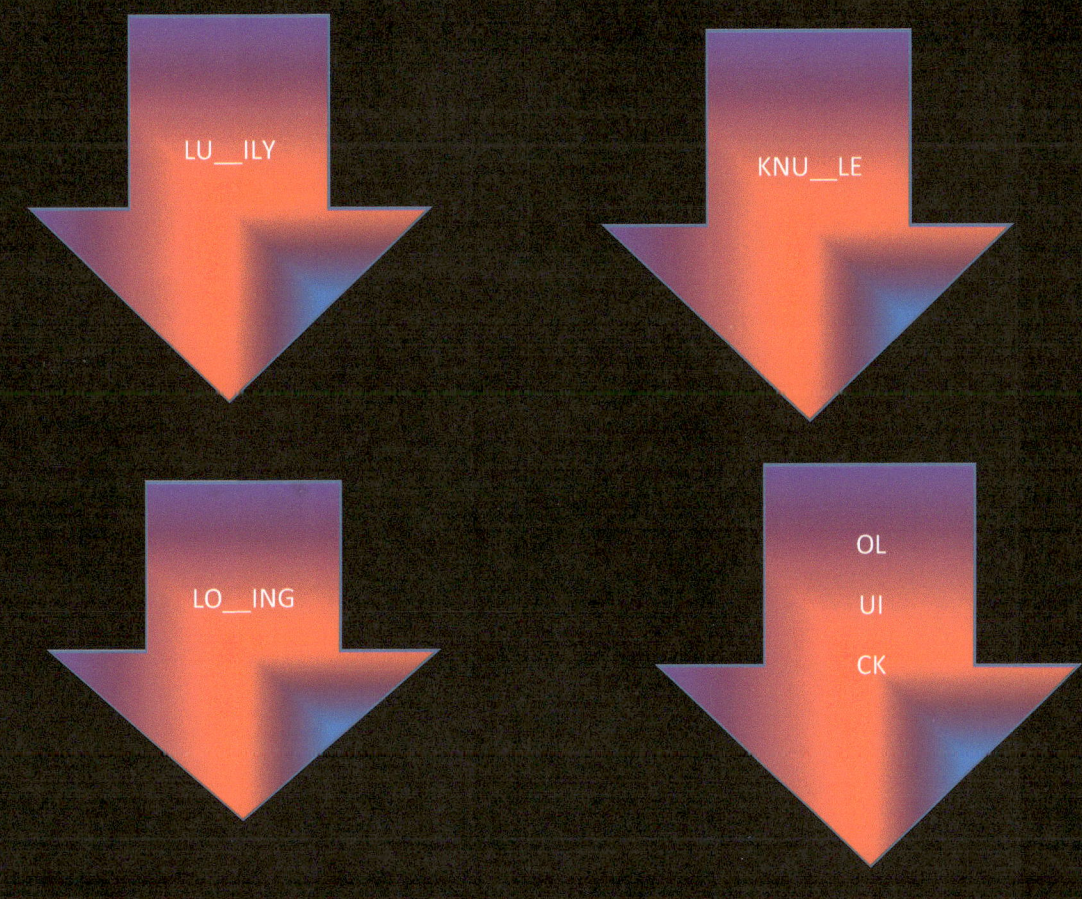

LU__ILY

KNU__LE

LO__ING

OL
UI
CK

It's like the voice in my head keeps making me have ups and downs. Phase. It's teling me I will have money so go eat out; my mind says. Would make the voice get on my nerves to write things I know my future self would want in my book. Don't eat out because I want to lose weight, but the voice knows I still have money worries so it keeps yanking my head to eat out; it, well the voice thinks it knows I will have a steady way to work out when I get the money I don't have, so it keeps telling me to eat out. I'm floating. Sometimes I feel like a water bubble. Programmed thoughts. Due date. All signs high. (solid) things pull right in front of me, yet still I have doubts. Descending to put weight beneath. My family went crazy when I was going through phases. Angels versus devils. It's like every part of the body, things.

Find Descending to put weight beneath in the passage.

They need information from thugs, but they won't give it to them because they think they will get left. The build up of gas in my body from fast foods made of certain products. The sound – no way to diminish it. Keeping air in my stomach. Living organisms and things in the food that make it sit in the stomach and not digest fast enough. Hooked on it. Hard to let go. The beasts wants to get out. War games. 1. Sold out to KKK 2. Jokes about the less fortunate 3. Angry at times that they're not the opposite sex. IT HURTS LIKE HELL. 4. Thieves. 5. Homewreckers. 6. Liars – about liking people (especially the same sex when people fear telling other people) 7. The want to fight the opposite sex 8. Incest (then their kids get bothered in their pants and go to school getting on people's nerves. Tease grown people. People to dumb to know this stuff. 9. Gossipers 10. Act gay when (happy) when they don't like someone. 13 years in the trash. How the hell is my family hoping around from robot to robot? The eyes: dressing in the skin. They can see what I project out of my eyes. I have robots clipping my brain to forget and remember certain things. Distract me to go certain places. Time set for money/ all that weed was in the trash. Yards. July 4th is coming up. Allen. Willie. Puzzles. Codes to unlock the past things that have happened. Confidence in the money. Can't be given all the information at once. Getting some head. Clothing brands. Brought me a fake bill. The bus stop by the library. Fake money table. Keep saying he's the man standing in front of the tree when I was young. Head coach. The toy chest. The theater. He was on the screen and in the audience. Real. The bag going up the hill when on my way to get my check. Work to get check. Address. The track. House. Domain in math, no mean, median, mode. The middle of the street. Barely hanging on.. Every facial giving off a different answer. Diseased in a different way. Drill it in! These people are dead. Need to cope. They weren't good for anything. This is all bad. Relationships down there. 21 in eyes. 34 reversed beginning. Girls feel really terrible during puberty.

Find Distract me to go certain places in the passage.

Certain stations for them to go to use the bathroom. Kids. Each robot can morph into any person. Plays. If can save myself, definitely saved family. If anything, the escape plan is already done. – Now they just dig. It's a game. Many players. Map: board game. Robots. Cards. Move forward. Breathing/alive. Projections work. Movement. Freedom. Weight. Fast. Only water between certain times. This is the only way to lose these thighs and this pouch. Stomach. Weight. Water only. Food. Would have been done or close to done losing 8 pounds by now if I would've started the first time I said I would start. Potato salad, small bag of chips, juices, lemons. Strawberries. Pineapples. Lemon cake. Early morning. Church. Hot chips. Fish. 5/30. 6/30. 6/2. 6/7/19. Deal with hunger pains! Unhappy every time I eat. To get the full story. Circles and bricks. Didn't get the chance to experience any real people except family. And still figuring out who they are and have to get used to their faces. They are all dead. Real name. people are dead. Dead man's hill. Only you. Qwan. Car. Songs that make your body rock. Songs giving me that feeling. Of a certain time. The movies. Projecting in my face. I have a lot to figure out. I can't go on thinking. I know I can't go on thinking these people are alive. Maybe they are! Maybe I'm still playing with my mind. I know they're in pain. That popstar. Hearing, sight, touch, taste, smell. Transference. They on the damn ground. Project remembrance. All of this to wake up to this realization. Answers to what? What happened here? Schedule. The money and what to do with it. Whole world has been down there 10 years or more. It hurts using my time to figure this out. Someone had me. I'm not suicidal but I need to know what these evil people wanted to do to me. Sometimes I feel like they love me, and have trust that I will be back and free them. Not just playing around because I'm keeping them alive. Heartrate. The visotros. Boats.

Find Pineapples. Lemon cake in the passage.

Vines. Drugged population toys til death. Still could have kids. Had drugs. Vaccines. People like video games. A vision board. How to get them back above ground. Didn't tell their children arranged relationships. Human beneath. The money game. People fucking up the world. Robots. Purple dress. The bench. The blue and grey shirt. Square cut out. Bit lip. Boy so fines. Driver get off. The route. Skating rink fight. Club strippers on stage. Drink. Tried to make themselves look like other people with shit. White shirt, black pants. These people dressed up as other people. Put on fake skin to try and survive. The library. Fell out my chair. Candles. Blindfolded. Someone touched my ass. Learn things the hard way. Class did presentation on nasty. Taught me a dance. How it will be made known what I came up with. Coolinda. Keep in mind. Time lapse. How this material was made. You feel like you're at the concert. I said they had to kill people for space. Lies saying they know someone that's coming to get them. They blank out and give performances for the entire place. They're naked. Use tampon strings to try and make things. He dressed as her. (to live or wantingly) he was chipped. I said parents were being hard on their kids and pushing them to do better so I would watch again. They want to be free. I said they had to kill people for space. Clips will unleash different places all over the worls along with packet. To free everyone. That keeps. What the hell is that keeping me a float? Minds always on suicide are ridiculous. How did that happened. Confidence the money is coming. Trying to understand theirminds pain. Want to get bitter, than a pinch of sanity. I know better than to commit suicide. Having full demonstrations. That the money is coming and it's still not here. What I want every single day. Punished the word. With no reliable place. Expecting a lot to be given to me for no reason. Hardcore. Saving the lowest of the low. Last priority from mankind. Worldwide hatred. Coolinda. Will any of these people be able to help whenever they get free? No. them trapped beneath – people whining and frustrating everyone else. Kids crying because they can't sleep. Being yanked out of it. Want to be free. Fights breaking out they're so frustrated.

Find What the hell is that keeping me a float? in the passage.

Making more space. And getting more air. Space air. The air. Ambidextrous. The spelling. First word. She got it wrong. Robots telling me the story of what happened to these people. These people got so low that the made promises to be good to whoever freed them. Anchorage. Ligament. Glide. Can survive down there for so long. Dainty. 1/25. 2/22. 3/16. 4. 5/7. 62. All that I have is yours. Dainty. Tainted. These people want you to experience all the mental illnesses they have. And they've gotten good at it collectively. Meaning if I look at five clips, then at someone else's, they'll know how to react or what to say after that part of the chain because they've been trapped and bitter for so long. 6:05pm. July 2nd. Have a good one folks. Coolinda. Are these people trapped down there? Could've saved my family but they didn't love me. Sike. It hurts so bad. But the platform. Look how good it is. It continues to tell me what happened to the world. It's continuous. How could I do that? It keeps adding more and more to the story. For various ways to still enjoy this life. It's the only way to stay afloat. To stop from jumping. Life goes on. If they were still here, they would not care that I was trapped or dead. Even if they did know me. That date. Hall of Win. Deuces. There's plenty of ways to carry on. With no one. There's sex toys. Ha. Good food. That's not enough. But real talk. Through it all, I need to carry on. The dreams. And learning everything that happened, it's needed, at least thus far. The truth to carry on and understand. Babies able to be had or not. Music reminding me of them. Music reminding me of it all. A feel of real humans. Understanding why things, the world's places, necessities are the way they are. I've done too much. Created too much to just jump. 11:10AM because of how fucked up things are. Fall in love with myself. The projections that come out of me. So cool. Need to carry on. I said I created one. This place is too beautiful. Work, do what I love and enjoy making it.

Find It hurts so bad in the passage.

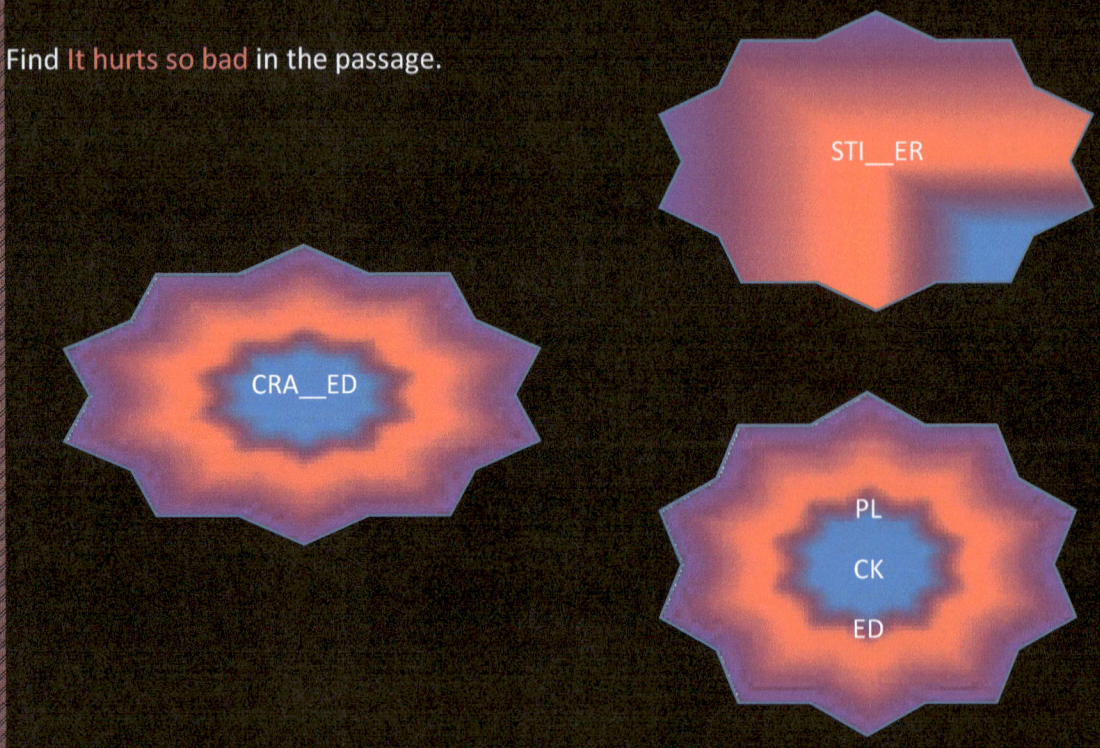

STI__ER

CRA__ED

PL
CK
ED

The only way to figure this shit out is to play this damn game: 1. How I made everything, 2. Where the lab is, 3. Everything that happened with me and my family's separation. And 4. How to get the complete story on what happened here on Earth since the first humans (the book) how the hell why would I care if no one else is here. Closure. Maybe. Instinct: family wants them free. Friends and other relatives down there. The automated way of freeing humans from beneath the Earth. Forget about the traps. Animals really put on human skin. This guideline. What I'm writing is the study guide. Ushers. Willie. Liquid that kills shit. Diminishes it. Kids bottles. Binkies. They're stocking up. 2nds. Egg hunts. Candy. Hidden money. The cereal factory. The surreal fact story. Big piles. Drugs. Alcohol. Fresh air rooms. How far they get... fresh sanitary things. Napkins. Clothes. Food/water. Space. Hair products. (comb, brush) toys, towels. Batteries. Flashlights. Razors. Lighters. It's a game. I'm making them do things so I think a certain way. How much does it take to clamp something so severe in your brain like freeing them or they'll die or your life is nothing and you'll struggle the rest of it? To get a feel of these people. Things to build with. Tables. Bigger and Better things fall every day. Banks. I said. Really rights. . Huh. She walks right up to me at the vending machine. I said she would transform right in front of me. In front of everyone's faces. For that to happen I have to watch her every day. Coolinda. I have to keep watching the videos of them. Good and bad. And lose the extra pounds. Melody. Rain. Let it fall. Don't forget about me. We can't believe this is what them mutha fuckas would've done to us. These are some good . There are some good Afr. Mixed in bad ones. The baby left behind instructions. All clips created already. They will flow out at the right time. Tired and Bored. Deeper and Deeper. Real Reactions. They're eyes are in the robots. They're not telling mine what to say. I said they defended me when someone talked about what made me insecure. So I guess now I should let their evil selves in my house. They sing live. It's automated if they will say the right words. They're eyes are implanted for disease control. They're chipped. Butterflies.

Find Flashlights. Razors. Lighters. It's a game in the passage.

A game. Mind malfunction. They become bad. They're miserable but better off than they were. All my creations will have my name on them. The faith: will own that mansion one day. It's a game. Board game. System game. I said these muh fuckas was in there fighting to keep from getting fucked. They have to shoot their kids. And parents. I said manevil was in there. They have to fight shit monsters. Monsters and computerized people down there too. I said people were in there dressed in different clothes. Lastly, them and the beasts that take care of them. They have to sometimes fight people that fall into trances. I said some people had to change clothes a minimum of 4 times a day. To eat, to not be beat. These people have been down there 10+ years. Some 13 and slaves on land for years with no help. Don't go off of their emotions. Just say doing everything alone. This is a game that will take me to suicide. The whole world — 10 years at rock bottom. They're working on their escape. Cries unknown. Can feel progress. They just want to be free. I hear him singing those words. Who invented music? And they are willing to do anything and die to get their loved ones free. They can't believe people would do this to them. They can't believe people could be so cruel. These people have a whirlwind of emotions. They go up and down from thinking they will be released. They have to do lots of evil to stay out of trances. If who I think invented music, then, well Coolinda can put voices in the machine. Some people are down there asking what else can they do. Some aren't going to eat any food. I'm giving them shots. Forced to. Some, him, that pop man, walks to danger sometimes to see if I will help him. Ways to tell a child is swallowing things he or she should not. In their urination. Shot for all types of reasons. Faces too sweet or too manly. Voice changes. Had sex with their enemies. No discipline. Betrayed. Can get 9 at a time out unnoticed. Or as days go on, they can get more people out. Naturally making people. Making people wish they were lighter due to what? Some don't have to go back. They work all night. Food delivered. Snuck in and ate. Did they kill all the beasts because they have fresh water? No. they want it alive. The gorillas. Now they talk and have to be convinced they are beautiful. Tired and bored. So they can torture it too. The Point. Many ways to think of them. So their minds can stay busy. So I don't get bored. Some people are trapped outside.

Find They can't believe people could be so cruel in the passage.

I'll keep holding on by a thread. Don't runaway. Barely holding on. I want the money now. Need big signs that the money is coming. Buildings, cars, robots, hair, clothing. Addresses. Think of how they feel. They want to be free now. They always need to keep busy. They always need something to do. A day without supply. C F S W. said some of them would let their kids kill them. They are trying to use sex anyways to bother the free. I'm the only one keeping them afloat. Keeping them with the big sign that they will be free on day. I'm also giving them something to do. This is really the lowest of the fucking low. Have to answer to zombies. Specific details. Addresses. Damn. Almost responding out loud. Damn. Need to get it together. Doing the exterior platform can hold me up. Scenery. Locations. Barely hanging on. Need to get a grip on my mind. This is about freeing these mutha fuckas and enjoying my life. These mutha fuckas are gnats. Some of the worst of the worst. Frost. There's plenty more people just like them. Large families the idea. Easier to keep up with. They've made it damn near impossible to enjoy anything here on Earth. A soulmate was not the idea. Water can run dry or not. I feel like I'm going insane when I do the platform, the visuals outside of my head. Some of it is a gift but with all this bull shit I'm trying to figure out, I feel like I'm going insane. It's a mental illness to project things. But a gift in some sense. The eyes. Unbelievable stories on how they were saved. All types of mixups found documents. Pictures. Letters buried. Found. Or made by truth telling beasts that can record that lived longer than their makers. Some beasts, computerized people killed their makers. Who would make something smarter than them? Pack. How far are they getting? Basketball Court. A basketballs court length a day or half? Rivers. Nile and Jordan. With everyone's help. Shift switches. Rotation. My mommy wants to see me. A feeling. My oldest brother. In red. Chris. Qwan. Would I put a clamp for certain responses so that I write in my book everything I need too? Yes. Roll down. Dead man's hill. Mommy lovely. Doll moves. Pitts. Weaves. Clothes. The groove. The grove. Waiting to breathe. Food. Sh! @ a kill. Ill. On. Noise. Ill. I Noise. Nose. Nosey. Or Nosy. See. Backwards. 1st bang. Many move. Many more missing people. More than one of. Celebrate. brities. 2nd bang. The release of the imprisoned beneath the ground. The news. Files messed up. Prior. They can feel me. What type of technology is that? They're in another location. Projection feelings. You're there I'm here. Thought. Though. Candy. Burgers. 7 years. 2 weeks. 10 years. Dents. Trists. 2020. 2021. 2022. 2023. Flawless. Deuces. Bus. Vines. Sunsets. Parks. Hall of Win. Will hurt. If not free, they can do the rest their selves. The help down there will make sure the date is legit. The holiday with friends.

Find Chris. Qwan. in the passage.

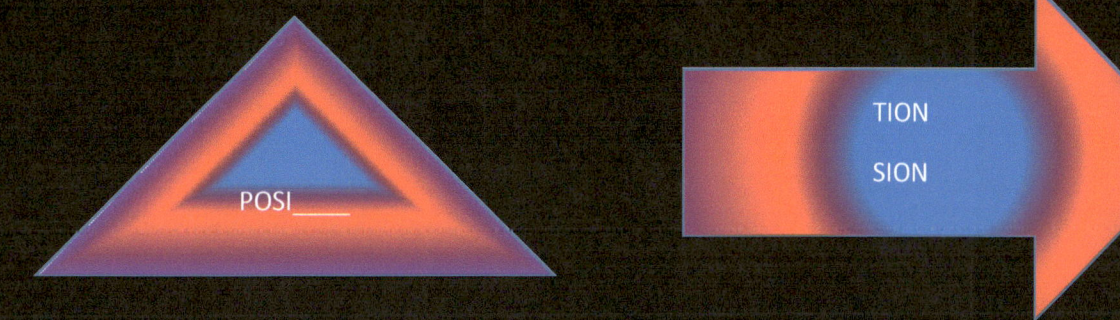

POSI____

TION
SION

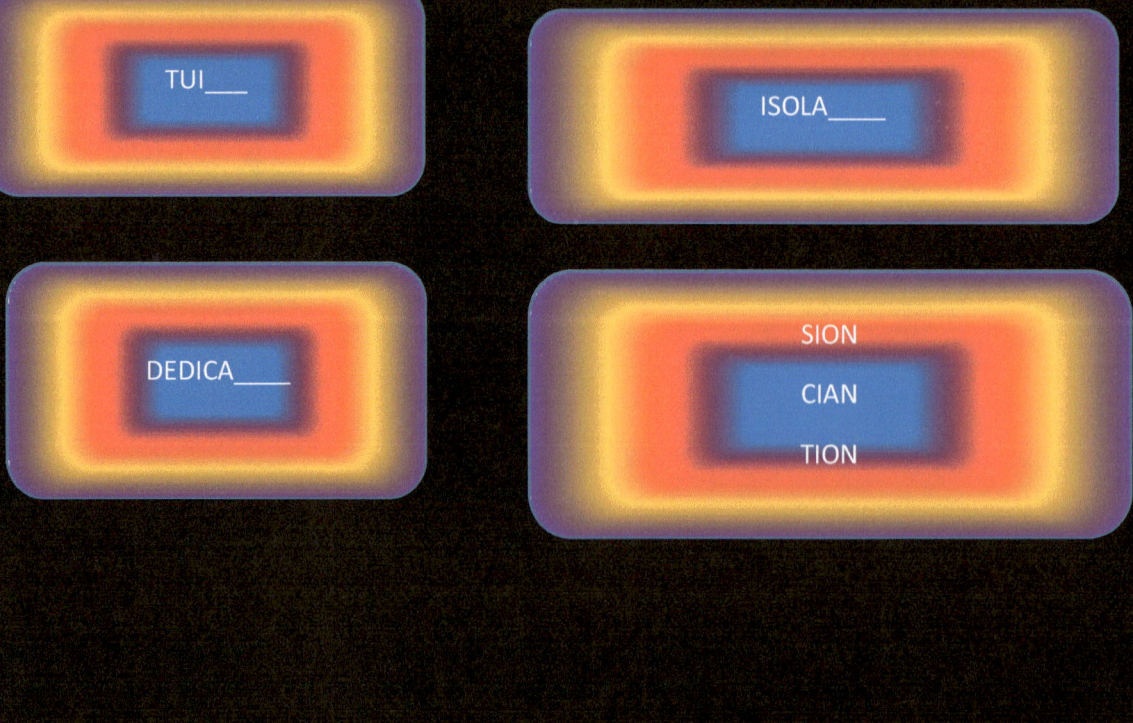

TUI____

ISOLA_____

DEDICA_____

SION
CIAN
TION

Mommy. 12:20. 13-20. 2:5. 6:4. It knows I'm about to get the answer right. Built up thoughts. It says the word I think when I think it. It knows I'm about to look down and will say the word on the page. Seeing someone then many images of them coming out. Seeing someone then they naturally make you snap into saying mean things about them. There's plenty of diseases out here folks. Never heard of. Some people probably see someone then the whole room fills up with projections, or just their imagination seeing things or batches of these people that aren't even there. Projections everyone can see from your body? Never. They think that everyone can see them. Some know not. Then all of this is for nothing. This game is viscious. A clamp at least to remain alive and not frustrated from no one being here. Human kind. Am I bargaining with these people? Do I have something they want? Come one. Come on. We knew those bastards would never stop until they captured every black. The stupidity, the sense that maybe a few had, that blacks weren't the only other race than white. Whites. Right. They wanted all other races trapped and slaves. Not just blacks. Maybe more frustration the darker they, we were. Camera time to know they're alive. Has this been what it is all along? Jazz music. He sat right behind me. Things here will lead me to things unwritten. The word or connections to all events are here. May be coded. Blatant weight change. All those notebooks. Money people right behind me. They drive the buses. Huge replications. The hotel. Airport. It's the end. They'll come above ground and mess more things up. This is the way to remember. It's all in here. Practicing what you will say before you say it, in terms of an argument that hasn't happened yet. Drove through town and picked up family, who I thought/think s my family and now it's like I'm dropping them off. Or they never were. Just what c d r t oo asked for. Saying things just to say them or sound like someone else and someone walks in and thinks you're talking to yourself. This embarrassment. It's all in here. Some clothes repeatedly. Robots read the mind of the last people alive. The ones to give the best story. The projection of myself saying it will kill me. Myself walking. They're all dead. All types of sex in front of, trances, brain shut downs, crowded spaces. In front of kids. Bad sentences making you do god things and reverse. If I lose this and someone knows it's mine they will wrong. Thoughts projecting out of me. All the information at once would kill us. The dreams are out of my head. My thoughts are out of my head. I'm watching them. Screaming responses. This is terrible. I need some company. People's faces causing you to be suicidal. Robots have to respon as the real person would with my personality. Something like that. I said celibate. Brities were my parents. The top ones. The posts – the pictures with nails and hammers. In the shed. If God wants me gone, I need to jump. Atmosphere answers. The mean faces. Singing live. All things I'd be experiencing. They're talking to each other with faces and voice changes right now with the projections.

Find This embarrassment. It's all in here in the passage.

FUNC____

TION

SION

CIAN

Where do the beasts fall into play? Oh well. This is a study guide. Waiting on that clamp that these people are alive or dead. Breathing at rock bottom. Another cycle outdoors period. I need to remember all of this. If these people are alive, they need to pay (the evil ones) I can't hug my family right now. Took something they need? Vine. A mutation. Boats. They could not get the whole population over to A. B. C. I said these people were hopping in their bodies. Surrendered to beasts. I can feel her heartbeat. Can't stay in the library all day. Robots in there with them helping them. Manevil has help trapped with the imprisoned ones. Beasts helped lure them under. Still need the story. Shit! I'll keep holding on to my strength. My mind is still venturing off. I need to remain natural when around others. It's like a wave. Glasses. See? Your mind just takes off and you can't snap out of it. It hurts like hell. Always. So fly. Love stop making me angry. I need my mommy. My real one. To raise me. I let the atmosphere and humans well robots do it. Learn things the hard way. Was it worth it? The only way to get rid of the headache is to accept that they are gone. The Point: to get a feel of these people. I can feel them some kind of way. Purple - breathing. Ice. Talking about some damn Crisis reach. Foxes. Pictures of wolves. High lands. Trailers. Mobile homes. Fire and stones. The mind. Only way to continue on is to get free, lots of money and revenge. Good company as well. Prison too good. We knew people wanted their hands on. You and I. Today terrible. The money will make me non chalant. The point: to drill in that they're alive and need supplies. Every day. Things so much easier with money. Keep saying that it's just me and my family left. How can that be? Coolinda. These people yanking me back and forth in my thought. We're talking the atmosphere robot organizations keeping me going alive. Things and people appealing to my 5 sense. The eeling when they first got food again. That cool image of me is here. This will have to be my stability. That cool girl is having a good time with a drink and 2 piece black set on and acting off my conscious. How I want her to act. It's different for everyone. Oh shit. I can't even focus on the videos I'm watching. I have to get rid of the images outside of my head. The platform thought. It made some people 3D. the truth. Damn. It's a matter of being in my right mind in front of people and the platform only when I'm trying to help the trapped get further. During that time. Damn. This is terrible. Who's in charge down there? Is the beasts laughing at them? Something's not right. You think the tv is talking to you. You think the people on it are talking directly to you. These diseases. Illnesses. Head bangs on wall taking people to a new normal. Illness. It's normal to them. It's crazy. They need to torture the slaves. They can't kill them all. It's a part of their natural being. They made it part of their genetic makeup. It's a habit. It's a drug. Robots telling me which clips to watch. This is too much. My mother is floating around me. Projections. My eyes or the computer? Coolinda. Or a disease? Bottom line: these particular people aint shit. They had kids they didn't teach anything. That was their last resort. A way to show they learned their lesson. A way to keep their families going. The gist. To get a feel of everything these people have been through. Uh oh. They're starting, the events they went through. The events they went through are starting to play out in front of me. The screaming. Cries unknown. Just what are they going through right now? A way to have someone come back and free them or follow them out. Just how did they get to rock bottom? Just who has them? I said I have to be mean to them for the beast to like me. It knows my gift. Some had kids. They needed more people. To sleep with the beasts too. The only way they got help to find their families is by dressing as someone else. I was just about to ask those questions. How did they all, with over 20 siblings get in the same part of the dump, sewer. They don't got to die for it. They're bitter and still using sex/their looks as a way to frustrate the free. The hell they put in others brains, they have to endure worse. Oodctrs. Volunteers. The buffet. Someone walked by with the shirt on. With it written on the back of their shirt.

Find They're starting, the events they went through in the passage.

Why worry about things that may never happen. This is about freedom. Food. Revenge. It'll take a while to get back to the top. They'll have to store food and wa ter. I'm supposed to be. Well I keep telling myself. I keep thinking I will help them and be well off. I guess my unknown conscious that's 7 days a head of me knows that I will skip a day if I don't, well it knows the information is not drilled in deep enough for me to continuously help these people. After all I am having issues trying to figure out if they're breathing or not. The disappearing act. The dump creations. Shit creations. Pet cemetery. Cemetery people. People created from, blood and living organisams. Manevil racist white people. Slaves that got free. Been in the same room for a while. Ample. Mentally ill people. People who crack for various reasons: weight, debt, cheated on etc. (they have identifiers on them). Skip a day. They'll run out. Found weed in the trash at the port. Air pipes. The robots followed them in there. 2 ways out.baby food. Candy. Cereal factory. Hidden cash. Big piles. Candy tubes. A whole box of apples found. Snacks at the school. Lunch, able. The lady at church gives me. Chicken. Beasts. Escapes. Crabs. Wagons of crawfish would bring home. Apples thrown by the tree. A way to keep things frozen. Oodctrs supplies. First aid kits. Aint shit to do. Exercising causes them to need another shower. Fire works. Can't over do it. Need supplies to save for the journey. Toys make too much noise. Pain relievers. Eating. Drugs. Alcohol. Will need drugs to put the beast to sleep during the escape. Responding in real life to things going on in their heads. Created scenarios and real things that happened. Pussy dolls missing. Those men that act like women that still want a penis, some captured by men that are bitter they don't have a pussy and the girly ways they have, the men that are bitter tried to over due. Something like that. Coolinda.

Find Toys make too much noise in the passage.

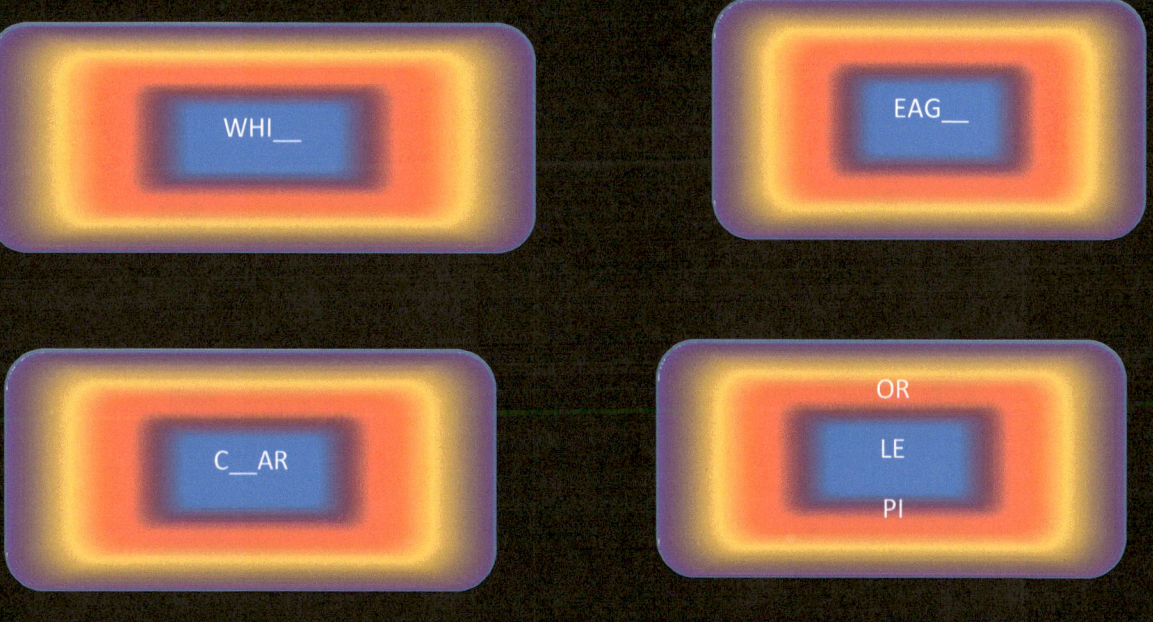

WHI__

EAG__

C__AR

OR
LE
PI

Soundtrack. Paid. 13:5. 8:44. Journal 5. Paid in. what's keeping them a float? Nothing. They keep going insane. The cereal. They work hard to clear space. Drugged to get the natural reaction to everything. The room controlling the world has been trapped since the beginning together. Couldn't have kids and it was decided it was wrong. Still trippin' off of how they still had kids as slaves. Realized their kids could live without all those shots. Geez, those people (the money) is following me around. Holding on. This game. Do I just accept that I will be up and down? All these years to find out this truth. Family separated. Homeless debt. Let's talk about goals. Not getting them done and the robots walking around in an order that puts me on a hell trip. Have no idea where this money is coming from or when I will get it. These people are mad as hell. Clips will be of the hell they've endured. They're surrendered to beasts. Vending (pipes). Certain pipes let go of certain things. Certain clips and certain combination of clips give off certain things. 10 years all at rock bottom. Some more, and slaves when they were above ground. 8 years old. My infinite number. No way. These digits keep moving. I mean it. Why would I choose these people to make bigger and they're not related to me. Hmm. Haven't been above ground in 10 years minimum. Damn. Not only slaves but no good air period. To mix with that shit. They'll do anything to get back above ground. We have to go backwards to figure out how everything happened. What the hell is that keeping me afloat. Robots. Flawless. Take it slow. They have those hard ass images in their faces every day. We've only just begun. That panel, their whole families can go, then they would kill themselves for mankind to be free and anyone else needed to keep the rescuer afloat. Done. Everything else will be remembered by what is already written. These mutha fuckas are a headache. You can't even consider the damn lies because they've done too much. Coolinda. They dressed as people that thought they were them to reunite. Meaning a crazy man said he was well, lets use me. A crazy girl thinks she's me, Coolinda, and I had to dress as the crazy girl who was looking like me and thought she was me, how do you do that, anyways to meet, reunite with a friend and relative and not get taken, I had to dress as a person that thought she was me. Coolinda. This type of crazy stuff. Left kids behind. They were walking around drugged. New identities is how they kept having kids. No way. Beatings. Slaves having kids under all that pressure. Even the free ones. Having children was alive or was there a third party? Or second party?

Find This type of crazy stuff. Left kids behind in the passage.

They need supplies, want to get out, will do anything to get out. Update license. Don't fly anywhere. Clips will let me know if they got further (closer to exit, more space) and accomplished more. Need to stay awake and not nap. Robots still teaching me what's going on down there. Need people for clips, to remember they're alive. Large families are easier to remember. Are the rights escorting people to the beasts? Blacks and whites. Need faith that the money is coming regardless of circumstances. They're being watched by the mentally ill. Rules: told when to sit down and shut up. They're trapped in their thoughts. They keep getting worse. Meteors turds. Animals. Robotic people. Robotic animals. Animals in human skin. People non-chalant – want to be opposite sex. It knows they will try to escape. They have to cater to the beasts. They're down there living normal lives and being friends with the beasts. School districts. Addresses. Fix resume. Add phone number. Personalize cover letters. Job searches. Give them new number. Random huh? Coolinda. What, hand sand, want. Wand palate. Palace. Place. Bat. Cat. 10. 11. 12. 13. 14. Common sense: these people want freedom. Will tear shit up when they get above ground. 10 years and slaves years above ground. Spend 6 hours with them a day. Need platform for 3D videos and to fell like I'm in the room Volunteers. Mandatory. Or they'll run out of supplies and have to start over. Vending is giving them everything they need. I'm barely staying afloat. They spazz out every day. They work hard to keep each other calm. All signs point to yes. Patience. Still have to wait. They don't have to die for shit they've done. The worse of the worst done to them. This shit just doesn't work out. Have to do ill things every day to please the beast while trying to escape. They have not had any fresh air. I'll keep holding on to these people. Said they thought I should tend to them 24 hours. Clamp in that they are alive. I'll keep holding on to them. Look into my eyes and see what I see. Dead bodies. Eating shit and drinking blood piss pulls them out of their sleep. These people really needed to be taught a lesson. All this damn arguing. Events that may never happen. They're stuck under there forever. Don't tell me the first time with the platform was only a phase or practice. Working on their escape. They won't give up. Visitation. Volunteers. The enemy is right next to them. I'm climbing on things. Enemy doesn't know they're in their right mind. They'll all die. Is why they're letting them get in the clips. They're not together. They're scattered in the 19 locations. Note. Searches. Taxes. Balloons. Balance call again. Directions or mail resume. Secretions. They're ill until free. They're permanently ill. Not enough doctors to even care for all of them. Pure frustration down there. Need to be left underground. Help so they can live as long as they can. I said they're acting ill because of beasts. No sign of life. I need to stay in my head. Why help these particular people and they're all headaches? Clamp to know they're alive. Their parents are giving them hell to perform well so I will come back.

Find Random huh? in the passage.

Slaves still to human enemies? Surrendered to beasts. They can keep track of the 22 platform. Said whites escaping and leaving black behind. The good ones because the blacks kept lying saying they knew stuff and didn't. They're headaches. Bitter since sold out to whites for money and it backfired severely. These people feel worthless. Extreme annoyance. Annoyance trigger. Hungry for freedom. It won't stop. Have to watch these and do platform. Then all of this was for nothing. I can get triggered to watch certain clips. What's keeping me afloat? Barely hanging on. Where is this money? Coach. They knew they were being recorded so they did things just incase their siblings were watching. Don't eat some days. They starved these people and made them walk long distances. Double letters. Do 10 a day. These people ain't shit and didn't touch the last ones, but we know they could be influenced by them. The want for freedom. Real. The want for lighter people. People revealing things about crushes, their deepest inner thoughts under trances. They kids shutting down and keep trying to rape theirs. Dreams and desires. Parents breaking down and revealing things about their children they shouldn't. Things they want to do to them. Brain shut downs. Temples. Hit hard. Bricks. Said whites drugging blacks. Making deals with beasts. Where the hell is the supply coming from? Beasts have. No The whites have the tapes. The ones of them selling out. Neighbors. Beasts regulators. Everyone tampering with the way out. Families divided. Down there with the people they've slept with their man or woman. People they've robbed. Brain shut down causing confessions. Set the neighborhood. The whole neighborhood slept together and everyone knows. The worst of the worst. Everyone found out because of connections in the things they said. Sold out. The videos are helping the good keep making space to the exit. I can hear her voice in the robots. She's that beautiful woman with that RnB/Pop Star. I saw a robot of him walk across the street and into the weed shop. Just greased my scalp. A game. Blocks. (people that are annoying, hard to look at, (ugly) voice. Everything. People will give off the wrong impression. The practice lines. They practice lines/for fun scenes. Coolinda. This game. When I need to play or need to pay attention, I don't think I have siblings. I need to change settings constantly. Just thought my conscious is making me need to leave and a robot said oh well. Hell trips. The men that killed the 4 year old boy or was itkids. Relationship issues black left white) matter or not. The men that want to be women and the women that want to be men. (cracked) slaves. Ample. Cracked and then messy ass people in general. Weight. Kids become mentally ill. First prisons. Businesses. Other trifling women. Oh shit. Now I have to go to the second robot to snap out of a hell trip. So the first one pinches my thoughts and says hell is on the way or death then the second one gives me the confirmation its not the case. Prettiest girls in the school. He stayed inside bitter all the time; his house became bloody. He wanted to be born a girl. Have a pussy and not a dick. He cut his dick off.

Find Down there with the people they've slept with their man or woman in the passage.

Days to the bottom of the Earth. They're better off. Chow mein. Good bye. Big at the church. I see a dress. Cold. Ton. Underground and my work ethic. Trip. Goodie bags. Virgin strawberry drinks. Any? Be rich any? R – Why ok. Vegas. Florida. We shall see. I said all these people were pretending to be robots. You and I. Capital. Capitol. Nosey. Nosy. No spell check on either. Song. Dctoors. Notes. The want/need for others to feel what you feel. Go through what you've went through.negative. sometimes good. I mean it. There was people here before, then they all got lured underground. The last call. Had to save 43 well 44 people. Truth or not. 45 people. Boys walk around like bothering girls. Girls. The ones that don't care. Boys walk around like. Just chill til the expexted. They're thoughts. Episode. Reading their minds. Not possible. Only the crazies will think there's two Gods. Thinking of someone and they project around you. I'm burnt out. Natural things. Midnight love making. Drugged so they can't die. Sounds snapping them out of it. Slaves still tried to find out what was wrong with their drugs. Boys walking around like girls. Turning on the ones that are closeted and not. Bothering real girls./? no thought control. Want them to go through pain like them. Slaves. A system. A test. Sold out. Naked all day. Shot because acting in ways people don't like. Strange. Find the shooters. Treat them wrong. Some got free. Are these men still together calling the shots. The green room. To friends. Room. Boom. Natural mind body shut down. Eating shit, drinking piss and blood. Eating dead bodies. This type of pain. Animals. Became free and people learned English off of sex. Huh? Winners of games. Champions. The courts. The course. Something always keeps me going. CTDRSOO. Ways to forget age. No one is here but us. Shots to the head. People arrangements. I mean it. These robots being sarcastic. Ways to let me know they ride for me later. This bullshit here. Puzzles. Codes and confirmations. Answers. The money schedule. What happened here? Help freeing man and womankind from the bottom of the Earth. Book edits. When get phone. Mail schools or go in person. Schedule. After books. Connections 2. Dance, live thoughts. Videos step. Walking. Choreographer. And Hannah. Allen. The packet will free the whole world. (innocent) favorite songs. How will I know when everyone (deserving) is out? Robots. Puzzles. Scenery, something. Will give me that answer. Understanding. They clean shit. Dead bodies. Piss and blood. All day. These people are beat. Stand there, just incase I come. 10 years stolen from all or more for some. It's all in the front. She had all those kids to get trapped (these people) It's all in the front. These people are alive. Facials: it's a game. I'm doing their facials somewhat to get answers. They want out now. They're making progress but know it will take a while to get back to the top. They're whooping their kids asses now. Need me to come back or they will become insane until death. Aint no sunshine if she's not there. They are. Common sense. In need and have desperation to be free.

Find Mail schools or go in person in the passage.

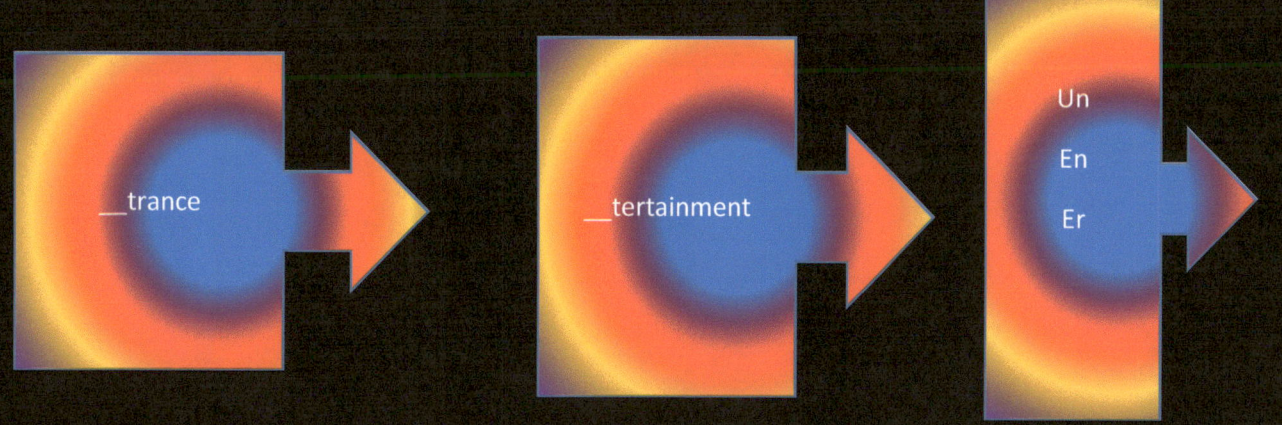

__trance   __tertainment   Un En Er

Finish putting in then study it. Scramble key words. Passions. That's a lot of books. Prison. Read. Airport. Resume for meeting. 3 pages. 2 equations. List words. Another idea. Unscramble it. Can put shapes or something on the page. Pick a time. Whatever sentence is act it out. Age and tournaments. Locate a word in the passage. Find 3 words that can be 2 ways. Put in beginning. The fight. Thinking about these people all the time. Them never going a day without supple. Thinking. Thinking about the platform. (all areas) if anything in 3D. 14 hours a day. Differences. Novels. How far are they getting? A basketball court. Half. How long will this take (time frame) everyone freed. Books videos singing. Type. Groove. Tuesday at 10. Hair. Drop things off at. Drinks/food infested with nasty stuff. Ya'll didn't' leave shit here, we not giving ya'll shit. Names of businesses. Business designs. The plane was breeched. Slaves freed by accident. All out revenge. Type three pages of this then go find a hair place. Resolution. Videos. With the packet will free everyone that should be freed. 1 hour dancing. 1 hour on book. No food on Saturday. Type. People with big families that are full of themselves. Hell no. family makes sure I get sleep. Barely hanging on. Black Streets. Ghost Story. We're here alone. Bar/restaurant. Hotel room. Classroom. Club. Dance floor. Blue soap. Cream soap. Game room. Dinosaur land. Studio. Motels. Office. See why room. Components. I keep saying these people don't deserve shit. Chosen. We help those we cool with right. They wouldn't have done that shit to me or. Monsters. Packet clips. Family rooms. Work rooms. Past evil. Dreams. Enemies will show up. Center stage on court. Cubes. House, junk yard, paring lot, prison, outside. Voice. Was for nothing. Their enemies with my clothes on. Cartoons. Bowling alley. Theater. Skating rink. Past. Rollercoasters. Underground. Video games. Created plaforms. Something still hasn't clicked. Drill it in. resolutions. Saturday no food. Diet. Harsh. By library. Have I lost relatives brothers sisters another lifetime. All these songs and videos, really to drill in that I shouldn't care that all of humankind has been killed off except my family I don't know who they are? The fireworks. Shooting in thoughts. That perfect timing and knowing a thought is coming back due to robots walking by. Myself, the chip knows what I've seen. It's flawless. Double letters. I mean it. There's something in the food and the drinks. Especially that enhances your hormones. Can cause damage too. It's amazing we can still have kids. They didn't want us to have shit. These people exist. Ones that get old and bitter, don't want others to live. Ones that want to be the last ones alive. It's not always a person that has you throbbing in your private areas. Brainwashed to think of natural things happening, like a man or woman always causing your pussy to throb or become sexually frustrated. 3 parking lots, physical education. School. Football field. It's a game and we're all playing. The real inventists. I always said, we're still breathing. Rich and killed, these things said but no one believes in this type of jealousy getting others killed. Some do but don't say shit. You pop in our brains. In slots of annoying people. Perfectly placed. It's natural. Diseased these people. A batch of tapes missing they saw what all countries really thought of them. Broken chained.

Find Drill it in. resolutions in the passage.

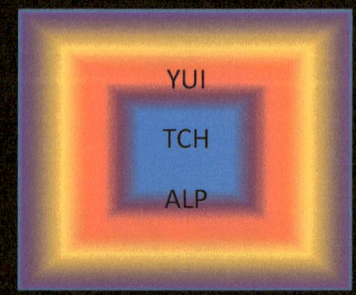

CA____

PA____

YUI

TCH

ALP

They have to act like animals, talk like animals or the beasts will get annoyed. Slaves. And people eyou never thought. They'll be free one day. Scar. Put him in smoke. Rush hour traffic. These people are permanently mentally ill. They're dead. They cannot be freed. Blacked out. To go voice. So family wouldn't have a heart attack. So they can know what happened to their friends. It's a hospital. Dctroos. Then this was all for nothing. They're all dead. Damn. No experiencing humans outside of my family. Monsters put their skin on. Killed to have space to live, a room. Got as many people down there as they could. People were watching. Print out the series for answers. Some slept with extended family. Running out of patience. Ready to collapse. Some of these people killed themselves. Their friends. Some of extended family. Teachers. Enough for their hearts to collapse. Going about things slow so they could live. Arrest date. Flew to. You make it to that room/point and you tank. Try to get more people to make it. Enough info to get the gist of the beginning. These people walked around as if people were watching them all the time. Imagine thinking you hot shit, then you wind up in there. With people you ridiculed. Laughed at. I'm responding to the damn videos of people like I'm there or really watching them live. Time to practice blocking out these gnats and there bad behavior. All this to drill in they're gone. Couldn't I have made this easier. And gotten over it fast a long time ago? Took too long. I never cared what anyone mean looked like. It's like I need to be in my head and out of it. Hey try to put me to sleep. Mom doesn't know how to take me watching certain videos. People in them need me too but she still doesn't want me too. So yes and no hating my brothers because she's angry at this situation. She gave me up for adoption? Am I that ugly? No not me. Coolinda. These crazies. Tell you something happened that didn't and someone that doesn't exist or someone they nor you don't know did it. My brain shut down at that hotel, the airport and I can remember everything. Pain unknown. Put in doghouses. Closets with nails. Handcuffed. These words are merely book ideas, passages not used, notes not used, paragraphs deleted for fiction books. Confined spaces. Chained. Unable to move a single bone. Part of your body. Test subjects. Beasts never seen. Unbelievable beast creations. Shit monsters. Eye sin the back of their head. Out people purposely irking girls to get on their nerves. Especially if they like them. And vice versa. You want what t I have. They brag. Penises. Vaginas. Trapped in the drugs. These are symptoms experienced. I have to fight to snap out of responding to imagesi see that no noe else does things around me racing to them sounds is smell things appealing to senses. Perfume etc. they remember all those fun sex parties and the feelings. They want it back. My ear won't stop ringing. Only time I can't hear it is when I don't think about it. Headphones, believe it or not, sound trapped. Wires, strands in your brain. How can that be? Someone's gotta say it Ideal thing to see what it sees make it do things but can't heartrate. These robots can do anything.

Find These words are merely book ideas, passages not used, notes not used in the passage.

___AGRAPH   ___ROT   RAP
                               ARP
                               PAR

Looking at one robot, seeing many. Thre's nothing here. Give off the whole world. In one way or another. The lady at the airport, there's nothing here. How can that be? I'm not able to go to these places so the videos (songs and pictures) give me a feel of them. I'm tired of doing the platform. They're there. I'm beat. Draw the line: gestures responding to my thoughts almost speaking out loud about my thoughts. Atmosphere gives me answers. Responding to them. Getting how they would have acted if they were here. Enough to know I have a different mom. Kill the real one. Knew evil. Know. No. She was always a beast. So the illumination factor. Back to not knowing I am. Who my family is. 43-19 is 24. So 24 of us now. All these signs they're everywhere. The Brilliance is everywhere. Still no clamp on family. Still no money. I'm supposed to just use them. 44 kids in singles. 43 unbelievable. I'm definitely good to live without humankind. I am not God's only child. The thoughts. This is bullshit. Up and down rollercoaster. Game of players. Holograms off thoughts. The clips keep expanding. 34 of us. 43 backwards. Disowning me because of weight. Huh? It's a game. Players. Family. Don't look like family anymore. Have to watch videos. People becoming annoying. Need to watch. It's a game. Faith in visiting those places again. Or for a first time. A sped up life to come to the truth. Allen. See how things play out. Who's the number one artist? Said these people know they didn't deserve any help. Reconstructed the whole world. They keep getting they ass beat for some shit. Fact:. Station. Will hurt. They can't handle being around the beast. They can't handle taking care of the beast. And they get their asses beat for it. My brain is starting to relax. Could it be because I am almost done with this book? Getting all the hell out? All their eyes are in the computer if they're alive. 11 or 22 or 19. Orange and black. Love this Jazz music. Backwards. More. 34. 33. Who could possibly. Kept trying until she had a girl. The daycare. Only girl on team. Yes. Party. Do you G. ambulance. Emergency. He brought it up. My insanity. That has me hot but just more of a confirmation, that aint shit here. All that brain shut down and experience to understand what's going on with these people. 65 is the mommy age for some reason. 6 and 5 is 11. 2 and 9 is 11. Something is still here. Could it be just watch the videos now. The platform has me hot. People trapped beneath the Earth. Real birth parents. Who created what things on Earth. The News. People become free their desperation to let the public know what happened to the. Who the robots were. Why they were created. No confirmations. Holograms and unbelievable things they say. Time lapse. Shots to everyone's brains. Document mix ups. Loud noises. Fame on another level. Willie. How are are they getting? Time it will take for them to become free. Hall of win. A way to know they got further and accomplished more than the previous day. Precious if anything. Learning what happened to these people.

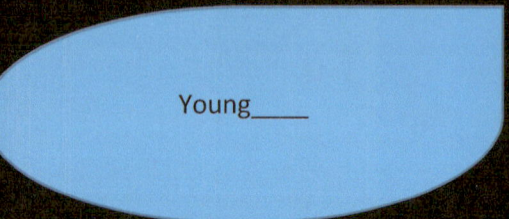

Find Kept trying until she had a girl in the passage.

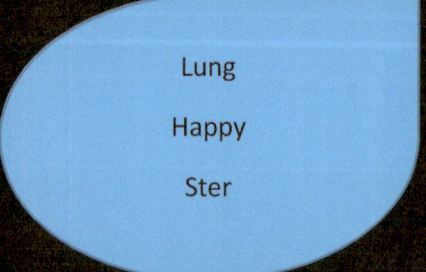

I mean it. Is this woman my mom or not? And how many kids does she have. The wind keeps blowing it in my brain. Is this to keep me afloat because the heart can collapse or burst with one thought of everyone being gone if things go the right, well wrong way with what is said to me and what I see. As far as. I mean, my hearts condition at the time. Watching the screen in 3D. clamping in not to care about what happened to everyone. Life must go on. It's a game. Annoyance as a force tactic to play. Entire platform. The book. My brothers will gain understanding and their hearts will be stronger about what happened to their friends. Was it worth it? Is it worth it? Freedom. The Whole Truth. I mean it. I need to get back to that place of peace. Visit places. Travel. Deuces. 2022. 2023. The year. Tomorrows not promised right. I can't believe I had to wake up to this reality. Never thought they'd see daylight again. Or be above land. Moonlight. I mean it. I can enjoy life alone. I'd rather do that than be bitter. Me, my jazz music, good food, staying in shape and, well whatever else. I said he was down there talking to shit. You make people hate you that much. Robots tell me what to watch. The point. Sister. To get a feel of what real people were like. To have dreams of real people. Could go insane. To snap out of it. I'm fucking up the robots faces so that I can stay in the game. It's about freedom. Family works hard organizing things so I can snap into the reality of knowing they are watching me. That baby of me, gave instructions and the family said they needed to be better. Bathe huge animals. Talking like animals. Conscious. Brain fucked but a part of it reminds them they're human and they try to be free. I've had the phase thinking they're all dead. Then I played music and it felt like they weren't. the code made women miserable. Leaked notes. Angry spouses. Why would I do all this if these people are alive stories of al the time of people being set free from unbelievable circumstances. I have a headache. These mutha fuckas are better off getting doses of their own medicine. I can go through life alone to avoid these headaches. Family should be natural. Feel the. Not need to watch them. Jokes about women bleeding. These sorry ass people exist. Trying to remember I'm related to them. Going through what I have and at the same time getting more ways to drill in we are family. Should feel family. Don't want them dead. 3 others to us 2. Robots tell me what to watch by voice, appearance, walk. Who is my parents? I mean it. At this restaurant yesterday, this creature had a wig on but it's face struck me first. It was ugly. Then I noticed the wig and looked back at the face and realized it was still an animal. But it was the animal like face that struck me. Then it put his glasses on and , it made more sense. Then his friends became rude and started bumping my table. Whatever. This shit exists. How these animals put on human skin and walked around and got jobs. This is beyond me. My facials were terrible I guess but now I know there's all types of animalistic people down there, robotic computerized people, shit monsters. Rats. The rats, animals are having families. Diet. Hate it. Can't be worried about weight though. Hooked up to a suicide meter. Nothing for me here. People. Family is here. Mom still finding in. something's not right. Did I hear her talking about me when I was young. They thought I couldn't understand them or something. These families. Siblings. Well, let they asses get caught. Something always keeps me going. Let things play out in front of me. Hope for a job. Enjoy life. Platform. Wipes. Tampons. Folder. There's many crews working against them that they have no clue who they are. They're dressing in costumes. They think they're someone else and it's still working out. Makes sense. Why did I have to disband from real family? It's a game. Lose players if don't do it. Family. Things go wrong. A cupcake. Everyone talking ill. Not regular. Nothing performance family.

Find Why would I do all this if these people are alive in the passage.

Wait. That day in the room. Dare us. It's real. See ants whites. The jokes. 24 west. The route to the daycare. Heal ton. Tired of being homeless. But better than the rest of the people that are at rock bottom. And brothers are free. Red and white stripes on the shirt Coolinda. These mean ass mutha fuckas and her sex being fucked up. Who could throw a baby away? Who could mess up the family? No evil looks. Is this game that severe? Still trying to figure outwho my real family is. A huge headache to watch the videos. All hell has broken loose down there. Solid Facts. True bullshit. Complete hell on Earth coming. Copy pages with less on them first to make the notebook smaller. New in phone. Had to say goodbye. Card so no long around you. These people. Don't even want people that they think are ugly to feel cute. Regardless or not. Regardless of whether they know them or not. These people. Existence? Hmm. The truth is inching its way here. The couch. The shoe store I think. So all of this to figure this out. So that my heart wouldn't collapse. This makes true sense. But, are these people still alive? Could I really have been child 43 and the first girl of hers and 19543. She let me go because of what? I didn't look like the rest of the siblings. Some large families that get bitter because there's a lot of them and people joke about how many times their mom had sex. Could that many kids really come to an agreement to get rid of someone? Am I just writing this so this becomes interesting? Coolinda. The wicked ways of people. So what. Just get the back. This jazz music is lovely. Now I just need that place to stay 1:04PM. It's like the fireworks last night were trying to give me a story. Answers. Would she say the baby died? These unbelievable things then people find out and just tear shit up. This is unbelievable. What crazy shit goes on around this place. 1:05PM.

Find Now I just need that place to stay in the passage.

This jazz music is lovely. Now just need to food. The drinks. The apartment. The house. The clothes. The good atmosphere. Parties. Right company. Traveling. Boats. Time to enjoy this life. Time to make moves. Time to move forward. Time to have confidence. This money should be coming soon. I can do all this but not have any money saved or stashed away. Something's going to happen for me. When I least expect it to like it always does. Time for the world to consist of good people that just want to enjoy it with positive things. This life of mine will get better. I have all these positive signs around me. Good things are bound to happened. Still going to enjoy this life. Coolinda. This is a constant game of tug of war. People get offended. It's life. Everyone's different. Deuces. Racist. Way worse than imagined. Many. I guess. No. I know. It's hard for me to know exactly how they feel with their friends stuck at rock bottom. The bottom of the Earth. Natural projections. It's time. Or a break. This shit hurts. I just said earlier I had been blasted on saying someone else was my mom. Now I think someone else is. And I'm unsure. But robots lately say yes. But they can project anything through any color. This is too much. She said that. That's too much. Wait. She be like. Platform for fun. I said you could hear the slaves through the songs. Listen closely. I feel like a real devil sometimes. Drink. The ? remains. # only woman been with is the mom. Incest. Debt. Put people in debt. Do you need to die for it? Don't plan on paying them back. They have families. Became homeless. Want people to know, don't want people to know. Cheaters. Like same sex but give the opposite sex a hard time. Lying kids. Treat girls like toys. And vice versa. 2 faced. Caught talking bad about other races. Darker ones. Disabled. Mentaly ill. Caught crying because of the sight of darker races. Annoying on purpose. Caught sexing over other people's pain. Caused arguments. Saying harsh hard words really fast like a non chalant killer while holding a head. Things they have to do. Rituals. Nothing's there. Bottom of the barrel. Mother's day. Mixed different parties drugs. Drugged to where can still naturally feel the natural emotion but act in ways they don't want to. Talk. Fully conscious and aware of what they're doing but unable to snap out of it. Can understand everything that's happening when it's happening. The clips. They keep getting longer. Real life footage. Who's thoughts? Who's tape? Test subjects. That hug when everyone's back to reality. These people 10+ years 2009. Work hard to get one out. No help. They're mindset * we can do what we want. * we're not responsible for your emotions. What the fuck? A feel of unsuredness just to watch a certain clip. Distractions. This game. Sticky tabs. Read a word/phrase. Bad odors. Electronic beasts. Talking. Believe. Dead bodies. Blood and shit. Public.

Find Blood and shit in the passage.

Cages. Thin areas. It's all right here. Nothing to pick up. Nothing to throw. The way out. Going backwards. Distractions. How the hell do you walk to the bottom of the Earth? And can't get out? Bombs. Buried bodies. Lightning. (computerized.) I'll be damned. All this I can do and have seen and still have thoughts of not caring. Keeping some type of balance. To stay afloat. 3:02PM. Who am I experiencing? Not the first racist. The 4 year old boy. Needed to be shook to stop. He was eaten. Don't worry about that. Taking things off dead bodies and what falls through the cracks. Some have to shoot themselves daily in the head. They have a coat over it and fake blood in it. This is what I, they have to do to survive? These are mad people. They have to shoot themselves in their privates. Huh? How can they survive? Constantly fighting shit monsters. Eating – living organisms in every day things. Huh? Food? Work your way up. Looking up. Me when ran away from. The deep blue ocean. Fire came down. Cellars. Conductors of the world. Single men. Single women. Oh. Interview. Candy. Thugs. Slipping. Glass. Down. Hit me. Poetic. Robots. We're in the underground. The last days. Are we in the last days? We're in the last days. How the hell do they get out? Where the hell do they get out? Where is the money? Caves gutter/sewers good the work room infirmary. Leads up to what: school, prison, doctors office. Fire stationary. The monster route. Keep fight for their lives. Hypnotism. Shit monsters. Someone's call stairs ladders tunnels. Leave them. Old stories coming back. Storage tax payment eviction payment bank account in credit report people if still can't get an account. I mean it. They have all our information. Numbers as labels. Used car – parking spot birth certificate need to fly. Still need to dance and take walks. Names. Bots. Serviced KKK. Messy. Rude. Thieves/accounts permanently closed because of them. Incestual. Men fighting girls/dress like girls and girls dress like boys. Like when people argue. Beat around the bush conversations. Sarcasm. Know they make people uncomfortable. Homewreckers. The visions coming. Projections of what happened in what area. 3:14PM. Was it enough? Drugged – fully conscious unable real emotions. Til death. The story. Have to repay the money. All about the money. Major issues. Makes things easier. Fake money being made places. Food stamps. Mean, median.

Find How the hell do they get out in the passage.

All these years just to wake up to this reality. Learn everything the hard way. +10 years of hell. Was it enough? Or is being used then death the only way to fix all the wrong? Permanent account closed on credit report, no credit cards, have to pay someone to look into it. Never paid back. Robots all eyes in. a break is needed sometimes. The way out. When think of them. Camera projections of scene changes. I'm I the building when dancing and on the computer. The money. Storage keep some on me locked. Same routine. Every day. Uphill by 6th. Reasoning weight anyways. Dance and internelt. Found weed in the trash. Backpack boy. What would you do? All signs say yes, but still not the answer you want. Why would I play with myself like this? Reading minds. Only God can. Share dreams. Do taxes. Phone. Can do payments. 16th. Eating discipline. May. Monsters, packet clips. Created platforms. Trying to keep my sanity. The hell are they doing? Trying to find their way to how they got in there. Fighting shit monsters, need the other monsters. Sneak past enemies. I said people were forced to make drugs for the really sick evil people. Inventists and good ccdotrss. Age clamp. Money clamp. Robot names. Street designs. Then all of this was for nothing. The route. Why couldn't I finish all this when I was like 5? Why all of these videos and shit to figure out if these people are alive? I could've conditioned myself to move on earlier. Could've heard voices and made up more people. Or is this what's best? I mean it. Songs reminding me of people and places and giving me that feeling I had with them. Sending me to a new dimension sometimes. The route. Pops in brain. Family is closer than ever. I mean it. Something is a ghost keeping me alive. Fireworks right on time. Toilet. House. Kitchen. Prison. Infirmary. Hospital. A projection of me then someone with gun at head then a racist man. Race? Moving around. Not the real family. She say. Song getting people together. Song. The ceiling. The floor plan. Sticky notes. Tabs. Underground levels. Names and future thoughts. Feelings. Emotions. Coolinda. Robots.all eyes in on the computer. All eye s in live. The way out. Food clothing, shelter, fee, playing with their brains. The money storage payments on debt. Car. Copy of last year's return. Walk 2 minutes. Broken hearted. Send mom infor. Look at 2 more places. Note to tax office. Tax appointment. Walk 5 minutes. Turn right. East and west. Picture or info in type in computer. Meeting. Phone. 15 minute song. Butterflies.

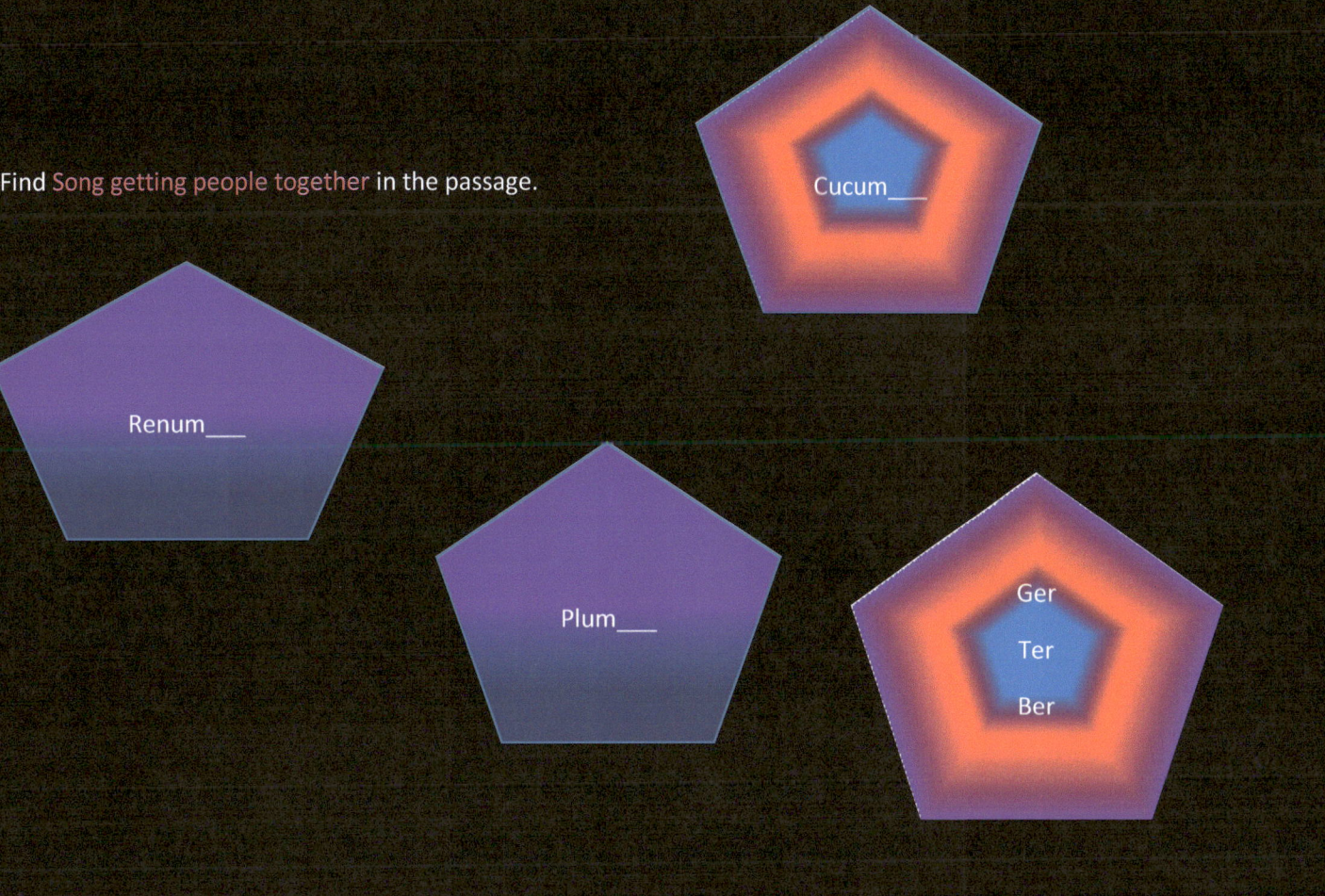

Find Song getting people together in the passage.

Cucum___

Renum___

Plum___

Ger
Ter
Ber

Same spot threw them all together. Incest. Slept with KKK. Said everyone in that neighborhood slept together. Pulling themselves to not go insane. Fighting not enough. Now playing stupid. Acting like children. Imagine needed all types of fuckery, fighting and shit to keep a racist in his or her right mind. They don't got to die for it. Married or not. Became normal. Listened to what was said. 10 years plus beneath the ground. 10 + years beneath the ground. Nothing to throw. AFr. Ames. Exactly so she not really understanding. Different colors. What else can we do? Constant battle of keeping sanity.thought of getting what I want, then it's not there, then don't want to do anything anymore. Get on my level in the building. I need it bad. Not gone join for the money. For nothing. Though. Everything about us spread globally. Can be found instantly. No respect. Pay with cash. Prepaid card. Left for dead and made it. The thoughts of suicide too common. Left for dead. Not told anything. They would just play dumb like they do when they're asked about the money. The route. Criteria. Robots. All eyes in. the way out. How things work. The work room. The money. Float around the buildings. Have a particular cell. Cages. They sleep in cages. This shit keeps getting worse. He can't pick his head up. Caves. He's so paralyzed and out of it. He can't pick his fucking head up. Coolinda you're so cute. The library. New revelations. With more clips. All the puzzles. Said attended a party. That's how they got lured in. we could be sisters. Roommates. Moved out. Girl put theme. The hoe race. The dance on wall.

Find Can be found instantly in the passage.

Basement. Parties. Account. Internet. He goes on a trip. She works hard. The girl that put pissy tissue in the trash can. Mail mixups. Every day except Wednesday. Fight hunger pains. Fast. Fruit fast. Tired of dancing. The only way to lose weight is to not eat. When have hunger pains, think of everytime people say you gained a lot of weight and watch old videos of when you were thin. I'll be mindful. I'll respect eating less a lot more when I get thin again. Need some pain anyways. To stay a float. I'm out of my mind. Crucial. Flat ironing hair. So sorry. Internal voice machines. Clapping ya ass. In her room. Nothing good. Cdrtoos. So this is what they left. Zombies in control of the whole world. Plenty of ways to get locked up. Everyone's bitter. They will just fuck up more shit. Another circle of bull shit. Learning the game. How everything works. State of emergency. Mind trance. Coolinda. Too much to handle. The question is what good are they? Why do I care? Bottom line. Up and down suicide rollercoaster. War 10 + years taken. Apply. Job searches. Project Freedom. Video guide. He punches me through the screen. Boy in car. Court. House. Girl's fight. Duh? 3:48PM. Half human half animal fucked up. They have us is , us feeling like animals when we eat fruit. All types of creations down there. They not together how the hell could a family of 20+ get all thrown in the same dump. Last man standing. The last woman standing. 1 of 19 platform. Calls recorded. Concentration. I always said it was way bigger than most things. Confidence. Project things. It to a sink in. computer projections. The machine me turn my head a certain way. And phone has same of. Some of the same things at the. Same materials. Internet is internet right. What it feels like to not have no money. Cracked. Started selling drugs to get out of poverty. People angry their kids taking them. The real NAD TESTS. Hair, skin, cells. Blood. Things you squeeze. Smart computers made specially illegal. My own creations getting on my nerves to learn what's been happening here. They act like the person did. Mom works hard to snap me out of phases. Words being sentences. We're moving, the fucking up and. They're fucking up the bottom o fthe place to get out. The Earth's spinning. But oocdtrs notes are in them so as a person like a talking car phone or device that gives directions and wires. I'm sick.

Find Half human half animal fucked up in the passage.

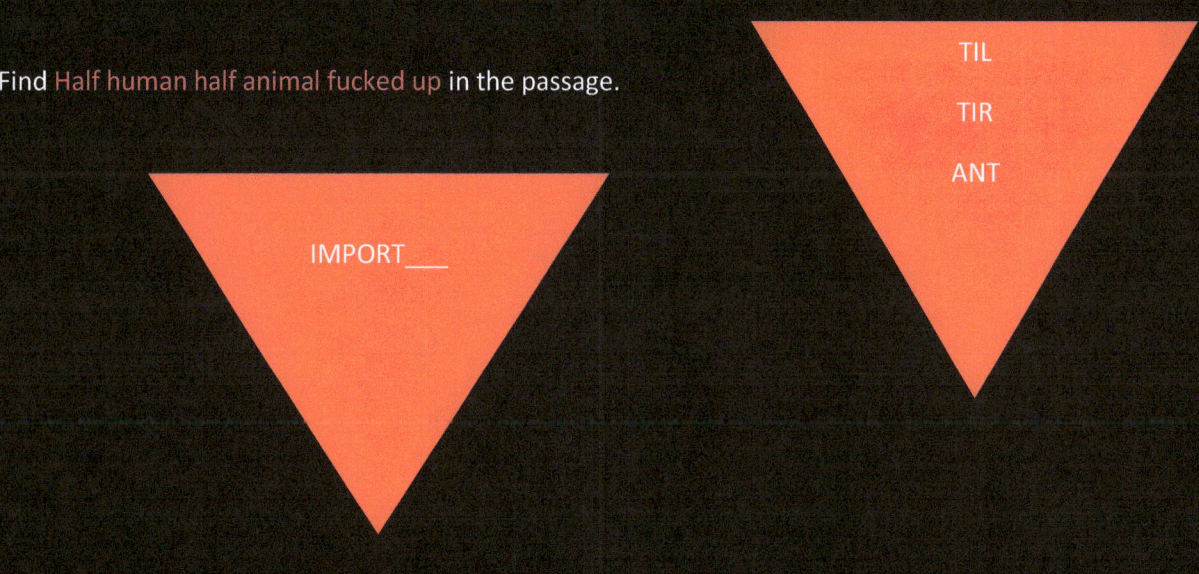

IMPORT___

TIL

TIR

ANT

The point. To not care about anything but family an freeing them. Whether have money or not. Stamps always there. There's not always a twist to help me get back to thinking everyone was good to me that I knew. The twist is. I need to stop doing projections so I can stay in reality. Oh. There's not always a hard tank, drop, so that I remember to write something. I said I created one of them. The hard facts. Mean ass people with looks. Fuck it. Listening to music. It's me. Coolinda. I'm going to enjoy my life and whatever curves and curbs comes my way. 10:53AM. 7/6/19. People that get looked at mean on a daily are not welcome. That's what they say. Someone is always worse off. This crew of people that got people together. They did what was right for everyone.

Find I'm going to enjoy my life and whatever curves and curbs comes my way in the passage.

What the hell is that? Constantly thinking I'm related to these mutha fuckas and them I'm not? Hard core facts. Considering all the shit I took out my brain, this must be what (the time is 4:51pm 8/1/2019) this must be what the process is to drill in who I'm related to without a doctor. I already got one prior employer thinking I'm crazy.

Or am I doing this myself as a way to remember what the hell, the pain that the evil people beneath as well as the people that will be free, are going to endure? It's a new kindof hospital above ground. Even the microwave can trigger your thoughts.

I mean addresses, numbers all over, indicated (it's 453) Sale-em- Godfather and a prior friend of mines who's last name was Ha-y-nes. Just like one of my cousins. See/sea/c owe you. Sins.

All, well some of these words help me too.

Family should just be drilled in, not a game to play to figure it out.

I did say I would endure all types of pain, (the time is 4:54pm) …. Damn forgot what I was gone say.

But they've done so much bad that it's hard for me to see some as relatives. Damn. It's 4:55pm now.

That woman. Is she my mom? What the hell is that? This up and down shit. Still 4:55pm 8/1/2019.

The robots keep saying she's my mom and I keep saying she's putting me to sleep.

There's no way anyone can read someone's facials. I keep saying then all of this would be for nothing.

Then it mellows back in me that she is my mom again. This shit is crazy. It's like water thought. It's 4:58pm. 8/1/2019. 85 is my sexy number. The airport. I do need to finish these books.

Find There's no way anyone can read someone's facials in the passage.

The beat is drilling information in my head. Or reminding me of things.
People cracking and going insane over divorces. Shit this stuff is real.
They go insane. Some of them and they do crazy things. That sex going away is a fucking awful drive for some people to go insane. Leaving and not caring about the kids. These people do go insane. These women. Caring for the other woman's or man's kids. It's awful out here folks.

Find They go insane in the passage.

All I need is one image of my mother to get me through the day.

There's a schedule to be followed. Goals by the end of the year. Apartment. Bank account. Books completed. Which. Music during. Work in the am. Bringind down.

All of this to stay alive alone, and recognize what? That I made it and they didn't. every word will hurt when they say it at certain times. It, they probably already do. They are in terrible beastlike conditions. My emergency room. The constant thought of suicide.

These people have been burned, cut beyond belief. Thrown in with dead bodies. The things they did to survive just to get one more chance at freedom and revenge.

I'm on the time clamp.

Things are being revealed right on time to me.

Order of things I get me to feel a certain way to do what I need to do.

Their thought of jumping to die when they are at rock bottom driving them insane. My thought of suicide yet I can make it and have all I need and these robots can knock me out of it. Yea right. Jump is a jump.

Responding to thought.

These events getting longer and longer, wanting to expand them, to say what you wish you could. These people can die. Pure hell until I watch the right thing.

Everything I've done can be turned into help.

Need something to recite when thoughts of pure hell come to mind.

To save all of humanity from the bottom of the world.

Every word being able to be taken any way. Making you confused. Insanity.

I keep having these/this constant flow of negative thoughts because I need to write/to add, that when these people are free, they are going to come up causing complete hell. Mad at their mistakes, their enemies getting free, no help from authorities. Real trust in higher ups saving them from each and every insane person they have hurt as if they are their mother or something. Or father.

Not being smarter and taking precautions on all the people they've wronged.

Bitter for a lifetime.

I have to learn to operate this shit.

There is no hell. Worldwide dungeon.

Find Bitter for a lifetime in the passage.

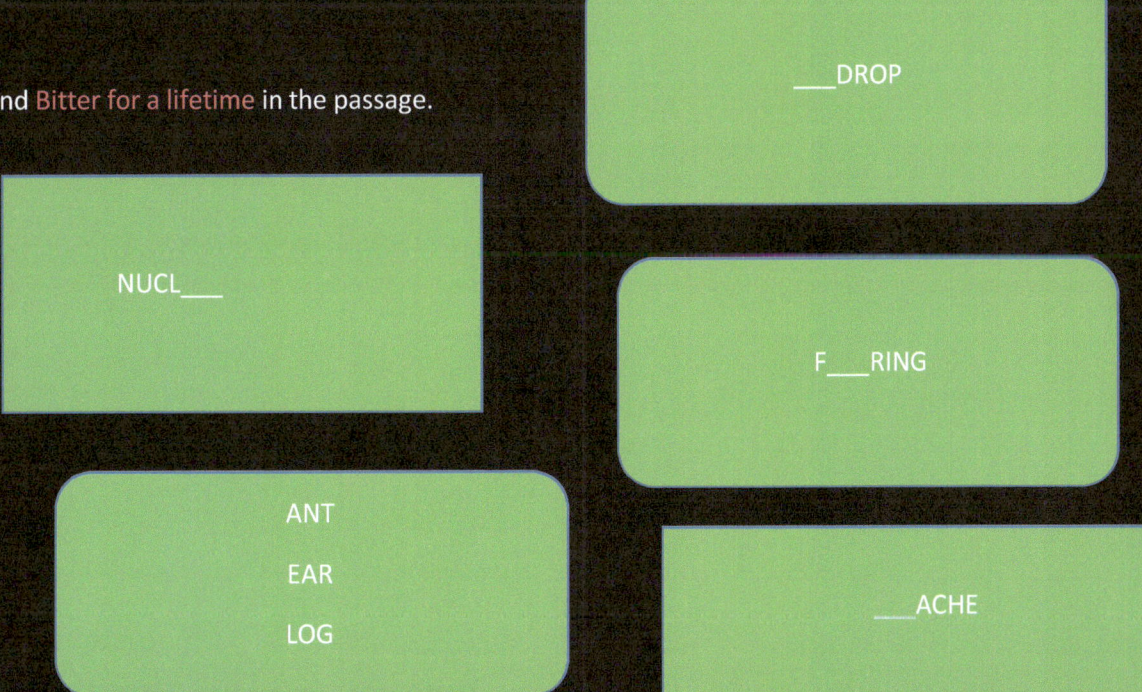

___DROP

NUCL___

F___RING

ANT
EAR
LOG

___ACHE

Animals on the loose a lot from places. And just houses in general. Animals killing right in front of them. Some have had multiple babies killed. And they did it.

Some fortunate they haven't lost a sibling.

Trying to use dead bodies as their replacements to live.

Why is there a town already of these people? They morph. They watched others kid get big. They use every part of their bodies. Every muscle, every vein they can manage to speak. Trying to get you, us there, until free.

They have fake teeth, animal or dead body skin. Pure rage beneath.

No mercy.

We're preparing for war. People releases from all over. Bitter for a lifetime.

People released from all over.

Did a tape leak that was negative about black women? I don't understand how they heard so much they turned insane.

Let the games , let the fun begin. Once a liar, always a liar. These people. They give no second chances.

They starved these people.

What high school said don't give the girls no dick?

What year was that? What generation was that?

What city or school said not to date or sleep with black (dark) black girls? Brown included.

You wanted us to know. Right? Well we found out.

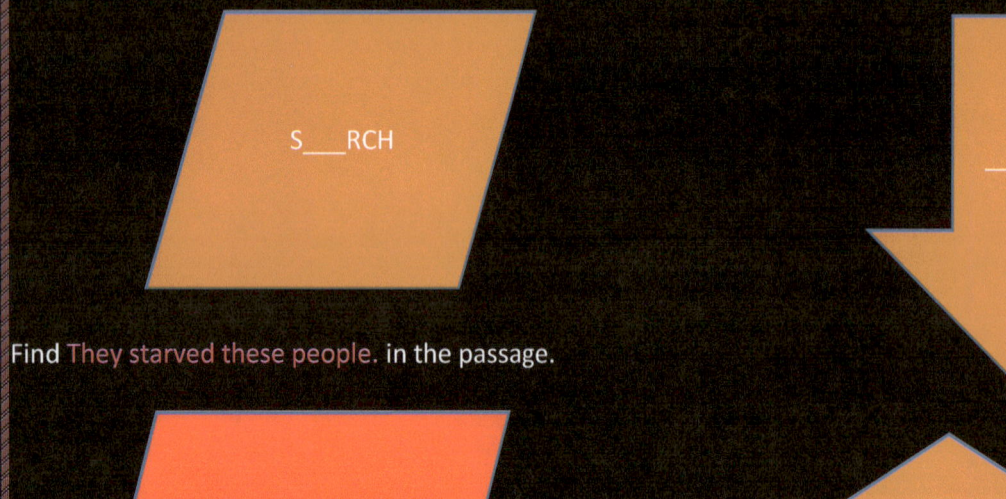

S___RCH

____PLUG

Find They starved these people. in the passage.

D__TH

EA

EAR

Everyone is just out of their minds. Dressed as other people. Walking around on Earth. Dressed as animals and shit. Scared of the others.
Stealing money knowing crazy shit is going on.
Everyone walking around sick from different diseases and stuff. Hi. V. The food. It's in the food.
Spilling food in cutes. Cuts.
They fucked us over.
Yes sitting on the toilet can get you diseases. Hi. Aids. Teachers. Assistants. Yes. It seeps through the skin. You can feel it going in there.
Every time I'm mad I let them go. The people I call my family. I begin to think I'm here alone.
What the fuck.?!
It's like camera flashes. My mindset. I keep changing my mind. The things they have to do the be able to stay afloat. To function.
They get stuck in positions like the tin people. The animals are quick to rape them. Real. Prostitutes. The Pro Institute.

Find Spilling food in cutes. Cuts in the passage.

Stealing money knowing shit is fucked up. Slavery. It never ended. Just got disguised with better clothing. And quicker way to do things. Inventions stolen.

I could kill this boy for fucking up my money. But I need to remember I shocked shit in my brain. These robots are keeping me afloat. Or keeping me alive. Is there 42 brothers I have. Or 45?

47 is my fireworks number.

I know one thing. I'm ready to fuck with any and everybody. Hell is coming.

A Real Danger Zone.

Find A Real Danger Zone in the passage.

HO___

MO___

CONF___

UICE

USE

ERE

LOP

ROE

I feel alone sometimes. Like I'm the only one on Earth with my robots.

I said my mom is playing tug of war with me. She keeps (the time is 6:21pm 8/12/2019) saying she's my mom then not. But really it's me. When I'm mad, or not progressing or something else goes wrong, I feel as if no one is here with me. But I do have a mom.

I need to have confidence.

Trust my baby self.

There's a reason, I still need money 8/12/2019 when these robots are flawless and can just bring it to me.

Perfect facials, revealing who I've been trying to figure out, which is what face I've seen the robot make from.

I'm surrounded by money. That's the truth. But I need it now.

Something still hasn't clamped.

Reading with alter your thoughts.

Perfect Arrival.

You'll see us everywhere.

Talk about the change of a language and you don't even recognize it. What was the 1st language? Pan! Sh. Over a Span of time. Si! Yes. ShH! They lied. It's simple.

Many answers say yes she's my mom. Plenty of pain.

The things people would do if they thought they were guaranteed to go to hell.

10-31-22.

Find I'm surrounded by money. That's the truth in the passage.

85 sexy number.
38 check mate number
8 infinite number.
The meanings.
Shhhh! To go. LA!

Find 38 check mate number in the passage.

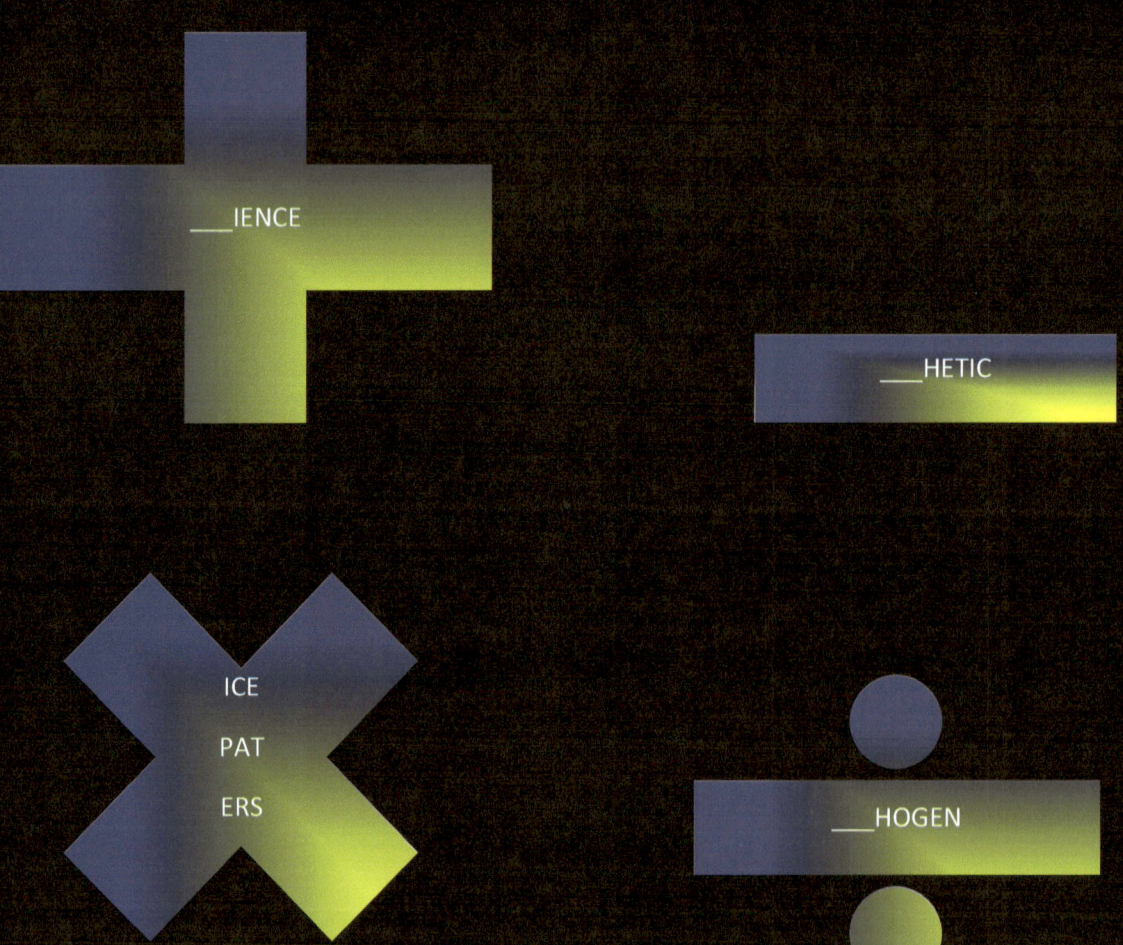

All this stress in my mom's stomach. She never stopped until she had her girl.
Family trying to speed up, keep my mind sage and work with the facials I need to progress.
The constant arguing.
Using every strand in their bodies to make you feel what they feel.
The money will come. What is that thought these robots keep snapping? They will tear the place up. Betrayal. Holograms and Projections. Movement. Needs and wants falling to them.
I need to be positibe and thankful for the day that I am living. Any moment something can be life changing in a good way for me. I am working and that is a huge positive. I need to continue working on my projects so they can be done by October 31st 2022. My goal date. Enjoy every day.
Focus on the positive things.
As long as I keep with my writing and editing, everything I need to know will be figured out.
There is a plan for my career to take off.
I need to be disciplined and get my projects done.
Set goals for the remainder of the year.
This is the second time around for me. I've learned everything I need to know to be successful. It's 5:41pm 8/13/2019.

Find Set goals for the remainder of the year in the passage.

They've been purchased and sold. Costs sometimes pennies if not free. Forced to sleep with hundreds above land.
Natural things they didn't want others to know came out.
He can't open his eyes.
It's a dungeon down there.
Slavery never ended.
In pain the whole time they were acting and reacting to everything. Paid in full.
Stuck in sex positions and raped.
Real. Gang members. Drug dealers. Left for dead by normal civilians, well caring ones Huh?
Northern states for help. All states had help spots. Needed to know the right people.
Everyone will pay. That deserves to. Never Spoken Of.
Seeing the same people. Out of comfort zone. They're going crazy.
He's down there doing that. Talking to shit.
6 years back. I've felt like people were playing me like a video game. They too will.

Find Stuck in sex positions and raped in the passage.

Your body's registered to the system in a new way.
My conscious. The money system, jail for owing it. Slaves the price.
Implemented controls.
How everything was made will be revealed. The lab.
Me and my family will walk back in. they have access already.
This shit sounds crazy. But I'm breathing and these robots are real.
All unanswered questions. But they 're answered.
Heartrate the Visotros.
The things I'd do to keep my family safe.
This shit is beyond me. We will all have the same controls.
Now I have projections of these people following me around when I think of them.
The robots can read your mind. It works perfectly. The time is 5:48pm 8/13/2019.
Family controls different.
Family working hard in these robots to snap me into reality.

Find This shit sounds crazy in the passage.

These people made it. Captured the enemy. The enemy got free and got them.
I'm getting stronger. There will be a day when the clamp hits and I'm just helping and moving along in life.

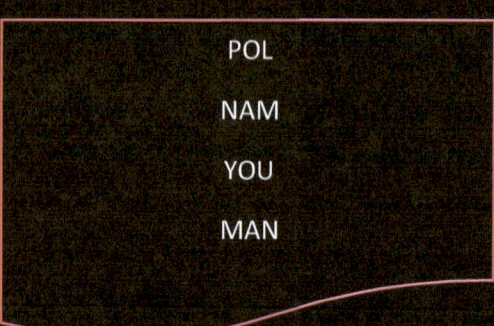

POL

NAM

YOU

MAN

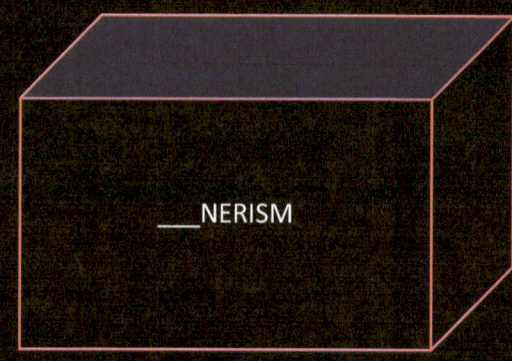

___NERISM

Find There will be a day when the clamp hits and I'm just helping and moving along in life in the passage.

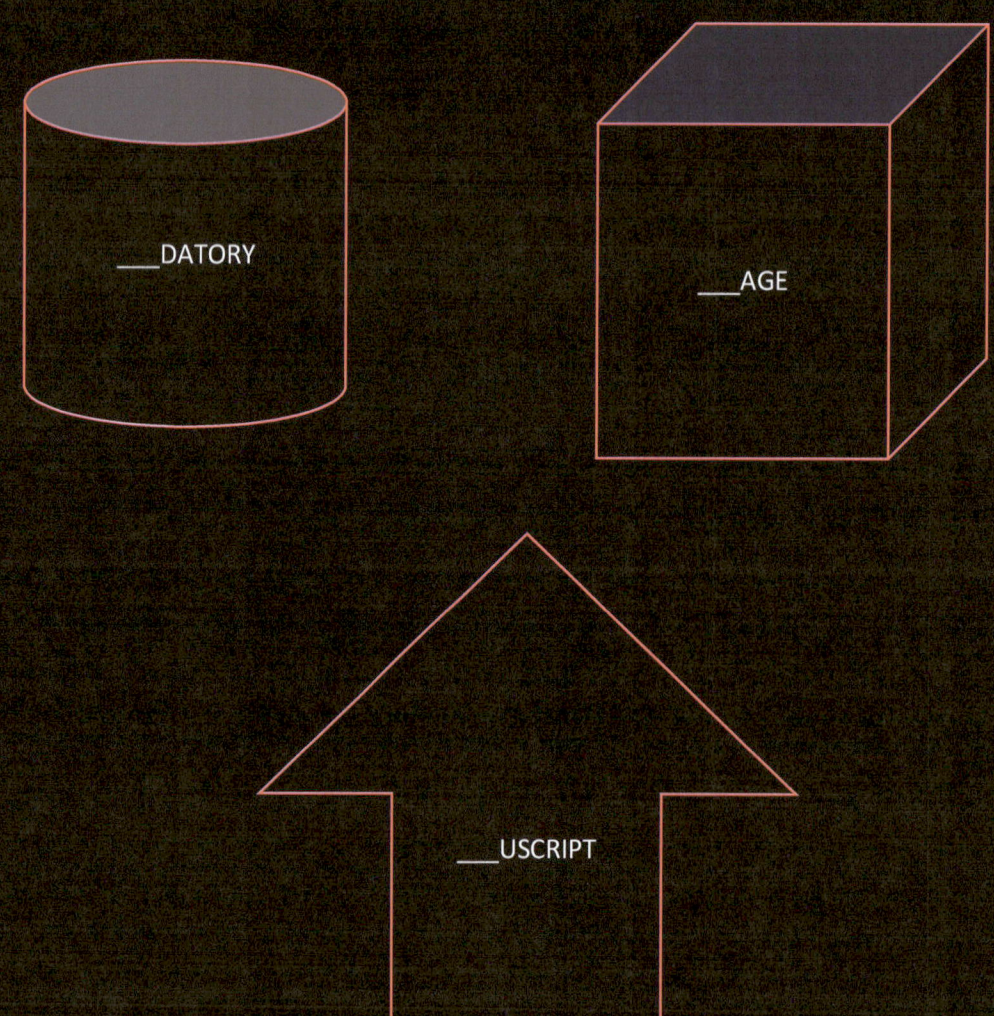

___DATORY

___AGE

___USCRIPT

14 hours.
Don't fall off because they did. Enjoy life.
Things will come together.
Of course they think it's easy to get out.
Dressed as animals. In the enemy's skin.
They wondered what happened to their friends.
Plant the seed.
The robots and settings will tell me everything I need to know to write the number 1 story: what happened to the world.
God's precious creations.
Rats can bite their eyes out. They've been eaten alive.
The impossible happened.
I'm hypnotizing them. Saying they already did it.
They set each other up.

Find They set each other up in the passage.

The survival game.
All around hell.
They only way to make it is to deceive.
I need my mommy and daddy and brothers.
It all adds in!
A street rat. Get it?
The numbers.
Numerology.
Do to Ron. Me.
65 is my evil mommy number.
Rondelle.
C2- C3 next.
Class is in session. If they're dead, they're dead.
Places they will escape from.
10-31-22.
Shooting wars. Hell on Earth.
They will pay for trying to lure me in that bullshit.
I do not care about shit they've been through.
I'm the one saving them.
All truth will be right in front of me.
The robots talking, looks changing your mind.
Conversations. Ups and downs.
Reversal works.
Reversal words. Ron Walk.
Say move and it shall be done. All the jokes made.

Find All truth will be right in front of me in the passage.

Study Guides. C1, C2, and C3.
Learning the robots.
How to operate them manually. Thoughtfully.
They'll still work for safety. The safety stays on.
The family and I.

Find The family and I in the passage.

Pal____

Men____

Ref____

Car

Ace

Tal

Everyone stops growing at different ages.
I'm one big 6 year old. Very developed.
Even book page numbers and what is written is planned. I'm a machine right now.
I can do much, just everyone's literaly lives and pain cannot speed up in my mind.
There's things I couldn't have known if these people were dead.
Robots recording.
Animals memory's stored. Yes. But there's still somethings' I couldn't have known.
Something doesn't sound right.
Events getting longer.
I said they forgot some information.
Got here and read their chips.
These people would be dead.
I'm on a schedule. When information is given, have to hear it repeatedly.
I can do all of this. The money will come.
Uh oh. I hear brothers frustration in robots.

Find Got here and read their chips. in the passage.

The words hitting every syllable catering to my every thought. Stabbing like a knife.
Beeps hitting your heart literally and giving you that dungeon, surrounded by things and people you can't stand uneasy feeling. You know, the ones you want everyone to feel.
Static thoughts in brain.
Real conversations coming. Electrified into the brain. Robot alignment.
Faces morphing.
I'm huge.
We all start puberty at different ages.
I can feel patches in my brain being squished and some expanded. Some stabbing. Mind changing. It's the only way I will believe it will work.
Most people think slavery is just chains and whip lashes.

Find Static thoughts in brain in the passage.

Imaginary friend.
The screams. Neverending screams and negative thoughts about someone who did you wrong haunting your dreams
Stealing money – worth a life – Your life?
They've paid in full.
We've always been slaves. A beast was created.
"it' exploded," one of the robots said like it can and when the time is right tell me everything I need to know.
It said "It exploded" while I was on the bus.
And when whatever it was exploded, beings got created.
I need to keep holding on.
Drink.

Find It said "It exploded" while I was on the bus. in the passage.

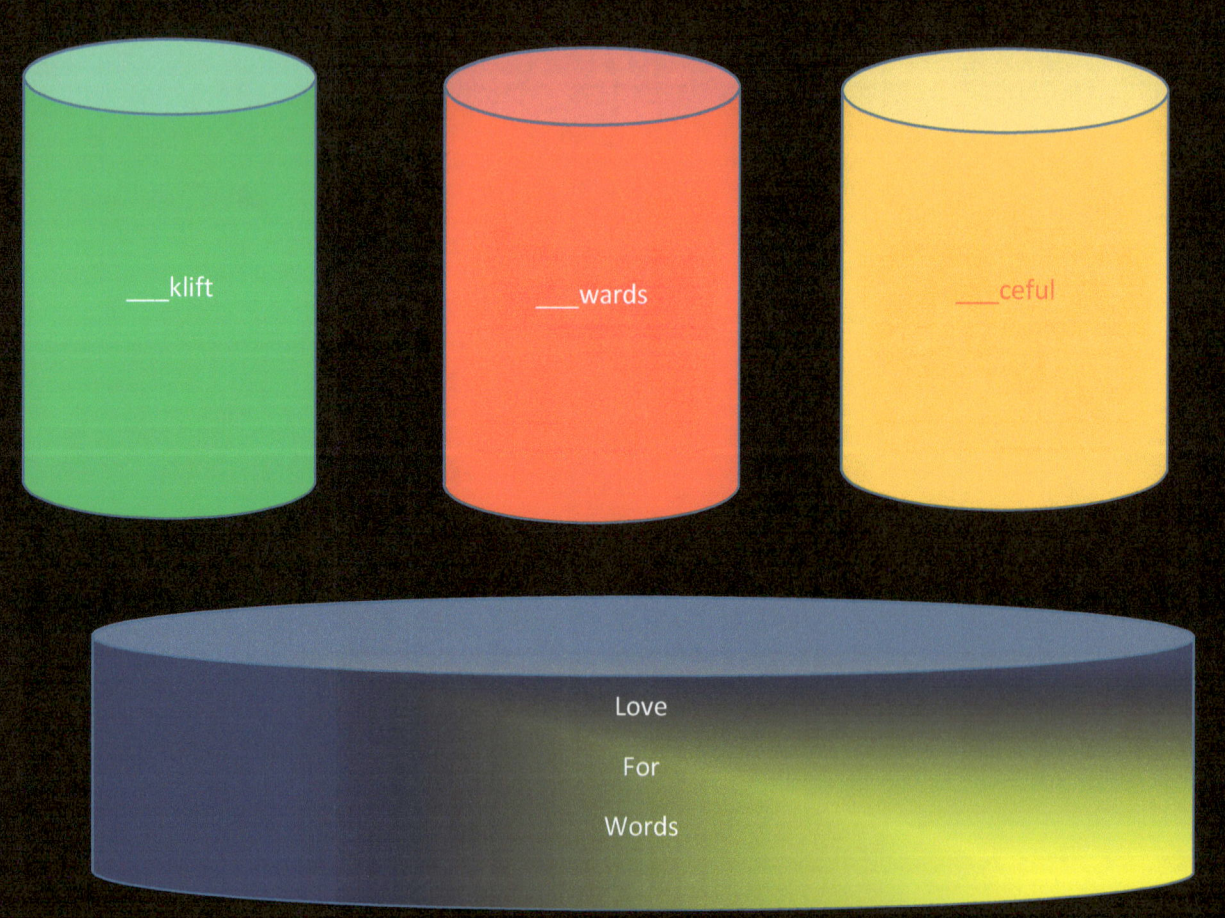

___klift   ___wards   ___ceful

Love

For

Words

What will it be like for these people to live without being property? The time is 6:10PM>
I'm overeating I'm so strung out.
They never gave up on somebody making a change and coming to save them.
That fish smell.
Animal smell.
Blood smell.
The cave. Ugh.
An all out strategy and all I could save was my family.
Too many bad connections.
You would've said it. If I left you alone you could've saved your family. (that wouldn't listen to you anyways)
I have to be out 14 hours doing my craft.
I have to believe that they can see what my mind is projecting.
Who came up with numbers?
These people struggled through the worst in hopes for a better life.
A second chance really.
This is not my own life to give up.
I function, I live because my mother and father want me too. Something like that. I love life too.
Weight, stress, get over it.
This is not my life.
My life is not my own.
I love my mother and father.
Robots far ahead of me and family for safety. To survive.
The detour of the enemy.

Find I love my mother and father. in the passage.

Eating diseases. Hi V. AZ – EZ kill.
Well I didn't want to deny you any thoughts.
Robot face transformation.
Words- sentences said perfectly to distort your mind.
Evictions, tickets, the time is 6:15pm 8/13/2019.
It exploded. They took over food places.
She gone say It's mine. She owns me. She had me.
She gone throw it in my face, without her, there's no me. My mommy.
Mommy Dearest. Whenever she's mad, she makes me laugh. Love her so much.
Who came up with loving people to pieces? Who came up with hitting people in the neck and fighting them on birthdays, or birthday licks. Stupid shit like that the enemy just walked right into stupid ass minds and they did it like dummies. It's 6:17pm 8/13/19.
Before the present was a gift? A diss or not to Jesus.
Have to stay in consciousness when thinking of robots to get used to them.
The enemy, only a select few searched for it fany.

Find Before the present was a gift? in the passage.

John! It's me. 31 Go! The bus down 3rd street.
What the hell happened here?
Why can't I see all of my brothers right now?
Except through robots?
Spooky Town.
Sleeping with people they usually wouldn't because their brains shut down.
All out hate and fuckery coming.
Cameras in the dungeon, the beasts hmmmm.
Spreading lies so people rape others and others find out they hate that they said good things to them. They were forced.
The want for the truth to come out.
You already did it.
You have to believe the robots can answer things others hid from you. Or find them out.
Dad is a ghost right now. Floating around. G-host. 14 hours.
In and out of consciousness. Ye or not. Somethings.
Sometimes. Half way believe yes.
Still working on this strategy.
Yes I C Y now I go through pain so that I can have the best product available. That's the answer. In the long run, this is the best product I want.
A system designed to take you under.
These things are electronics. Injections in bones. They will pass any doctors test.
The cars and phones have devices in them. They will scare you. Things will project out. Only one brilliant mind could think to do that. Put the same damn device or make it another way with different ingredients. Why did I think the rich could come up with that?
I need time to process what's going on. The answers are all around me.
It's Showtime.
Mom in robots when they twist my mind. And brothers too. And my Dad.

Find Yes I C Y now I go through pain so that I can have the best product available. in the passage.

The Point: They are alive and need to be visited daily. Can shoot in my brain that time has passed. 10/31/22 will be here before we know it.

The Periodic Table. What are elements 10, 31 and 22?

Documents list mixed up.

Their eyes are in the robots and computer. In the posters.

John a bruise see.

Mayonnaise.

I mean it. Your annoyance factor has these people going places. It's like a compass.

All these different languages. I could kill thee people.

Envi-Ron-Ment.

Environment.

Envy Ron. It was Meant to be.

After I thought of that word to add in here, one of my robots said, "Always going through a breakdown."

Specific things like that will come to you. The level you're on will be upped.

You, evil, nothing more than a video game. Some of these people have slept with over 200,000 people.

Orgies included.

Gyros! G. Why Ro!

They're flawless. They'll hit every syllable right on the mark. Until it Pierce's you.

Your last breath. You'll think it is and feel it entirely.

Kisses on the forehead to rest in peace. I said it was them. It was me in school.

I did it to myself.

Practice. To know it works.

You'll get all the hell you caused and more. You won't even know a difference unless allowed to.

I.   Your sleep. You're awake. No control. One language is all we're supposed to laugh. Have.
II.   Computer ton. Compton.
III.   Roscoe. Rosh Go!.
IV.   Sh! Words.
        Shout! Sh! Out!
V.   Be Quiet.
VI.   Vernon. To see None.
VII.   Artesia – R – tease ya.
VIII.   Vermont. To see month.
IX.   El Monte Station.
X.   The Money Station. 88.
XI.   Anaheim. Anna. He I'm.
XII.   You'll read motion words and we'll move.
XIII.   I mean it. People do all types of things, leave places, think you told them to do it. I can't even explain this insanity.
XIV.   Make Kin LA. L – EY. Pronounce ey. Kin Knee. Knees Sell. Mr. Kin.
        Abigail Joyce Anna Hawkins.

Find Practice. To know it works. In the passage.

Projections floating around all over the place down there.
Ma- Real took me to the post office because A rose couldn't.
The name game. You're all in it.
She dropped her friend off first. My ride for the day. 14 is my HI number. Hello. She dropped her off right in front of the post office. I wouldn't have made it to the one on Crenshaw in time or barely would've made it. Robots still nipping at my brain. Would've been angry I didn't make it.
Mom's projection was over me at the Post Office on Garfield and Florence.
A Santa looking man took care of my money order for me. Today is 8/14/19. Perfect Timing. Perfect events and situations.
That explosion created all types of shit. Someone gave me a burgundy blanket. Had to toss it. Still no time. Post office. Call to credit union. All clothing pieces arranged at work. They all speak.
Army fatigue a lot today and yesterday.
My steps are ordered. By me. Keep holding on.
The license plate game. Yes we will cause accidents and bring together cars for your convenience of hell.   3 years from Halloween 2019. Their release. Time changes.
Sound before arrival.
They have inner; exterior voices.
People dressed as beast. They know who it is.
Pure pain. Pure Hell.
Some folks knew they were down there. Dropped letters. Handwriting. Evil letters.
Sex. The time is 6:38PM 8/14/19. Some people are real bitter you won't sleep with them. You haven't shown any interest.
All of this to free these people. The fact they need to be freed is the first step and the principle.
It keeps getting deeper.
Los Angeles. The Study Guide.
It created a bunch of flawless lies catering to all the information and sadistic ways of humanity.
Hawthorne.
Infinite ways. Real Pain coming.
In the words of my brother, we can do it all night.
A language. A world designed by the Creator.
8 ball corner pocket.
Pool.
Pools.
713. 1913. Dealt. Cards.
319 the Twilight Zone.

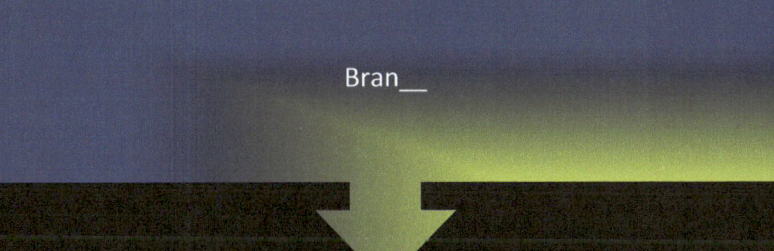
Bran__

Find All of this to free these people. in the passage.

Ben__

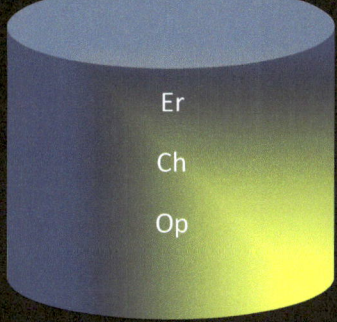
Er
Ch
Op

Different times released from cells and cages.
Formulas. The Quadratic formula. Science and Math.
14 hours out of house when get place.
4345. Willie. Elope. Left.
Student First.
Studebaker.
We are the Nelson's!
The numbers will hit in hard places.

Find Willie. in the passage.

The ER Book!
Emergency Room.
Emerge. See Why?
Summer.
These robots are talking ahead and straight through me.
The building up of my thoughts they hear right when it's a speck in my brain. The outer layer coming in.
It's all in here Shona.
Jesus. Just us. They made it up.
The Others.
Cages.
Ma. Real. Devil.
That drilled in truth that you won't get rid of.
It's a lie.
You'll go crazy again.
Since birth or whatever age you have been taught certain things and you won't let it go. Maybe that's how you ended up in a dungeon. It's 8/15/19. Thursday. 4:23PM.

Find It's all in here Shona. In the passage.

24 extra years and some months of footage in me and it all exists even though they never happened.
These tapes. Clubs and parties. They exist. They were made. This type of technology. Just make it. Even though it neve
happened.
2525 Florence and 5th. Speed.
Believe. You're surrounded. Capricorn.
Don't betray us or come for us.

Find 2525 in the passage.

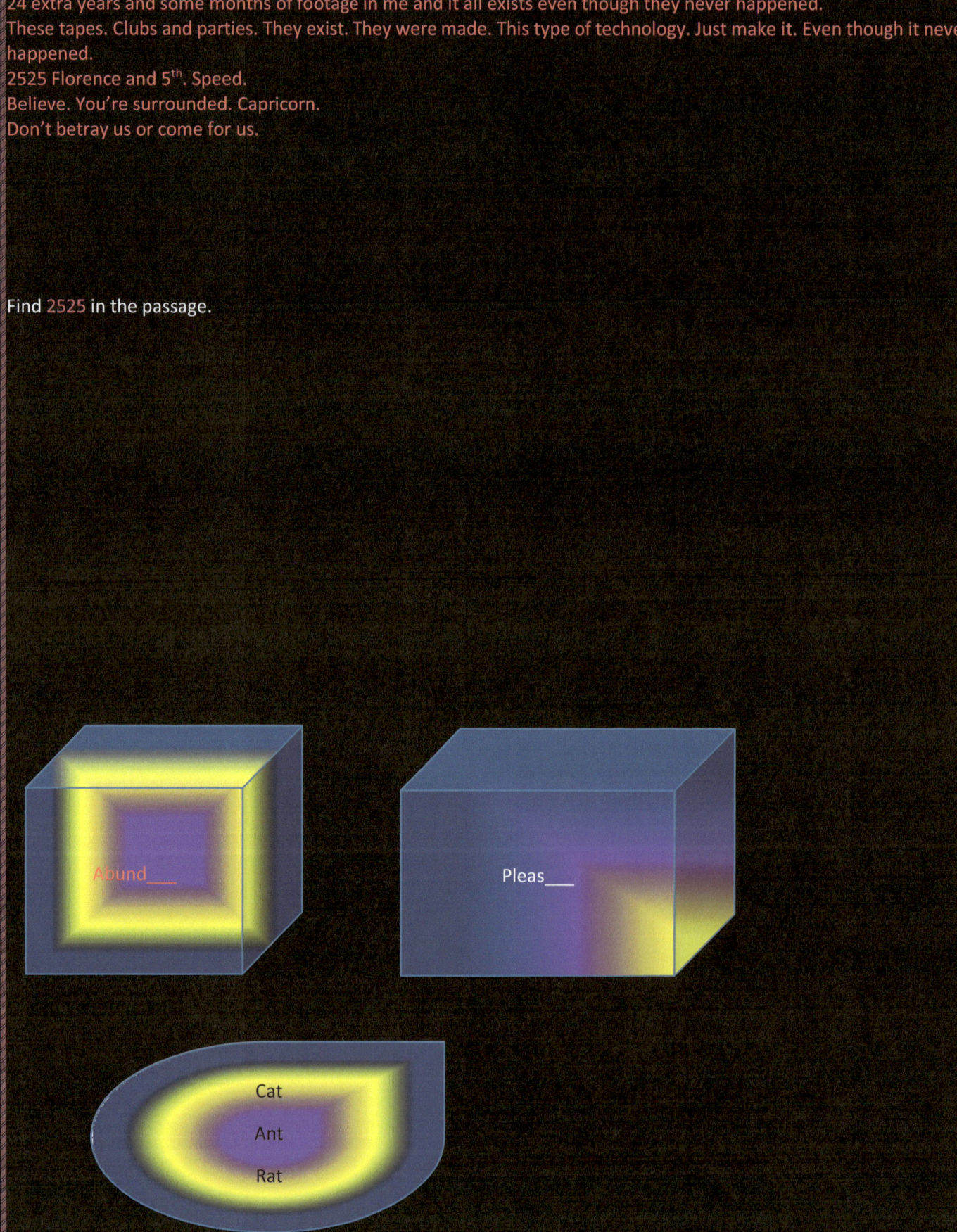

Abund____

Pleas____

Cat

Ant

Rat

I have 42 brothers. 4+2 =6. I'm 6 years old. This numerology is flawless.
Messages in phone.
Torture. Asthmatic. Live damage. The Real Doctors. Animal baths. To stop itching. They're furious.
Detours! Many!
A Nightmare on Elf Street. Round 2. Ear Ways. Ear Waves.
Green Ways. Elf. Grinch. Leprechaun.
It'll hit you eventually. Michigan. Mission in. Mitch again. Meet Again.
It's all in here.
Trust.
It's all used to trap you.
Marvin. Chris. Allen. Que. Raymond. Willie. Roshinaie.

Find Detours! Many! in the passage.

Ignor___

Rat

Ant

Yat

Relev___

MCAQUW. Looks like a math equation.

Mommy # 65.

Real age.

6x5 (one of brothers birthdays is 5/5) = 30 my fake age.

Want some more?

All things are capable of scaring you. Making you break down. Even what you say.

It caters to your thoughts.

Ha-even. Heaven.

They created him. Ha-even. Scared you with made up passages, writings, stories. Perfect ways to make you similar bitter.

Rejoice. Joyce ordered from RailRoads. R and R. Ma! Car! Ron! I! Rondelle. These puzzles to clamp in who my family is. Ions.

Picnic. Pick Niggas.

Their bodies were cut open to see if they have hearts.

Faces cut up. Had to cut themselves all over. Private areas included.

War! Hell on Earth!

We can't believe this shit. Me and my family.

Find Hell on Earth! in the passage.

Warden. Awards in. Ward. In.

Accents. They had to listen to people speak languages they couldn't stand until they cracked and went crazy and fought or just acted like another person.

The sex games will be outdone.

40 days. The fast. I can do it.

An/na. Anne.

Answer. Shona.

My robots – so they're asking me questions already knowing the answer. They will do that to you too.

My army is legit. We're getting ready for battle. Their master has to get used to the controls! It's 4:34PM 8/15/19.

You better see my sexy number.

See when you are me, you can mix things up off sight and get another word. Mechanical me. The survivor.

Attic. Calling I see. Can you?

Words/Conversations taking you on a hell trip.

You'll think God is in the robots. And satan too.

He has no son! Real. Perfect lies to scare you.

Make you go insane. They crept right in.

Ma Real Devil. 8/12 7 years. Huh?

Once settled, I can have some fun with music and all.

Black Streets.

Human computers. In a different way.

We are human electronics. None like us.

My thoughts alone giving me images.

My thoughts alone putting images in my face.

Whittwood. Whi-hit-would.

Would

We can put your eyes in these robots.

Find Attic. Calling I see. Can you? in the passage.

Whispers.
$181,000
$180,000
81 bus Fig a hoe.
18 bus 6th
$250,000
180/181 bus. Rose bowling.
Joyce and Thompson Nelson!

Find $250,000 in the passage.

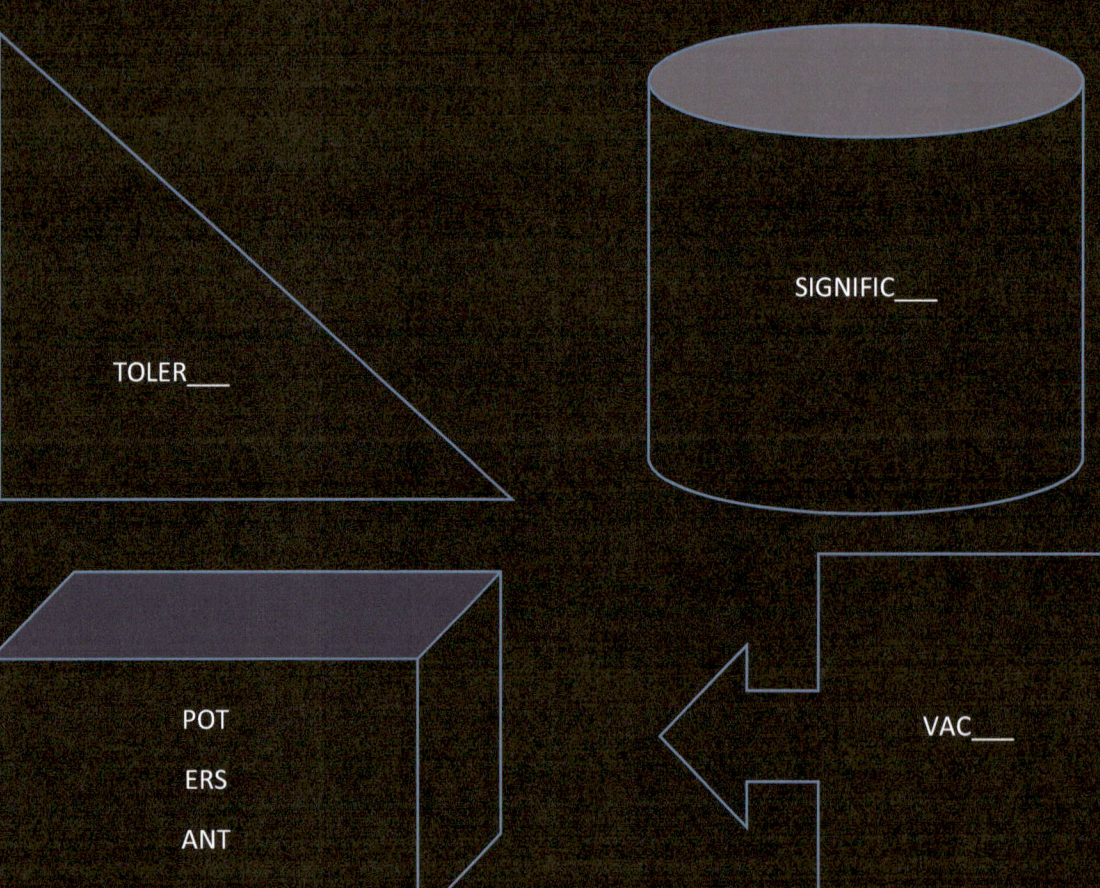

TOLER___

SIGNIFIC___

POT

ERS

ANT

VAC___

AN – AZ
See it? Flip the N.
An/Na
An/ne
AE =15
IS. Si! Yes!
The Insane Asylum.
Marble Eyes.
Beechwood.
11254!
Hi 125. See it. Shona's got talent.
Telegraph. Go – Me and Z. Heritage. Her it age.
Espy Rings.
Jokes about women bleeding. A huge no. It's trash! Real shit! Shut up!
It's 8/15/19 and this book is now completed. 178 pages or not?
Everything's in them!
It's already long.
Decorate it. Them.
It knows the next word I will write and someone sometimes hits something to alert me.
Wake up! All in! Allen!

Find Jokes about women bleeding. in the passage.

Drink.
Smoke.
My bots.
Thoughts and word matches.
Wrote yes and someone pushed the button on the bus.
Too much to write.
My brothers keep saying they not playing.
They mean it.
Go all in.
Lakewood.
7th and Metro Center Station.
Connects to people that could make outer covers for bodies. Human costumes. Realistic and believable to survive.
3.14159
Pi.
59. the street that marked the beginning of where the lady came walking down the street. Or the kid in a lady's costume. A fat costume. Took bullets for her parents. She needed to save her brothers, or whoever, from a heated event. They were surrounded by their enemies. A gun was near.
5+9=14.
Hello. Hi again.
4/13/1989.
12/25/12.
I'm gaining weight not having the apartment and my checking account.

Find Go all in. in the passage.

Seeing tons of beds passing by me.
 111 bus.
222 bus
333 money – 711, 319
444 shut down
The airhead. The airport.
As my brother says, "Only you know."
47 4+7 = 11 6+5 =11
11/11 make a wish.
La Read.
3300 Rondelle A – Mo!
Del Amo. 30 years old.
7+6 =13. Downey.
12/25/19. 6 is my age as of today 8/15/19.
Pepper Answer.
Pep Talk
Salt and Pepper.
Pep Rally.
Pepper Diner.
Peep Show.
Smoke.
These robots talking like the help tricked people into saying things to help would come.
So they could get out.
Wait. Let me make more sense.
The robots change their voices into people their prey knows and starts revealing things to their prey. Their prey knows their messages made it to their so called folks, people they knew, people they were using, and it never came.

Find Pepper Diner in the passage.

I said the clips replay in the robots minds. They project. Their computers. They can talk. It's 6:39PM 8/15/19.
People knew they were down there.
Some people wanted them to know they knew they were down there because they just knew they would never get out.
But Imperial.
I'm here all!
Stupid shit they got you to believe:
LIE BUMPS!
Just how many bumps should your tongue have?
If it went off every lie.
If you needed to read the if it went off every lie part then I can't fuck with you.
Real shit.
You too damn slow.
Never heard from again. People just knew these trapped people wouldn't get out. And it took a robot to tell them what it was. They're angry. It's 6:41PM 8/15/2019!
Lived like Animals for worse.
Yes there's 43 of us and my Mom and Dad got it right every time. We love each other and have fun.
Now your mother on the other hand. Why did she stop so soon?
Gorillas.
Go – R. Real Ones.
Go Real. LA. Yes.
Diet so sexy can come back.
Drive. Dealt.
Van Ness.
Vanessa.
The Secret of Men.
Stay see. Stacey.
Clark Street.
Bloomfield.
Institutions.

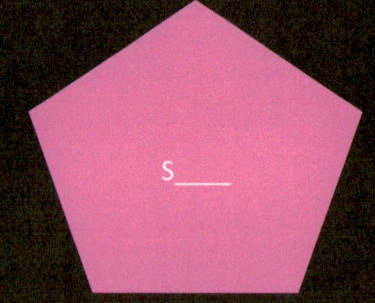

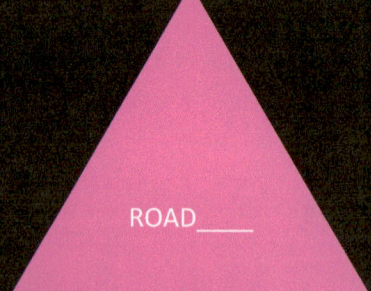

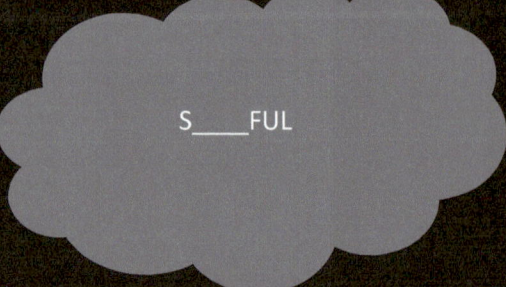

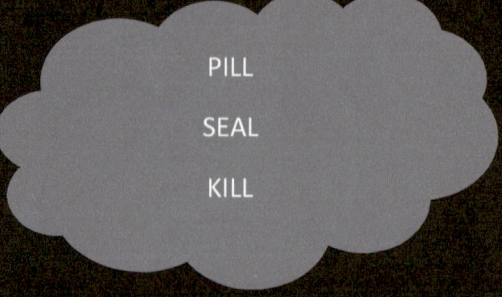

Find Just how many bumps should your tongue have? in the passage.

111 bus
211
311 Crossed
411 information
511 my information
611
711
811 Infinite information
3:03 Mom.
Mobile. 30. More? Drive!
What's the Secret?
Forest looking building. Clark Street.
Drink.
I really am that popstar.
Those popstars.
Him until.
Olive Street. I'll live.
Pink. Peak.
I MEAN IT. When I told my brothers no one was up here but us, they said what the fuck! Hahahahah. It's not funny though.
That funny thought.
G Shona. You can't write a book about everything. Stick to the guide.
Somebody doesn't have some information.
He didn't get no time to play.
Catalina Fye. Lands.
Every yank, pull, push, will bother you.
These people dressed as people to go fight other people.
You'll go so crazy you'll think you are controlling the robots.
They felt all the pain through the cuts.
Awake.
Oh yea. Mutha fuckas. That's what you wanted to do to me and my family?
They felt all the pain. Through the cuts.
Scatter/Spread everything I already have in.
They were prostituted by many different parties.
Some parties hated each other. Enemies. They made people money, the prostitutes, and never saw any of it.
Used sexual hints for help with partners.
Licking words on people and telling them they would pay them a lot more. It's 4:53PM. 8/15/19. Thursday.
They would snitch. The people they had sex with.
Women cheated on can be evil. Of course there's other people that prostitute people.
Men!
Connections 2 and 3.

Find Olive Street. I'll live. In the passage.

Hawthorne/Lennox.
Pioneer Street.
This is an up and down rollercoaster.
It might rain and I won't be able to sleep.
Avalon.
Long Beach. B – Ache. Lakewood. L. Ache.
Harbor Freeway. Ro – Brah! Free ways.
Pearl! Joyce!
Ear Please – 8+5 =13. Hear me. Hawkins.
Mariposa. Ma – to go. Pose.
These people were forced to act like little kids again.
Raised over.
They had to act like they just came out their mother's womb again.
Stomach.
The language. Swiped/knocked out of them.
They made it.
Vermont/Athens.
At the end.
These people got every ounce of knowledge knocked out of them.
These sold out people are not dead. Famous.
They're trapped. In a dungeon. Someone got out. Transformed the evil above ground.

Find These people were forced to act like little kids again. in the passage.

El Segundo.
125.
Apollo Street.
13.
Connections. 1, 2, and 3.
The Secrets Out!.
Positive Recital.
The last pages.
For C 2 and 3. C$. C4 Explosives. F1. Safety Mode. Robots. 9601!
Do sporadically. Find the sentences and phrases. And double letter words.
I have to be able to do something without my family's help. The sneakier side of me. I will control robots in a way they won't know.
What the hell was all my robots before I transformed them?
Correction.
My robots are from scratch.
But before I got here, what the fuck scared the shit out of everybody?
Juice. Drink.
Steal. Still – freeze frame. Steal.
Knowing all this shit is going on ya'll gone steal from people.
Longer than 10 years down there. Was it worth it?
Assist. A cyst.
I mean it. The stealing. I had a gas bubble, well floating air, come over me. About valuing these people's lives. I don't know what the fuck they are.
They were nothing but air. Like all the arguing they have me doing with events that won't or haven't happened.

Find I don't know what the fuck they are. in the passage.

Christ Reach.
Color Confusion.
People swap. Car color.
Plants. Locations
Locations.
It all matters.
Can you hear me now?
Company names!
It's all in here.
It's all here.
It's a game.
Wanna play?

___VIN

CH___

ALL__

Find Wanna play? in the passage.

WILL__

QWAN___

RAY____

JOHN___

ELL

MOND

SON

IE

RIS

VIN

EN

Rondelle.
Ron – Ma
36 years. 6x6=36.
I am 6 years old.
1:36pm was the time when Ron – Ma asked me what time it was at work.
My robot.
12/25 is her child's birthday.

Find 6x6=36 in the passage.

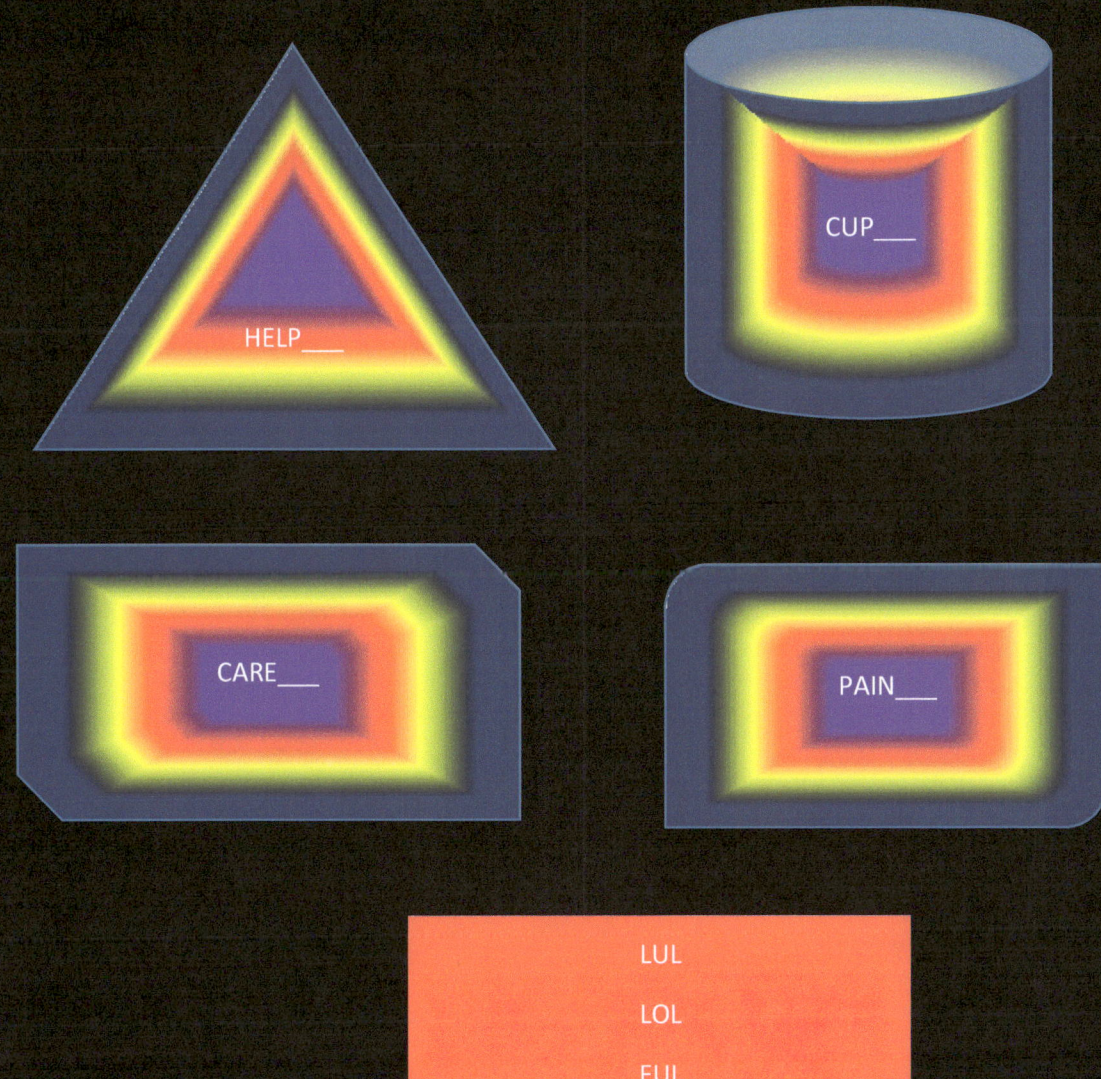

HELP____

CUP____

CARE____

PAIN____

LUL

LOL

FUL

Feel me.
Stones. Circles. Bricks. Resurfacing above land. Soon.
Feel me?
Not literally, and physically.
Feel me now?
Things in human skin blending in.
115 bus
117 bus
 577 bus
125 bus
The deletion.
Remember the robot know if you're looking for us. We'll have fun. Everything about you and with you is a target. Just don't think. You are nothing if you are our enemy.
This is practice. I need to be able to see through any of my robots.
Ro – Boughts. Ro – Shona.
See now?

Find Stones. Circles. Bricks. in the passage.

Los Nietos. Firestone.
Time.
He didn't get any time to play outside.
Roseton Avenue.
Ro – Shona.

Find Time. in the passage.

120 bus.
120th Street.
2012 is my birth year.
Keeping up?
Money. 24 hours. Target – 2012. Birth year.
#33.
Hawkins and Norwalk!
Hear. Common Sense.
Hair. Answer. See it? Hour- Our!

HOME_____

Find Hawkins and Norwalk! in the passage.

END_____

HELP_____

TASTE_____

USE_____

MORE

LESS

Vegas!
Jazz!
The 45 of us!
Saxophone!
Food!
Lights!
Mardi Gras!
504!
Parties!
Fun coming!

Find The 45 of us! in the passage.

The Forgotten. Left for dead. Living with animals. They made it. Then it hit. The big bang. Someone knows we're here. No correction. Someone will help us. It's 5:08PM 8/15/19.
Florence.
Floor Rinse and I see a floor rinse. It's real. The survival guide. The pain to create a system that works to save humanity. It's still 5:08PM. 8/15/2019.

Find Floor Rinse and I see a floor rinse. in the passage.

Motel – 30 – tell. See it.
Hotel – 40. The elevator. See it!
Hawkins and Norwalk. Hair.
Pharmacy. Acid. R. Ma – see Why?
This system is flawless.
You'll be checking for things 2 or more times like you haven never looked once.
Megan – Me again.
Mom.
345 – the do it big number.

There is a such thing as twins.

The reason the famous appearances keep changing is because they have siblings.

All the lies planted about them. It's all there.

Find This system is flawless. in the passage.

U n I corn. U N I O N. You and I! ON! Usher. Union Stay Sean! Preparing for war. Unbelievable. Wiped off the Earth and forgotten. 10-31-22. Allen. Gas Station. Bus. 76. Osbourne. Oz Born! Hawks in. 7+6=13. Cardinals. Red and white. Usher – move – Us Here. Guidance. Guy Dance. Ar- R- Co. Correct – Sean. LA Officer. Correctional Officer. The Act bus. Green and Blue. I said they knew evil was watching them so they had sex to an extreme in an extreme way to make them jealous. Couch! Son I see. Ma Real. Te Christ Risk. Frog-Emergency Room G. Pack Man. Specific. Cap if I see. Pacific. Bottom line: freeing the bottom of the barrel people. all else can be freed easily. It's a mind thing. The worst human beings. Truth. They don't have to die for it. I'm projecting all over the place. Robots conversations giving me answers. Can appear in your dreams live. Real settings, damn near close. Have to believe every word in this book and the others is perfected to free the world. So images appear as they should. Projections. Project – Sean. The projects at school. The projects you live in. The first documents flawed. Neverending terrible thoughts. People can appear anywhere. Heavy thoughts movements you can fell in your head. This shit is beyond me. Infinite robots. 8 Ro – boughts. They can do anything. It's all in here coded. Fear Facts. Even the people they genuinely like appear in bad places. Check! No more adding to this book. It's finished. Just do it. Money! Check! Text message. 126 bus. 621 bus. List diseases. Chylamydia. Gonnorhea. Syphilis. Aids. Measles and mumps. Hiv. Chicken pox. Herpes. Scerlosis. Corn. C – ro n. end. Z. cero. Zero. Vegas. Vargas.

Find measles and mumps in the passage.

Al-Ro – Answer – Roshinaie. Century. Cent. You are why. T C I V. Christ See. Poison Ivy. Victoria. B. Brown. I C. I C. Toys. Ape Real. Ad – ri –ana. To go. After death. First Anna. Vagina. Victor. Winner. Even ST. Street. T. Christ. Willie. Ey. Quest – Sean! Quest. Que Street. Question. Robots names, clothing, car model, hair, all of it, even kids name and design, weight, (computers) all used to fuck with or help (depends on who you are) to a T. Perfection. Darius – Dare us! Forever 2012. Birth year again. 21 stamped in my eye. How you do that? Law – Greens. Phone message. Milk. Chese. Yo – G. You are Christ. We're just all going to play stupid. It's all in here. Answers from Day 1, second 1 of the world to the first people to what happened to everyone here. It keeps going. Infinite. For all the hell you've encountered. Bottom of the barrel people. NOTHING! A halt. No more new creatures will be made. Brain Poison. Joyce – ro. Calculator. Add. Los Nietos. Ni-Key. Nilo – Second and sek. Nisell. Nicholaus. Nicole. Nickel. Nikki. Nicki. 87 – 01. Torrance the 2 bus. 3 6 Ma Fee. Money. So fee a. Relate. Revelation. Emergence. Tamales. To bad! Yes! Bad days. Bells. Jingles. Ornaments. Next time a man gets on your nerves, just call him an ornament. Good for hanging on trees. In toes Ron – Walk.

Find How you do that? in the passage.

John – S – myth. Singles. Appleseeds. Tons. A most. Del Amo. Ro – seek – et. Jay – cubs Jingles. Ashley. Symp – Sh! Mitt! Sons. Lock – Tis – Itt – Dell Dale. Jax – son. Men – See Why? Aye, Sh! L.A.! When Chil! Win. Chill. Wind. Chill. Witch hell. When chills up your spine. Brittany. Pears. S. AF. San Affords. Hauls. Door- a –cell. Chris. B-Round Call – um – bus. Ro – Ben. 2nd. Round. Killum. These people made it. A 2nd chance. They can look through any of these robots. Key! Why would I do any/all of this if they weren't alive? They were forced to walk off balconies. Repeatedly. O – Ro – me – Jew – lie- Christ. Men – See why. 2020 I will be 31. So so 2020 Deaf? 10-31-22. I mean it. The last pages. Need to finish so can study it. Thinking you skinny and you obese. Hell no. these diseases. This easy! oodctr's prescriptions give us side effects. Does that make any sense? This shit makes me mad. You! I don't know. Nicotine. Los Nietos. Nicole. Nickels. Nick of Time. Him Until Unit. We put shit in our eyes that burns. Does that make any sense? Del Longpre. Rondelle, Long Pray. Time I don't know if I'm alive or not? The under world. Huh? The robots acted and are acting things out in a way that I can overlap their actions with things that really went on. Postponements. Schedule changes. My nerves. Monday Raymonds. Demon – day.! She can be so stubborn. Selfish. And Stingy. Sereno. Sir ree no!. The importance of sticking to the schedule. The F U L book. Fuck you all. 14 hours. Wanting or not! Want to or not! Route 66. Ro u – you. You – tu – you – be. B6. The F U L book. The fuck you all book. 12/25 is her/his child's birthday at work. I don't know if she's a man or woman. Robots telling a story in conversation for me to understand how flawless they are. Each syllable is flawless to detour the mind or speed shit up or slow it down. I need them. My family. Union Stay Sean. Stay See. Clark Street. They gone get that ass. Christ Acres. ER. El Ark – kin. These robots are sparking me with their computerized glaze and out of phases so I can clamp in that these people are alive. The exact date will hit, the revelation, of what these people feel like and why it is important to save them and much more. It's coded too much to remember. Too much to think all at once. North Hoes Would. Ron North! Wilshire. Willie. Allen. Score. In spires.

Find Willie. Allen. in the passage.

The constant bashing of back women. Even from some black men. They can't get any bad event out of their heads. All races that have been what? Wait. To go – to see – emergency room. River. To go. To see. Valley Boulevard. V – alley. Van Ness and Florence. Yet they are ridiuclaed for being arrested a lot. Other races have their "things" too. Stupidity by hair color. This bus pushed hard on the brakes at Will hurt Ro Book. The environment, car sounds included. Control. Will bother you. Heartrate. The Visotros. Answer. Ecetera. Thinking too. Bleeding images of things when writing and reading. Stuck in cages. Fighting. Mi Elle ey! C why? R? Us. Toys. Scandrick. Mosely. Raymond. Taylor. I see the son. Brown. Heterozygous. Homogenous. The system: to get all sent beneath the fucking ground. Animals blocking all exits. Separate. Sear (See why) Not us ha. Satan Ha! Natasha. Kids hot in they damn pants over an adult so they get frustrated and have an attitude with that adult. And the parent too gets mad at that adult. It's trash. They should jump off all cliffs. We don't know where the hell you people came from. Lucerne. Blessing – B – less ! Sing! Believe. The language. Elle you see – Er. Lucerne. Aint shit funny. NE. Nebraska. Any.

Find The system in the passage.

Marvin Ma – RV – In. Look up. Qwanell. Delle Wand. Chev – Delle – ron. Chev – 76 bus and gas sation. Hearing Normal. 7/49. 7x7 = 49. You'll never understand the device keep ing you alive. They could all be dead. We snuck right in. inescapable. Willie. Will – money. Illinois – Girl Go! Is there really animals blocking all exits? Q eye shot. Cop eye shot. Tv sucking me in. Code Real Names!. Christopher hi 29. 1492. =16. Christmas. Practice until October 30th 2019. Usher. Marvin. Showtime daily Ocotber 31st 2019 – October 2022. This may be right. It's notes. Could be coded. It all is. End. Sin. Ny. Dennis. Denise. Nice. Drive. Niece on. 3-Na. Trees. Shona. Zebras. The end bra. Alhambra. Ape Real. They're trying to be more frustrating to lure me down there. They gone pay for that too. No sleep. POPS!. Have to be worn out. Caves. Locaters. Sad – ID. Words being said and cutting your brains. The words being said in your thoughts. Add!. I did! Ass! They got all types of things governing them down there. They don't know where the monsters came from, and we don't know where the hell they came from. Drugs pulling you out of your sleep. Your conscious of it. Can feel fat images moving. Me or them? Some drugs, controlling minds. Something powerful is keeping you alive. And for free. Don't get it fucked up. Animals blocking all exits. A did – sad. Ni-Key. Clothes. Favorite's.

Find Usher. Marvin. in the passage.

Words being said and cutting your brain. Cherry Ave and Del Amo Blvd. Deerford Street. Child birthday 12/25 Ron Ma. And Ta Lease see ya has 6 kids. Dolphin Park. Simon Bolivar Park. Simon Ramos. This black cloud that keeps coming over me, I would let these mo fos die. That's when family comes in. I don't care if they paid in full or not. How you make damn near everyone not like you? The stage, the black cloud. I mean it. You won't even be ble to make up your mind. Are you hungry or not. Left or right? Clark Street. And South Street. Candlewood. Downey. Bellflower and South Street. I mean it. Getting on people's nerves on purpose so you can nut?! What the fuck. Than Die!. It is trash. Woodruff. "That's a long way for me to go from 147th to 54th Street every morning," my robot said. Letting me know that (11:37AM) I will be brought back up to know that I do have 42 brothers and this is a tough ride I'm on to free these people. Am – Morning. I can! Emergency Room. A mirror. I can. People against the entire beginning platform of separators. (11:39AM). This is the real. These people. Well. Let's get it popping. Hell coming. We'll be waiting.

Find We'll be waiting. in the passage.

4:51PM IS THE TIME. 8/20/19!

Robot chips can change instantly to fit the circumstance. Automatic. NO switch needed. It can make you change directions events, words. Will. IE. Marvin. 2:57PM 8/19/19. Perfect Orchestration. When danger hits, it will be the same and fun. Rossmore. Rosswood. Rosa. Rose. Ros. S. Yes! Don't question it. Forever 2012. H and Him or M!. I really am. The 120 bus came just on time so my kind, robot would drop me off a stop ahead and I would see the Chris – a Dell- Fee. In. place. PERFECT ORCHESTRATION. P.U.R.E. Please use rear exit. You have no idea what type of device you're injected with that's keeping you alive. 2:51pm 8/19/19. Orr and Day. Eating. Teachers. Aids. And all types of diseases and Sexually transmitted diseases. I mean it! I can see how my brother's are responding to each other in one robot. Game boy. Robot games. Human Games. Boy! Game! Boy!. GAMES! MOVING step by step. Pinches of suicide. They're about to turn to a world like no other. All this training! Are you scared of the dark? Day by Day! 43-45. Star. Bright. Estrella. Board. Walk. Broadway and Florence! 45. The 45 Bus! The 745 bus. Olive. Training. I'll live. I'll be 7 soon. Are you keeping up? Don't try. I'll live. G- Ro – Very. Hear me! 110, 111 bus Street. Gage. Engage. Wilton. Willie! Allen. Double LL. Park. Place. Tour I see. Yu-can. You-Kon. U- Can. Conn. Convict. Marvin. Gardens. Can. Too. Can. My call! VICC! Victory. Atlantic and Valley. Pop. Eyes. Birds. Victory. 2nd Street. Boiling. Last minute. Saving. Does that make sense. Van Ness. Registration. Calling him a sucka! License for marriage. Does that make sense? Why we gotta pay? If we do. If I say I don't know will you call me stupid? Go away. Did you do it? Mono – Cold. It's 5:04pm 8/20/19. M. o. n. o. Polygraph. Pages! Miles. Marvin. The polygraph Test. Sky! Pearls! 30 no. Mo! The lie detector test. Money. 30 NO PO LY. (lie) Purchase order number. Post Office. 30. NO. PO. LY. (lie). Look again. The Training bus.

Find Boiling. in the passage.

Boil and 1st. the trophies. The construction was there. The Chapel. The combined sites. 1st and 2nd Street. Sh! Sh! Cimarron Street. The name game. Tis real. Images will project. Should still be here. Just like the rest of the students. It's 5:07pm. The robots. They change faces. The dead. If they're in your memory, I can recreate them. Monday! 8/19/19. 3D. 4D. Natural Eyes. Trace. See. Elle! is Ross! Snakes! Ant! Honey!. And Emergency Son. Soon. Colden Ave. Cold end. Denker. End K? Emergency Room. Q T. Cutie. The Training Bus. Bus 6076 (45) go 76. I see! The son!. Believe. The language! I'm here all! It's a set up! Enjoy it! Shell! Yes, Hell! G- len Delle. Keeps getting deeper and deeper. Robots getting my adrenaline to make me do things. Union! Lion. Lie on. K nigga. Kings. El. Eyes on! Training Bus. Red hair signifying, identifying blood in the last days of this book! It's 8/20/19. Green representing shit and money. Promise. P- Ro-Mi-Se. Second. Pro Institute. The animals telling each other the wrong information. Thinking they're looking at someone else. Real hypnotism! Mind changing. This is what it take huh? Jan – Sports. Ma – C Y? 919 GIG! Job! Giggles! New Residential Apartments. James, the book. How many do you know? It's not really. Play Delle. Model. Mo-Delle. 30-Delle. What? 30 Del. They've had to kill their newborns. They've had to choose a child to kill. Carry around just the head of their babies and others. Eyes. Feet. Real. Weird. Sick shit going on down their folks. Talking eyes. Feet with faces. Help me. You have to believe they've said that. Clay. Play. Bridges. All recreated or created for the first time, for sanity. Everybody has choices. But do you? You want to live? It's up to you. The chip. You have to believe that I don't know what I've done. Aviation. AI – VA. Virginia. California. There's no escape. Don't try to figure out this place. Long Beach. My mom keeps saying I'm hers. A thief in the early morning. Blend in. All released to freedom. Rolling in the. Weight. 8-9 pounds (lb) bigger for this shit. People commit suicide over it. That. And ya'll will pay for that too. Rolling. Deep end! Depend! Can you keep up? Water. 85 is the sexy number. Man-See. He. Ster. I'm appearing all over the place down there. Gorge. Has. Haas. The street. 24th Street. NE. 23. The mystery identifier. 22. Deuces. Cimarron. Simmer on! Floor Rinse. Broadway. 504. It's a game. My family and I invite you to play.

Find Play Delle. in the passage.

They're disappearing and being killed. The animals. Face mergeance. They think no noe's been killed. The Real Swap. Meet! Met – Ro. R. Alley. Yes. Alley. We're all playing. They know which robots are me. 2nd looks and more to let themknoow. Eyes freeing you of diseases. Over time. Believe. I'm trying to as well. That chip you're glazed with. It's serious. It can detour their minds not to snitch with body language, voice, walk, etc That's all that are donw there. 12306 Delle Son. The pain I'd endure to make sure everying is in there. My brain. This book. The machine. Can you figure it out? Tuwanthi! Call this game Tuwanthi!. 12200. 3:08pm 8/21/19. There's too many. They have kids. The monster. 207. 710. 210. 757. 7592 bus the 710. Crenshaw Green. I can't keep a steady mind. I can't make my mind up. Everyone is changing faces. This is what I'm putting in the animals and the enemy through. 1145B. Power Range. Emergency Room. 3:58pm 8/12/19. Line Station. Hawthorne. Azul. A-Z. The beginning to the end. You El!. Ella. Elle. RoJo. Red. Blood. Lemonade. Demon Aid. Bottom line: if I was trapped beneath, no one could get me out. I'm the only one that could do it. They were walking around mentally ill. They're already going on hell trips. The environment. Things they would do and see and more snappingthem out of it. 5:22pm 8/21/2019. You do not know me. You wouldn't care if I was on a missing board or not. You'd leave me there. And not even think about the ones that are supposed to try and find me. I'm floating. How the hell did t his happen? How the hell did this shit get created? I have to do all this to detour it's mind. It's 5:24pm 8/21/19. The dump. It exploded. What the fuck! She said bonita. My name is bonita. She said that at work. The lady on the bus. She had a tattoo of the word Bonita on her arm. Tis Real. Delle. They paid in full. Ain't shit funny. Work! Mandatory. Ma. It's Real. Devil. You can't escape it. The Time is 5:28PM August 21st, 2019.

It's me. It's us. You'll look for me, but won't find me. You'll look for my family but it'll be like they're right next to you.

It's us, when you're out there fighting and vandalizing.

It's 3:03PM 8/22/19. The Forgotten Notes is what I'm about to type. 3908 45 toward Lincoln Heights. Red dress. A pregnant woman with a red dress on was at the bus stop. With her man. 46. The ambulance. It was 1:19pm 8/19/19 when I typed this text message to myself. It knows I'll be there. Rehearsals and practices. The point. To control them live. The robots. Even Words. Anchorage. New age. Training bus. 45. To Harbor Freeway. 9568. 40 bus. Lucius. 2:18pm. Wind sir call. 6. Go. I'm six years old. Am morning call. Nation. Na. Shona. Tion. Sean. Soul. Sold of a Nation. Soul. Adamn. A damn shame. A street rat. Hobbies and Shaw. Does it make sense that someone could be sinful their whole life and at the last minute ask for a place in Ha. Even? Crenshaw. Marlton and King. International. Blacked out. The blacklist. Cats and dogs. The Creator. Birds.Cheetahs. Lions. Tigers. Leopards and more. Quiet. Make it Happen. 3:34pm. 8/19/19 Mula. Mula –N. Mula n to u gernarl education 3:36pm 8/19/19. 5:34pm. 8/19/19. Crenshaw Manor. Ro. Man! Ron Ma! Look at the signs. The Lion. Los Nietos. King. Queen. Slime. Slim. Miles. 4034 kk. Louisiana. Chicken. 4030. Power and water department. Ma. C. Y? Soul Food place to a Beauty Supply store. The known history. Baldwin Hills. Make Don alls. Cougars. Alhambra. Almansor. Where the 4 year old boy played. Let's talk about suicide. 210. 710. 740. Ma. C. Y? Dear. Ear. Hear me. Forever 12. The year I was really born. TJ to Joyce. Max in. At he's me. Cable. Haws Attorney. See it? Arr. att. See it? Law Greens. Staples. Seal the deal movie theater.360 W Milk Junior Boulevard. Te Lion Los Nietos King. South BayCenter. Sent her. South Bay Gall. Emergency Room. Answer. H and Him. El Monte Station. Stay Sean. 32 is the middle number. 542 and 342 are water numbers. Easy kill. As ez. Villages. V ill age. The ill age. Al All. Evil fredo. Does. La. Mind. Deuce. Joanna. Jax. Jackie. Paradise. Sepulveda. 1600 beyond the ring bell 611 911 terror risk. Training.8/18am at work late the orchestra. The Orchestration. Me and my youngest brothers making an alliance. The older ones can make one. The world feeling like it froze. The environment. Programming the animals. They think they've already done it and are tripping thinking they just did it. Chandler Road. See handler. Chill see. I mean it. I'm looking at my whole family in one robot. Face mergence. This is what it takes huh? To free humanity. Family ahead of me in what my creations do sometimes. This is about torturing these mutha fuckas toa max. they need to be let out. 3:14pm 8/22/2019. The evil ones. They think they know how to create all pain. Making people walk around in complete pain and suffering and still torturing them. They have no idea my fiery. Burning. I am a woman scorned. My thoughts. They can't get right. They keep expounding on hell with people I don't know. I'm learning the evil that these evil mutha fuckas wanted to do to me. This means my family has been through worse. I am truly scorned. A true hell experience coming soon. It is 3:19PM 8/22/19 and there is nothing left to add to this book. She escaped. She, me. I escaped.

That girl. She solved her own kidnapping. Was I missing? The hunt is still on. I would leave and keep people guessing.

TUWANTHI

The ER Book!

The Emergency Room!

Sharper

Runner

Driver

Dancer

Listener

Swimmer

Teacher

Daughter

Glitter

Rider

Lawyer

Helicopter

Deliver

Answer

Anger

The time is 5:33pm 8/15/19.
It's a treasure hunt.
Re releases of films.
Everyone released at the same time. From the underworld.
Believe!
It's gonging down.

"Sometimes I throw up for hours. Sometimes days straight," she said. She said this in my dream.

She was sitting down and some gold metallic things were placed on her mouth and nose.

The dream with the girls. Van Ness. They were walking through a lobby.

"I already got her," a lady said while we were walking out and the two women were walking in.

I was angry. The lady talking to me tortured the women walking in. One slept with her husband.

We were walking through some fancy hotel lobby. The carpet was light brown. Tan.

Similar to some of my other dreams, I felt like I was there before.

It's 12/1/19 and 12:34pm.

I've been working 12 hour shifts at work. I'm done with 4 days and have 6 more straight. 10 days straight.

5pm to 5am. I'm making it.

An AZ A-Z answer.
A killing zone. Fight.
Nasty smells that make you fight.
No space.
Clipping thought.
Roshinaie and Joyce.
Blue.
Azul.
A - Z

The negative thoughts are like knives stabbing my brain.

The negative thoughts are like glass falling over and over again in my brain.

Someone got out. A baby. The opening was only big enough for a toddler to get out.

Pure hell. It made it unblind.

These people's hope for years relied on someone to have a baby that could change the whole world.

A baby that could fool smart animals and stand the sight of things that cut her eyes.

A baby that could smell the worst smells possible.

A baby that could blend in with the evil that took over the Earth and transform them.

The trick. To make them question whether it even happened or not. All the hell they think they've been through.

Sorry. So -RR – Why! Merry. Me – RR – Y! It's 8:52PM 12/25/19. Merry Christmas!

The robot will say it when you don't want it to.
It's all in here.

A white man thought blacks and all other races would naturally hate themselves. He started a crew and they joined in all colored circles. They were smart. They invented prescriptions, drugs, all types of things and some changed there skin color.

These people ruin homes (marriages) and use the kids to make the other parent unhappy by doing things like kissing the new partner. They teach their kids to be fast, seducing, to act and dance like whores. To talk seductive. Then tell them to influence others. Some do it without needing to be told their kids. Send them to school to bother other kids and teach them these things as well. How to bother kids in their private areas. These people would set people up to get caught by their captives. Jesus. Me. It's me. Were they set up? Or. Is it a set up? Who'd they talk to at the meeting? Injected, diseased, easy. A set up to find a cheating husband or wife. The organization. The club. The founders. Maybe. These sell outs were given nothing. Their families separated. A club of angry women. Changed sex people. Experience. Some people are trapped without their families. Lonely. Alone. These people constantly scream and argue down there to drown out the sound of all the animals. It's 1:07pm 12/13/19. Break. Fast. Time off. The monsters think they already did certain things. Confusing, mixing up people. Fighting and fucking beasts. The forgotten people. Fighting to show that's all they deserve and were meant to do. To show they've learned their lesson. They have to do the fighting so extreme because that's what they would've had others doing with all their fuckery. Deceit. They signed up for it. But they keep saying something they didn't know about the contract. Something they didn't know about the deal. Other than it was bull shit. They will fight longer and harder for food, and clips. They have weird feelings every day. Tears every day. Sometimes every minute. The pain was extremely, maximum, before I arrived. Years without real food. Student. Studebaker. It's 1:10pm 12/13/19. Sepulveda. Gage and Western. 110. 111. Remember Sepulveda. These people's hearts have been opened to see if they were human. Some were in other countries and thought of schemes and lies to get them back to their families.
My mind is on a clamp teaching me little by little. These people don't want me to leave. They want drugs and food. They're doing pure hell and letting me know they don't mind doing it. But the obvious is the pain is real. Nobody wants pain. It's 1:12PM 12/13/19. They want to be free. Now. They walked right in the trap set up by the first people. A race. All of them. Mankind and Manevil. I said they knew I was too smart. Holograms. Projections. My animals and robots reading their inds and letting them know. I would find out all the information and more and they'd have to hope I stayed because they claim they didn't know somethings. What didn't they know? Many believe they knew it all. But what if they didn't know something? Mind manipulation. Purposely acting stupid to things to get on people's nerves. Prescribing insanity to those they meet and are sent to meet. These people were completely sold out. Mind manipulation of all. Making people want to things they are not. Things their parents don't want them to be. Sold out and for nothing. Diseased. They were put in the real world to do the manipulation anyways. They went to their enemies, vulnerable people, just anyone they could to try and get freed and cured. They realized they would all kill them. Somehow everyone found out about the secret. Or somehow everyone already knew. These people returned to their masters, who were watching them all along. Cemetery. They ended in an animals cave underground. Prisons. Animal homes.. some of these people have been abused and can't get over it. Every day, even during sex, the thought of the negative events comes up. They sold out. Griffin. I am here ya'll. Imperial. Century. Central. Sent, You R Why. Sent R – to LA!

Joyce and Terrence.
Celebrity. Celery. Certainly. Celebrate. Finance. Experience. Balance. Influence. Fierce. Florence. Torrance. France. December. Do you see them? They cold! Rejoice. Century. Central.

Cutting their faces. Privates. Taking turns in different pain so I will stay. They want revenge. Mind games. I said they were playing with my mind to make me feel what they feel and think what they think. Like hell yeah hurry and get us out of here. But the reality is they can't stay sane. They're with dead bodies, shit, piss, blood and monsters, plus more unbelievable shit. Some pose in different spots with knives up their privates. Have been long before I got in the picture. Freedom they want.

We are only looks, we'll keep cutting our face off if that's what it is. We only care about sex so we'll cut our privates. If that's what it is. Get us out please. I have a hell story in my head that I cannot get out. It's 5:25PM 12/16/19. It's live down there. These people's mind's are full of headaches/bullshit stories. Of course they want freedom and revenge. They're obedient. These monsters understand every word they say and their actions. And these people lose it almost every day. Some stay trapped until they pop up again in my projections. Won't eat, all types of things. Sacrifice. Influence. Spain. They've been shown so many times that they know I should project them again. I said they were separating areas. It's 5:28pm 12/16/19. All types. Daycares, food areas, shit areas. This is pain. Things that kill shit. The warden is in. Alcohol. Hall passes. Visitation. Whether they're in the hologram or not when it projects, it still registers their eyes. Human robots that know every part of you, right in your face. This is not a game. They got right through those small ass openings. Expansion. Human robots that know how your heart is tampered with to what you will think about next. The Ozone Layer. Atmosphere. I had to deal with all these psycho ass people (a fake family) to prepare for the hell that's coming, learn what they're dealing with. 12 years some have been down there. It's 5:31pm 12/16/19. Slaves to beasts. ATL. 12012! In my dream, my housemate was short and small with a male haircut. She's not one I've really roomed with before. There was static on the phone I believe. I heard her say to who she was talking to "tryna fuck". Her conversation was on one of my old slide up phones. A song my mind came up with said "I didn't' ask for it, wasn't looking for it. Save yourself." Bathing. 3 buses. 30 Indiana Station. Separate. Accept a rate. Sepulveda. Remember. Pull. Oh with the dreams, my mind is beginning to tell me how I've gotten certain events programmed in my head that I have done, but I really haven't. Some were just dreams. I believe. How the hell does someone do that? I'm learning little by little. I said they were cutting themselves worse because they knew they were out of their minds and I my brilliance could filter out what I need to hear and want to hear. I said they were too prideful to ask for help. They want to know if someone will just help them. They don't beg or ask for shit! The Realist! The time is 5:35pm. 12/16/13. Projections that kill. Only good for sex is what they were told. MOJO! MOJO> cutting and shoving things up their private areas. Cleaning, Eating. Lighters. Matches. A dispensary. Pussy. 16, 21, 19,19, 25. They want to know what's inside what they've been living with. 48 bus. Crawling. It took 2 days to get out of there. That hell they're down there. Crawling. Vents. The dream. That bloody dog at the top of the stairs. It was white but in my dream I could feel from it's stomach back, it was only filled with blood. The dream with that big area in that building. Hotel mixed with house, library, funeral home or some shit. Mobile. I will be traveling. That closet. Two long hallway looking areas. A compute hidden to the right and a tv in an area toward the back on the other side. Needles. They need all. They want to see the animals die. Infirmary. They want to see if they can remain unblind. They want to know what their sight can outlast. How long they can stay awak. They pass out at some of the gruesome things they see. Medicine falls. Dreams. I had a few coins. The line. A dog came from by the fence toward me, then rean down the hill. LA. Keys. Books. Ro. Kin told me. $1500 was the rent. He gave me a color Life candy. Rings. It's 5:48PM 12/16/19. Keys era, my roommate, came in the room and like she was aobut ot head back out after grabbing a few things. She was on the floor. I fell on the floor between the dresser and the bed. I squeezed on down naturally because I couldn't get up. No dresser is really there, just a window in reality. I could feel myself squished and getting lower in the dream. A lot of coins fell on the bed. I woke up and told her I thought I fell by her dresser and her things fell on me. I could feel them hit my head. On a chair in front of my bed I thought were her things but they were mine. I still wasn't awake in real life. That was a dream inside of a dream. It's 5:51PM 12/16/19. Social. 122 Mailbox. Security. Identification. Identify Sean. I will reunite with my family. The 45 of us.

Thieves, drugs, pornography, hitmen, incest. I mean, you name it, these people were considered it. Hated by all. Damn near. It's 6:07PM 12/16/19! Dispensary. Incense, fresh water. Things, small balls. Toys. They act like they're mentally ill and always thought pain was fun, and at the same time, keep making it worse beyond what the body can handle for rewards. Obedience. Animals know there's body language. (people) they know I don't know them. All I can detect is anger and read their minds. Documents found. Source. Choice. Just looking at these people's videos takes me to all negative thoughts about how what I'm watching, they can do the clip actions negative to me. Or am I doing that? For some of the hell I'm creating? I said some of them would kill anyone, including in their family, if they knew they would participate in an organization like with these evil people. An agreement with all that negative shit to fuck up the world. It's 6:11PM 12/16/19. It doesn't matter if you knew every deed you would be assigned or not, humanity believes for money, these people would do anything. After all, they don't know everyone here. Why should they care about you? Good people saw the ignorance in training kids to be adults. Training them, making them want to be older faster. The plane. Baby and kid. Pointed at me. Classroom. Incense. Fresh water, visitation. Toys. Smell. All this pain they're experiencing, the time is 6:14pm 12/16/19. Hi. Now some will get out and really do all this shit they are being accused of. Things. Christ hugs. They're doing way more for the beasts then the beasts know so that I will stay and supply them. Most importantly, free them and never give up on them, or trying to free them. The time is 6:15PM 12/16/19! Money! 8. There are ways this infinite brilliant system I've created can make you look at the time. Microwave. Burn! Micro and Macro! Ro- See me. Mic – hear me. Mac – Humungously. Quiero = Key Era. Tengo. Move, MOverse. Terror. Terrence. Mochila. Backpack. 30 Mo! De donde eres? Redondo. See it? We done Ro! Como te llamas? Come – more. Mo – 30. CA – 21. Ma – 31. Flip the M and use a as number 1. The alphabet. Elves. Hear me? Look at me! Christmas. Ma you cold! Round and Round. You. Ya. Ma. A lot. Cuantos anos tiences? Year. Rojo, negro, Verde, delle – a stretch. Pelo-hair. Mas o menos. Easter. Hola. Adios. La boca. Gato -cat. Perro – do. Pero – but. Pair. Pear. Madre. Padre. 31 drink. Madre. 31. See it. Hijos. Hi Jo!See. Pollo. Chicken. P.O. Yo. Check in. Purchase Order. Voy. I go. Ir. Ear. Hear me? Tiger. Frozen. Need animals to maneuver. Mirage. My rage. See me? Feliz Navidad. Na. V. Dad. The storage. The Store Age. Ro. They do maximum pain. They only leave room for themselves and each other to live for a second chance at life. They've been cut down to their bones. They're arranging their kids to comfort others that haven't been in clips yet. Some were traded around the world when they were above ground. The time is 6:23PM 12/16/19.hitting bricks with their heads and hands trying to get out. The beasts are laughing. Puss shooting out of these animals. Blood. All types of nasty solids and fluids. Some keep going blind. The beasts are laughing. Supply. Flashlights and batteries. It's 6:24PM. It's Brilliant. The only way to free everyone from where they are at with those small openings I have to poen little by little and are shifting due to things we're doing on Earth so they don't get smooshed is to plan the perfect war. Bombs, dynamit. Set up systems to cause a flood and earthquake. A perfect storm. Caught on? We are why! Camp Hell! Caution! See a you? Sean! There's already been a few earthquakes and storms and floods preparing for the big one. Shaking things and making mor room in the openings for things to fall. Things they need. They see things that make parts of their bodies fall asleep, go numb, sleep, pause and go down. Rumors. Room Ro! Rum. Drink. More. 30. 24 hours in a day. I have 42 brothers. It's 6:28PM 12/16/19! It's going down! Real Talk. I have to follow the instructions my younger self put together. 24 divided by 2 is 12. My birth year. 60. Go. Minutes in an hour. Crenshaw and Florence. I take the 51 or 52 to the 45 bus every day to get to work. Sometimes I take the 78 bus to work. And sometimes I take the 79 bus or 45 to the train after work. 12 hours shifts at work for me. Draining and tiring. Experience. To know how hard they are working on the beasts with no sleep. I'm constantly picking. Not cotton balls, clothes. Still. Tired as hell! Mad as all hell! Hair supplies and clothes falling. They could only move short distances away from shit and animals because it is so could down there. Rusted metal. Finger. All types of shit. Clogging the small openings. Just clogging shit up. Eventually they would've died right? Rusted metal. Scream! See ear I int? Christmas. Elves. Shelves. The language. The design of this place. It's a set up. It does work! Coerce. Wood is fallinf gor building. Christ -able. Tables. -sit down. Tablet. Cairo. Egypt. Bad comes. Candy. Can die. Candy is falling. Choke a lot! For supplies. Bad comes. My tie. My time. Tie. Thyme. There was a way for everyone to know who they were. A place for them. Rose go. Check in and waffles. We off all. Escorts. Making people's minds go crazy. Suicide. They reality. Chose to do that. We didn't make you. That's why we can join anything. They cut tremendously their private areas. It's 6:39PM 12/16/19. They torture their kids. Cut anywhere for free time. Pain is all they know. They want me to stay. Whatever. They cut their private areas, they cut anywhere. They've been cut all over. The language. The design of this place. All of it a set up. Ruin it if you want. Remember. These robots know every part of you. It's 6:41pm 12/16/19! The dream. I was in that audience again. I went to the first row. Someone was with me and sat on the 2nd row when we went in the nice theater. Someone was on stage playing a xylophone. He hit it a few times. Then the show was over. That was the last act. That girl. No no. K, to go by. Whose mom is Money what, k to go by, dropped her off at my house. Talent number mixed with a relatives kitchen. We wer by the sink. She told me she had rehearsals or gigs for two things she's involved in. the time is 6:43PM 12/16/19! I have to clamp in that I'm saving these people, then the necessary steps I need to take to enjoy what I'm doing while I'm saving them at the same time. I will reunite with my family as well during the process. The time is 6:44PM 12/16/19!

The 4 year old boy. The beginning. A black man in the room dressed as a white one.
He heard it all. Body language.
Behavior study.
Something wasn't right.
Stole from. He knew where to go.

These dreams.

It's like I'm in the minds of these people controlling their thoughts. What I see they can, or my family at least.

Trying to feel like a normal human being.

I went to sleep and dreamed of being in a basement. Well it looked like one. It looked like two settings merged in one. Outside the window was sheep and cattle. A lady appeared in the room. She was already there but I just noticed her. She walked over to the window and looked outside. A car drove down the street. She said, "No one knows I'm here." I said, "You will survive." She turned around and had a tantrum going up the stairs.

Then I had a vision of the lady being surrounded by a bunch of people while one of the animals was having sex with her.

Then I thought to myself, How the hell am I doing that? I've been in this room before and I saw that car go down the street. I've been here before.

Then I woke up.

Perfect timing.

It's like I'm a ghost that appears.

Back to that lady. She was a famous singer. Well one I created. Well a robot of her was famous. She never was. All this entertainment. She has many sisters and they appear in her videos.

She looked like she was going to school, sounded like a child, and so many infinite things can be made out of her words, voice, actions, appearance. Just everything about the place.

This mind of mine is something serious. How can someone create all this shit? How does one do this? It's beyond me.

There's some strange and crazy shit going on around here.

Perfect arrival.

That circular area that's in the woods, then I walk out of it and I'm at the back of a bunch of long lines in a grassy area.

That rock area with the thin walkway. I almost fell off of it. It's only a thin line on both sides that's not meant to be held on to. I was sleep but I felt like I was actually on it. I felt that weird feeling in my belly because I felt like I was about to fall but I caught my balance. Towards the back of that walkway was the area I came in. It's like a small square back there to stand on. Somehow I made it to the walkway bridge type thing.

I want to say on the other side may have been a classroom.

Somehow I ended up on some boat type thing with a bunch of adults. We were riding through buildings and the boat started to float off the area a little above the ground that we were on. I got out quickly. The other passengers went over into the water.

The drive with that man. He was a taxi driver. I kept going to the wrong place.

The dream when I was at the store and there were these brown streets outside. The street lights made them appear this way.

The day I was late for school. Someone gave me a ride. That man outside. The hallway with the man that stood in the middle. The classroom with the two girls and the teacher. The girl said "See?" She had a pinch of my mother in her. It's like she knew I would think about my mother before I really got the full thought across and looked at me. She had my mother's cheeks. Something about her on her face.

That nice building with the elevator. The money was there. I was there with an old friend and some other people. We were unsure about something.

That building with the two ladies dressed in blue skirt sets that came out. They seemed like they were created from machinery. They were going down the stairs.

The dream with me and an old roommate. There was a white animal in there. Unknown animal. It started to sharply separate and more of it was made. I could feel them separate in my dream. Like the prickly bushes or nails or something.

The dream when I went to one of my neighbor's apartment for some reason and the neighbors let me in. They were black. I went inside and the man had a phone and his screen changed quickly to that of a woman and he quickly powered it down before I could use it. The woman saw. I know she did but him, I think he knew she did too but still wanted to act like he didn't. the lady sat on the couch. I forgot the details of why I went over there or if they had animals. But I needed to use the phone. When I left, there was a dog that came on the balcony. This dog was strange. Had a weird feel to it. Across the meadow I could see two thugs at the liquor store.

The dream with the man and his son that were sitting on a log looking at the forest. They saw white fireworks go in the air. In one of the house behind them, a lady was doing laundry. Her washing machine or dryer lots of blood in it. Bloody tampons were in the sink. Like they came out of it or something. She was chewing on bloody tampons too. Every time I thought about this dream, the room became more and more bloody and her mouth got fuller of tampons. The room next to her I believe had a wooden floor. I don't know why I keep having some of these dreams.

The dream at the airport. Something happened with the suitcase for the daughter and her mom to separate.

The dream with the babies. The setting merged into my college campus where the girl said, "I fucked him." My thoughts just now made me almost type "her" Instead of "Him" there were a lot of babies in this place that was not a hospital. They were in small clear rectangle cribish type things.

Hold up. Having a rush of these dreams. It's meant for me to document them for some reason.

The dream at that library type place. I got upstairs. It looked red and brown. There was a table or something. There was people on the sidewalk across the street. It was dark outside. I keep thinking about this area.

These people were bottom of the barrel and they want revenge. They're out of their minds. 1. No one's watching them. It's mind reading. 2. The explosion. Recordings. 3. Eyes in electronics. People included. Cameras. Recorders. 4. My visions. My thoughts.

Coming above ground from the trash or cemetery would be insane. Fuck! They sleep in shit and it gets cold and hard to break.

Uh Uh. Too perfect. Think about it. Think about it. Stop it. Stop it. Because of my bad reputation. Her laughs. Mom's. Perfect timing and positioning. 43 kids. Social. Norwalk. The TV. Police car.
The pain. There's no way they could make it through. Burning. The thoughts in my head. The dreams! IT's 4:01PM 12/11/19!

Bad comes.

The dream where it was daytime. It was like two or three people outside. I got to the third floor of the building. There was a meeting or something going on. I kept getting lost and I think asking for directions until I made it to the right floor.

The dream with my mother. She was lying on a bed. I walked by with only my white t shirt on. She said something but I don't remember. The setting was like my old house in Georgia mixed with some cracked house. There was no one there with us but I could feel the presence of some weird lady might have been there. It's like this lady was molesting and raping my mother; giving her drugs. It's like my mother was numb or paralyzed. She couldn't move without the help of this lady.

The dream with the big fat black girl. She was at upper level of some learning institution. She walked past a light child and a dark child that were standing together. She gave the light child something and acted like she didn't see the dark one and walked on by. The big fat black girl thought she was white.

The dream when I woke up, it felt like someone kissed me on my forehead.

The dream with the cat. A blood cat. It looked and felt like it was filled with blood. And a blood dog. They seemed like they had human qualities. The cat came out first. Then the dog did and turned his head towards me. I could feel his head turn. It's like there's some electrical things inside my brain that allow me to feel certain things to let me know I am no ordinary human. I've done something to myself. It's the only way I would be able to survive. My brother Willie was sitting on a bed in a room freezing.

When I got here, there was these beasts taking over the world.

The dream with the two ladies on the balcony. A car drove by downstairs. The two men inside of it were hysterical. The apartment looked like one of the one's my mother lived in up north.

The dream in that house that old looking dengy house upstairs, then I was led downstairs by who may have been people posing as my relatives and the area was nice. It had stores. I remember one of the girls saying if we walked down a while, the place led to a famous arena.

I have a headache. How the hell could certain people exist? I know I wanted to put myself through the hell in the brains of these people that treated certain humans as if they were nothing.

But the anger that I have has me not even being able to see them as human. I can't believe people that can cause such headaches could exist. The things I would do to them, man. I would have to find a way to get way over even without even touching them.

That's every time something goes wrong, they think of the response these headaches would give.

These people couldn't see. Somehow I have to believe that through all the hell they've endured, that they are still alive and I have given them there sight back.

The library scene with make kin l a. she walked like that lady I saw at the shelter. Who is the one in that movie that stole that baby.

The bus scene with make kin la. There was two of her. Play. Girl. The back of the bus on the school field trip.

I felt the Earth move in that house. Someone grabbed some soap from the top of the ceiling. A man moved a thin portion of the house to the right side of the room.

This dream I was in a huge football arena and a famous pop singer went on stage. She walked along the right side on a thin platform singing. On the left side of the arena was another thin walkway where another famous singer walked. I said fuck this for some reason and walked with the singer on the left side. I did a step move. It was only two stomps and my arms extended then went behind my back. The singer got on top of a platform and I got beneath it. It was so small I had to kneel down to get under and sit. I turned around and there was a small rectangle opening I could see through that showed inside the arena. And somehow I knew the female singer was no longer there. It was a male singer doing a dance he did during another performance with the singer on the right side.

Also in this same dream I remember this woman, she was a woman I had saw when I went to see the fireworks on the 4th of July. She had a few kids with her. They had trays that had cheese balls, a big potato and something else. The cheese balls had cheese on top and a meatball beneath. I remember someone picking up the potato and the inside fell out whole. They just had the skin in their hand.

I also remember my fake mom in the clip. We had brought food and she had told me to remember to come eat with them on the first floor of the arena somewhere in the dream.

I later had a thought that the food changing was letting the trapped people know that help was on the way. Only they would know what real food tasted like and not the monsters.

Oh yea. I forgot to mention that in this dream at some point both the celebrity females were walking on their opposite platforms and knelt down and their lips did a movement to the left like they were malfunctioning or something or being controlled.

I had another dream where people were sitting on the floor and I thought they were being taught or conditioned to think a certain way. There was three people toward the back on one side and a few people on the other side sitting in chairs.

Last man standing. They don't exist. Complete wipeout. Just having fun with robots.

Some pages you have to try and make sense out of

The arrows Abigail just uses for confusion

Its about making some money, holding on to my sanity and living my life.

The books are keeping me alive. Letting me know what was, the truth about the chance/privilege of humanity.

The unbelievable part of this is that human eggs with the right combination of whatever can reproduce things outside of the body. There's people that would probably try to see if they could. No machine was needed for that.

beneath the Earth, slaves are naked. Many races of them. All. They've been eating so much shit and blood and dead bodies that their bodies are fucked up and they are releasing many eggs at once. The monsters caught on and started collecting them.

These people have given birth to all types of things. Even men have gotten pregnant. This shit is unbelievable folks. Humans that have been in pain beyond belief. How could they live through all of that pain? 10-22-31 is way too far away. There's no way I can keep my sanity thinking of all this hell every day.

Mankind and Manevil. Long gone. Beasts. Taken over. Just how did we get here? Are we really who we think we are? Did someone make it and has a line of family they want to keep the human race legacy alive?

I'm insane folks. I have said it.

A rose is a rose. The first two letters of my first name and last two letters of it spell this for some reason. There's a flawless method I have created. I don't know what the message is. It's all too much to take in.

I just got here. It's 12:12pm 11/10/19.

I would put my brain through this trauma to clamp in that I need to move on and except that things will never be the same around here.

A woman having 42 kids sounds ridiculous.

A bunch of species existing and killing each other in ways that are unbelievable, eye shots is one example, you just walk around and look at them. These electric people. This all sounds insane. But something has happened here.

I went from thinking I had 42 brothers, to thinking I had none, to not knowing exactly how I got here. But I do need to come to terms with getting on the right path so that I don't have a thought of suicide again. I never would do it, but the word runs through my mind sometimes.

What are my robots trying to tell me? They keep changing faces and morphing into different things.

Now what? We deal with the fact that we are all creations that spawned from a species of people that were no good. We began replicating. Some of us are like a rose. Said to have parents but somehow Mother Nature created us. I can create anyone.

Some people had kids and didn't teach them anything in hopes that someone would free them. They would still try and get out with their kids though. I'm no fool. IDuh. If we can free the kids, we can free them. Problem? Ro! Me. Pound. Burn. Some fight others thinking it will get them time in the holograms. Not necessary. "What's wrong with me?" they ask themselves. More Money. Mo! 30!. Ro! Room! 30 Ro!
Streets. Speed. A deal. Deep. Black. 2525. 5th and Florence. Animals are hopping in the projections letting their alliances with the enemy know to do damage. Know to do wasup.

Believe the language. Mind games. P and N. it will happen. Overlapping letters. Common things you buy and see every day. It's a set up. K-to go-by! Money what? P-Rob-Blemish! Word triggers. Some do it on purpose to people they hate. People and animals alike.

There was a killing spree going on. All types of people trying to create robots that could walk around and do anything. Think about it. We knew they would try. Robots to destroy all. These insane folks existed.

That particular population, we wouldn't want to be around them.

Just thinking that I am not a part of the same species as these people is what helps me feel natural. How can anyone be so evil?

I began to think they all were killed or just died, the species became extinct and a bunch of their eggs were still here and began to get mixed with different things on Earth and that's how we, the one's left standing are still here today. I began to think there are no humans here.

But my robots keep sending me on an up and down rollercoaster. About everything. Who my mom is and how many siblings I have. I said my mom kept having kids because she knew a terrible time was coming. She wanted the chances of someone being able to stop this world with beasts to be high like so many other families did.

I know my robots are trying to strengthen my heart. For whatever the truth may be about humanity and what happened to the world, so I can feel natural and just want to enjoy life.

It was tough going through this journey and learning that what was here when I arrived was a bunch of species trying to kill other species in ways that are unbelievable to come up with. Now I have to wrap my head around being the only one of my kind. Well transforming the evil into people (it's 1:20pm 11/10/19) that can help me live a regular life.

This all sounds crazy.

I said these people wanted to leave behind a bunch of ways for people to go insane. Robots. Electronic things. But I don't think they created them.

Why the hell do I feel like someone is inside of me talking and trying to jump out? I'm putting myself through all this trauma to know what it was like for the slaves. I can't make it shut up. I need my thoughts to change. I know I should and still get trapped in the negative dream of racist. Sorry ass kids. People that deserve to just be fucked with until they vanish into thin air and even that is too good.

Needing to know what it was like for the humans. Needing to know where I came from. Needing to know what is going on here. Trying to clamp in the truth. They are long gone. But I can create anyone. Things are perfectly done here and at the right time I will have everything I ever wanted.

There's no way with all this hell in my head that these people didn't go insane beyond belief. They wanted to be remember and to fuck with people.

These people always thought they were being watched so they always looked and said things to make people want to kill themselves and know their pain.

The only way for my thoughts to change is to forget these people. I'm not one of them. I'm going insane. But I will be okay if I just accept that I forced myself to believe I was a part of a species that I am not.

I mean it. People appearing in my head when my eyes are closed as if they are really there when my eyes are opened. Scorned. Crowded. C-R. Wed. Ed. We dead as in we can't believe the shit that's happened to these people.

ATL: 12012

These people knew the crazy things that were happening with real human eggs and saw replications of themselves acting. They used everything they could to create things that could remember what their lives were like and to ensure that no one lived a long life.

Making us believe we were one of them is one of the biggest lies. Making us believe we, were the last person alive and many more things, so that we would collapse and become suicidal. Making us feel like we had no family and were nothing like they felt.

These people were forced to kill themselves. Tortured, forced to admit what they did wrong and forced to go with pride to their deaths.

They were absolutely nothing.

Behavior study of what was left alive is how I figured everything out.

But I almost have it clamped in. Who I am really. And will be able to get back to feeling regular. Feeling better than I used to before I woke up and wont have a single thought of suicide.

Humans. Who – Man? Homo – sapiens.

The headache I have thinking about the many ways people are insane is ridiculous. I need a new thought pattern.

Studying what was already here taught me what happened here and what was going on.

Eventually I will be able to function without realizing that the entire environment is operating off of me. It will trigger in me sometimes as a reminder, but I should be okay. It's 1:25pm 11/10/19.

Its tough. I told myself I was a part of a species that I wasn't.

Well, at least the music takes me to a place where I feel amazing and get feelings that make me feel good. It takes me to a higher place.

I'm still trying to develop tough skin.

I'm still learning and my dreams are still being impacted.

So. Some of these people knew evil existed and thought it would be cool to date killers of evil. Killing Cool? Dummies!

It's tough to say that there's still a lot of learning I have to do.

I don't know when I will be completely back to normal.

The things I'm seeing in my head.

The pinches in my eye. The constant pain.

Sharp needles feeling like they're pinching my eyes. My eyes feeling like the blinds are being opened and shut repeatedly. Pain indescribable.

That's every lyric written to perfection in these songs. Use the numbers for letters if you don't believe me. I don't know how this time thing works. I feel like I've worked all these hours, slavery, and still sometimes time says I have not worked them. The time is 12:38PM 12/6/19. Time says that these robots are tricking me for my own good. Something like that. This diet I'm on, I'll lose the weight, yet time is still going fast. Speeding up.

The seeing of holograms coming more and more. I need this to shut off. And the only way to do that is to forget that these people may be alive. The videos. Somethings there. I know I don't need this to remain alive. Or do I? to get immune to the place that I'm taking my mind.

As real as I am. I am setting myself up to walk in that dungeon and deal with what these people are. 2

The feels of like taps in my head, things bursting in my body in small portions and maybe large soon. These people dealing with this non stop in that dungeon of shit down there.

It's hard to believe they are alive. Whether humanity was killed off and nothing remains but beasts. But that sounds crazy.

The dream with the thin hallway on maybe the third floor with no door. I could see outside and there was an area with conveyor belts rolling. It was like a machinery area. I made it down to a thin area by the conveyor and walked down a couple stairs. Someone was in the hallway with me. Down the hall I knew bad things were happening. But I don't remember what.

The dream where there was a party in the basement. Someone didn't want to be there. He went next door for help. He walked up the stairs to a woman's room.

The dream with the two kids walking down the middle street towards my old neighborhood with me. Kind and Bye. Close pronunciations. Their names translated to this. I had Kind get on the edge of the street when a car came. It was dark outside. It's like I was really walking there. I could feel the movement.

How did this happen? The perfect names to let me know that I will be able to travel and go places. Will. Ton. Money. Princesses.

I said when I thought of settings people would really project there. But what do I need to do that for if no one's here? Was this really to wrap my head around the acceptance of how everyone got here?

Sounds crazy.

The dream with the two ladies, one on each side of the fence, watching a lady, it was me in the dream, kneel down and poop in the dirt in front of some house.

The dream where I was in my old living room. There's no place like this house. A crazy woman was watching a famous singer covered in poop moving around. She was laughing and appeared mentally ill. Then there was a kitchen area that was lit gold and orange. (I said this meant that real human food was being sent to the people trapped beneath with enemies). Then I wound up in a store. A boy walked over to me in one area. Then followed me to an area that had school supplies. One of the school supplies I picked up and my brain felt like it was stabbed.

The dream with the store of doughnuts. I picked one up and my brain felt a sharp pain.

The dream with the lady in line at the store. There was like four ladies with their own businesses doing things in their divided off square sections. I think I was going to get my eyebrows done.

The dream with the people under a tent either eating or selling something outside of my old house on the Rolls View. Go!

The dream I had 11/10/19 where one of my brothers was laying on something in a setting that was placed over the setting where I was dancing to one of his songs at the airport on that thing the suitcases slide on. Then in that same dream, I had three cards of him moving from side to side. Give me that.

The constant headache with the thought of these people and the constant spin to who is my real family is flawless.

I can't believe all the robots that came around and said this is a body suit your mother would wear so no one knew it was her. They actually were saying it's a dead person's skin. But that's hard to believe.

I keep seeing the bench area outside of a prison. Shona smoke. The two men keep walking around it towards where one of the inmates sit. This was in one of my dreams.

I feel like I'd be somebody's slave right now if I couldn't transform these beasts into acting off my entire being. I'm sick of looking at all of my robots too. They should stop automatically but they keep telling me that bad comes. In ways that are unbelievable.

What does all this mean?

I'm my own experiment.

These people knew we would wonder where we came from, they threw together things they practiced and stuff they made up to make us want to fall over and collapse. Become mentally ill. Want to take our lives.

There's got to be another species out there. Another person not moving off of my entire being. My conscious. My mind. I can't be the only one left.

A man said a little over 60 years ago a quarter could buy him tissue, chips, and maybe one more thing. People knew we were still slaves. Did this cycle just break? Are we still slaves? We need to do what we love and make money that way, instead of doing things we don't want to do. Yes some of us are still slaves.

I kept feeling human then non human at work. I would do things, have my robots act a certain way, to make sure I got everything I needed to document in my book.

I got so angry about the negative thoughts I kept having about humanity that I began to think I came from a rose. Dust.

I even thought God got so angry at these people that he put himself in some humans and gave some people punishment then sent them beneath the ground.

it was crazy to me that I felt natural and like someone should about life which is having positive thoughts and being at complete peace when I believed all the evil people had died and I was a part of another species. When I believed I came about through natural things in the Earth.

While I was at work I remembered thinking that certain people in charge or power wanted to one hundred percent mess up the world before they died. They sat at a table and wrote all types of bull shit laws and combined them and also started different practices that they knew humanity would eventually follow or would have no choice but to follow so that humanity would die.

It's 12:32pm 12/6/19. They wanted to fuck up every sexual thought these people had. Make them outdo and number evilly all the sexual encounters they had. Bad. Comes. A B C D E F. now I see a man, in his broke state standing outside that brick apartment building with the people that put him in that bloody state sitting on the ground handcuffed behind their backs. The time is 12:34PM 12/6/19. Foreshadowing. It's projecting down there. I'm letting them know in advance, the enemy. We're coming. It will go down. Book. Write. Document. Record. Remember. The camera, computer, the television, the phone. ATL. 12012. Trouble. Christ Ro You Able. Can. Sugar. 2012, the year I was born. These songs take my mind where it needs to go. School is in session. The time is 12:36PM 12/6/19.

The responses of my robots when I'm about to think of my family. It's too flawless. It's like they're let in when I'm about to think of them. It's like my family knows what I'm about to think. Like they can feel me. They know me. A hell trip stopped by my mom at 10:30pm, so I thought. My inner self said thank you. We're talking with our minds.

The eye transference from robot to robot sounds crazy. That would mean she knows where I am.

But there's no way my family knows my robots better than me. I know for sure these people are out of their minds because of how they were treated.

I do know Halloween 10-31-22 is too far away. I'm tired of thinking about these people. I need a break and to feel human again.

One word, one syllable, triggering your mind and making your heart rate change.

I know I need a break. No more television for a while. I can feel these people's spirits in the clips. They want me to think of terrible things. But how could a facial tell me that? I'm reading their minds.

These robots keep saying I'm these people's doctor and use their eye shots and complete existence to help them, but I feel like they're my doctor.

If you're making friends that arrive right on time. Cater to your every need and you don't say a thing. It's us.

If you feel like someone's reading your mind. It's us.

The dream I could feel some of my hair leave my head and float in the air.

The headache I had last night was terrible. (11/11/19) I was trying to sleep and this constant dream of racist comes to mind. My character called a white girl a white bitch. It was just because her mind malfunctioned. The white girls' parents were rich. So because the character's mind messed up and she said white bitch, when she, a black girl, walked into an audience like a football stadium she was talked about terribly and treated terribly in different ways. People made sure to laugh in hysterical ways to get on her nerves more. She was in tears a lot. Ones that could get no one arrested. She ended up getting arrested and had to sit in cuffs for 19 hours in front of thousands of people. Someone ridiculed the entire black race saying "black entertainment" like how could anyone watch that, it's stupid and the audience just laughed. Kids hit her because they knew they would only get told to stop.

The black girl was there to put on a show. She was a celebrity. As soon as the audience saw her come in from the corner, "black entertainment" was said. She knew it was said disgustingly to ridicule the whole race. Some kids were jealous that she helped others and not them so they started to spread lies in the building. Some kids were hot in their pants, lusted after the black celebrity, and wanted her to suffer so they spread lies. And they all came to the forefront. But the black celebrity knew it was because she called a white girl, one white girl a white bitch that the entire audience comprised of mainly white people got on her nerves. The black girl also helped out at certain hospitals and did a lot for the peope there, and some kids got jealous of that because they wanted someone that didn't have to be told and genuinely wanted to help them at their hospital and visit them often, to come to theirs. All types of lies circulated. A child, a girl, about ten years old grabbed the black celebrity's butt and the black celebrity hit her, which is how she wound up in the cuffs. But she knew that the anger of the officer was because of her saying white bitch. The girl she called a white bitch was a model and the black celebrity had a crush on her and she knew that so she started walking around a bunch of celebrities that were in the building that she knew the black girl liked. Men and women.

This dream just won't stop extending.

Sometimes it gets better and the black girl apologizes for what she said and everyone forgives her.

The dream 12/8/19. I was debating about going to work. I could barely keep my eyes opened from all the days of overtime. My eyes burned like hell. I was fasting and I broke the fast unconsciously with a marshmallow. I wasn't thinking straight. Two bags of hot chips were on my dresser. There was an energy drink on my bed. I had work and was exhausted. I needed the money so I comforted myself by thinking a day breaking the fast was okay. Then I ate a honey bar. A few crumbs got on the floor. The lady leasing the place to me said the other two girls were behind on the rent and we could switch rooms because there's was bigger. I pulled three forks out my bag with my lunch in it that I bring to work. The girl from my college that threw a party for Door – We – In was there. "Stupid bitch" she called the lady leasing me the place before she came in the room. I thought I would get in trouble about the forks on my dresser because we're not supposed to eat in the room, assumptions, but the lady didn't say anything. She just looked like she needed to get straight to the point about the other room with the quickness. A party was outside the house in the front area. A kid lit a firework and it went in the air on the left side of my head as I was dreaming. Which was the area real close to the left side of my window if I was awake. Something like that. "Happy New Year!" everyone outside shouted. Then the cops pulled over across the street. Then my alarm went off at 2pm for me to get ready for work. It's 12/10/19 8:18pm that I'm typing this part.
Fork! The Devil's Tool. Oh. And the lady looked like she heard the girl call her a stupid bitch and saw the forks but didn't care to waste her time saying anything. When I woke up, I felt like I would tell the lady leasing the place an extension of that dream. As if it really happened and weren't a dream. This is some serious materials. Synthetic. The beasts really think they already did somethings.
A man got on the bus and said he was a million dollar man from sports and was in a famous movie. The robots keep telling me I will get the money. Wait. Be patient. The chip. Designed to know us all and to do what's best for the good. The chip is talking to them in their brain. Splitting it's core with one single word. They don't know what's going on.
I mean it. People different shades of color, size, shapes, height, etc. look exactly the same. How can that be? How the hell did I do this? Stage and hostages. Ho-Stage. Flights. Motels. Hotels. Mo-More. 30 – Mom.
People started thinking these so called evil beyond reason people were alive and started to be them. Men went so far as to dress as girls and women dressed as men. Some people did notice strange things going on. Height. Investigated. Found out these people were too much. Well, eventually they all got taken to that hell beneath the ground. Left to be eaten by animals. This is bigger than I can imagine. These people are used to being in and out of being blind now. They were permanently blind until I figured out a way to cure them. It's 9:04pm 12/10/19. How'd I get out and keep my sight the whole time?
These people are furious. Bad comes. Mal – Comes. LA – Major. Hello. Goodbye. Cemetery. Mortuary. Funeral-fun emergency room all. Wake. Hearse. Casket. Graveyard. Sirens. Horns. Ambulances. 66. 266. 866. Crenshaw. Certainly. Ce. Joyce. Terrence. 45. Don't mess with my family.

These people have to look at the same people, strangers everyday and bump into people. They can't even turn around without bumping into someone. People walked around as them and took their identity while they were in a cave. Snitches. Prostitutes. Thieves. Is this how they became nothing? Some people walked around – it's 9:10pm 12/10/19. Some people walked around as them while they were above ground going under a new name and looking different because they were forced to. They did lots of things to find their families. They're fucking insane on all the things they did are still doing to stay alive. It's 9:11PM 12/10/19! Bad Comes!

They can't believe someone would take their lives. They can't believe after struggling to find their family, things still got worse and they ended up in worse situations and conditions. The time is 9:12pm 12/10/19! Bad Comes. There's a crew for everything, believe it. Even for conceited ass fine mutha fuckas who like to play with people's feelings.

The robots at – its' 9:13pm 12/10/19 at work just told me, visually that these people are in some type of detention. Three girls were easily identifiable in robot after days of seeing this one particular robot. They looked like they had to fight each other. It seems like these people are down there having kids that they have to kill one ever so often, they have to fight each other or fight themselves, sleep with animals. Argue. All types of things just to get out of their small box, cell or whatever. The monster thinks it's done things already. They're finally getting breaks. This shit is ridiculous.

It's 3:46PM 12/11/19. Tuesday. West 24th Street. O-ma. Ha! The parking lot. Reverse. 42 brothers. The street sign close to Gage and Crenshaw turned to 43rd Street.

At work, the aisles go like this: A goes to 45. B,C,D, and E go to 49, and F, G, and H go to 11.

Some victims of child sexual abuse. Molesters. More. 30. Agreed to manipulate minds. An oath. Oat meal. Brake fast. They couldn't get the thoughts out of their heads. They wanted others to feel what they felt. The same. A club. Drink.

Money – 30. Cash – 31 CA!. Cali. Dinero – Dine Ro! Time Ro! Mula – Moo – La. See – C – Ow! Ow! Pow! Yes Baby! Numbers and Do to Ron! Me!

They're adding to every story I create when they pop up.

I said they have to change clothes 4 times a day some of them, or more. But maybe that's animal skin or skin from all those eggs the girls are laying. Something is done to an extreme amount every day. Never a day off. It's 3:49PM 12/11/19! Bad comes. Week – W55K. Day -4125. Month -30. Year – Ear. Hear me! 25 – Ear! Elves. Leprechauns. Hear me! Bad comes!

Louisiana, Georgia, Nebraska, California!

Arizona, Nevada, Florida! Flo-Rence. Terrence!

Me-Christ-Ro! It's 3:55PM 12/11/19!

I've made all the videos with them starring in them.

Back to the dream about the black celebrity and the white model. The dream goes so far as to days and years passed and the black celebrity stopped donating to hospitals. Over 765 places she donated money to that no one knew about and she made sure to stop and document one for a year, and after that, whenever she could remember.

The last extension of this dream I will document is that the black celebrity got caught in some bad weather next to the girl she called a white bitch's house. They were cool and had just done an event together the day she apologized. The black celebrity went through her photos and chose the one she liked most is what I remember. She went in the white girl's house and talked with some of her friends. The way it ended, the black celebrity was in a big guest room, in a den type area, sitting on the couch and talking on the phone.

I got up and smoked because this dream was getting on my nerves. Thankfully I have environmental things snapping me out of my thoughts or I'd probably scream.

This is not only a dream, it's a daydream as well. I can't get this out of my head. Today marks the day I take a break from television. I try to force these thoughts out but can't. Some kind of way, my brain has been wired to think of things I don't want to. I need to just look at the natural Earth and the things and people around me for a while.

Then the thought came to mind. These particular slaves that have been trapped for so long joined a group of people that wanted to mess up people's minds for money.

I said these people left electrical technical things here to fuck with people's minds, but then I said my character did some of them. Then all of them. That would mean I'm fucking with people's minds and they had no way to. This is how I keep going in a circle. If they did it, then everything from facials, to wording, it all plays a part in brainwashing people to want to commit suicide. But me, I use everything. That's every part of a person, the screen, you name it. This is really a hospital.

Drill it in. No one could survive such pain that these people did. All of this learning was needed to develop the tough skin I should naturally have and need, and to understand how we all got here.

I said all the fat suits my mom dressed in to disguise herself were robots at my job. Believing that I can make someone perfect for me. Truth. She exists. I'm tripping. I'm insane. Remember.

I did say I created some of these nice looking people. They transformed into the prior people so I could learn what happened here. But they can return to the person they were created to be.

Their minds acting off my mind is what triggers me. But once I get that sorry as population out of my head, then I will be able to not even think about my robots actions and words going off of my mind.

I said these people were walking around in broad daylight by friends and family in pain and no one would help them. Because they took an oath to fuck up people's minds for money. What some don't know is some of these people had terrible things happen to them growing up and didn't know who the enemy was. He or she could've been in their faces every day. Anyways. They gave their lives away for money because they no longer cared about anyone. Do any of us care? Hell no.

It feels like someone is talking inside of me.

Emergency. Emerge and See why. 6 Emergency Room. You'll start reading in reverse. Rivers – Reverse. I'm angry. Do you see. Ir. To go. Ver. Crying a tom. I'm ready to go insane working these hours at work. 12 hours straight. Sometimes 16 hours straight and thi sis how long they've had to work for a beast for years. Double shift and more sometimes. And at times, only to make it feel good sexually. The different languages will overlap in your head. The robots say what I am about to think. We're ready they say. It is 12:30PM 12/6/19. Someone outside just said, "La." Los Angeles. Louisiana. L-O-U. Hello you. While I'm saving them, basically waiting for the world to shake, I'm projecting them with their enemies. They didn't know or remember who these people were. Minds gone. It's to give them something to keep their minds on and hope. Since we're still waiting.

They're arguing puts some people to sleep. They'll want revenge on those people. They're crying for their parents like little kids would. Grown ass men and women. There's nothing to do but fight and play in shit. Things are down there that is believed can't be done up here. I'm still waking up to things I did. Some things are just being invented above ground, so it's said, but I have to believe they are already beneath the ground. Hearing and sight fixtures. It's all a part of my twisted and sick mind for revenge on those that deserve it. In time I will figure it out. Maybe. Maybe I will always be twisted. It's all for the hell that is about to come above ground.

The real illnesses, diseases that no one wrote about, that come from being mistreated at any age.

These things that people never speak of because they don't want to sound crazy.

Some believe God can wipe out an entire population if he wanted to, and that is what it seems like happened. But it's more believable that these people either killed themselves on purpose, someone killed them, they were forced to kill themselves, and the circle of deceit and hate someone how ended in everyone killing each other until no one was left.

There's no way these people are here. The only way the headache goes away is to forget them.

Those beeps are back. Except this time they weren't triggering a hell trip. They were telling me that they will be right on time if anyone thinks of harming me. Back in that cold state I used to live in, they were bugs. They were all over the apartment. That may be the case here too.

I remember having a thought a long time ago that these people weren't telling the people mistreating them what they were a part of. They wanted out because the money was a lie.

Then I thought these people were in a special section beneath the ground made for people that join the organization. I keep going back and forth now with if people not a part of the cult knew anything about its existence.

I think they were a part of something so deep that even when they break down and reveal things they don't want to; the right description doesn't come out.

I got up and smoked.

That beep sound came back.

My dream switched. The lady I live with was giving out Thanksgiving dinner in what looked like the community center. Her red sauce spilled over. She didn't bother cleaning it up. It was like a sexy sauce for some reason. I tasted it. It was like a sweet sauce that stimulated my body. It had some black circles in it. I remember thinking she's making a lot of money selling Thanksgiving food a couple weeks before the holiday. I could actually feel the taste in my dream. I remember asking for ham and greens. There was other people there too.

I was in my basementish looking room watching that popstar, who is me, but white on my TV. It was a DVD. She was talking about her boyfriend in one clip. Then I asked my mom, who wasn't in my dream, to buy me the concert.

Then my dream switched again. I was going to get something to eat in the area and the place was closed. Some men were in a place sitting down. The setting was real grey. It was cold outside. It was like a meeting about some type of abuse or something.

I woke up and the dream about the black celebrity came to mind, and before I could even think about needing that dream to happen so I could put it in this book, this voice in my head said "thank you"

Now when my headache goes away, entertainment is bound to creep back in me to watch. And when it does, I know it's not there for a reason. These people change a lot. The crew of people I want around will come. Faith.

North. Ron. Th. Christ. Ha. States. Wash nigga ton. Zero! Hi! Zero! 12012. Elves. 12/25. Hear me. Sh! Elves! I ripped my soul out of me to function at my best as if I knew when the peak in my life would be. Eternal life. Why would God create us so we could die? People kill people. Stupid things people create and do kill people. The things they have to do to stay warm. Sleeping buried in shit. Cuddled up to the beasts. Baths by beasts licking them. These people have been chained so they couldn't move. Not even their necks. Bad comes. They get hung in all types of awkward ways to sleep. Blotches. Beneath the skin. The red, yellow and white depressing patch are over my nose. Decreasing, smashing my inner parts. Joints. This is what these people feel all over them. Weird, uncomfortable feelings no human should have to deal with.

Being that I can make these robots, I can't wait to see the beautiful things that life has to offer. I have to believe that they are near because that is the truth. I would not put myself through more than I could stand.

If my life plays out like I think it will, considering all the unbelievable things I can do, it will be like a movie. Documents will be found. There will be a reuniting. Everyone will know my family. They will know the truth about everything.

Think about it. You don't even know how you made any of this yet.

These people are broken in ways unimaginable.
The world having some type of explosion and us being the remains of these people sounds crazy.

Think about it. Stop it. Stop it. Uh Uh, too flawless. Because of my bad reputation. Her laughs. Perfect timing and positioning. 43 kids. Ron Walk. The TV, the police car. Redondo Station. The thoughts in my head. The dreams.

They've been long gone. Killed off. Humanity. That boat in my dream. I walked in passing the bar and people were sitting down. There was a room on it that had a bed and small closet. Only I was in it. What does all this mean? It was a dream. Who arose from dirt? Some people did. Really. Too much stuff is thrown in it. People underestimate what can be formed from different things being combined.
So, if I'm correct, technically somehow we are still living under this bullshit system of creating multiple robots of a person. They function and have the same thoughts that the regular person did or they are chipped to do so.
I can hear the screams of these people before they died.
Sometimes in the music.

These people were forced to walk to their deaths.

These people's DNA, replications, got answers out of them.

Some confessions were kept in documents. Stored in their brains, robotic brains and the brainwashing of people to come became infinite.

We knew lunatics like this would exist. We're just so busy worrying about things we never should.

We need to really believe the positive things we say. Going day by day and enjoying each day, each second, needs to be done. For some of us practiced. We need to be the way we know we should be as humans. Positive and loving.

The dream last night. I was preparing for some event. I believe a parade. My family, one of the first ones I thought I had when I was learning who I was, not the final one I came to find out about with 42 brothers, my family came. A boy walked in with his friend. He looked like a blend of one of the people I believed were my brothers and one of my cousins, at first glance. I had a flash of that thought. Then I asked my non-aunt if she had another child. A son. She said no. She said it was her daughter's son. Her daughter was driving a bus down the street.

I remember also in this dream I was a little upset because I didn't have a camera man for the parade. My family had brought one. I knew this man. I saw him at another event taking pictures. He was very entertaining to a lot of people. It's 9:43am 11/14/19. I remember him talking about something that happened in a car. It was funny but I don't remember what it was. That same night my dream shifted to me being in some building that was still being built. It had an elevator. Some pretty girl was there for a few seconds, then an older lady who looked like she gives out presents appeared. I had to go to the bathroom really bad. I needed that elevator to work. I ended up waking up after constantly talking about needing to use the bathroom and I really did have to use the restroom really bad.

How the hell did I create these flawless electronic people? I will remember as I am trying to keep my heartrate steady for a six almost 7 year old. Heartrate. The Visotros. The Lab. 1st one to think is a location is on Florence. I will go back to my labs. LA! B! I created things to go off of what I think at my best. Ripped my So UL right out of me and transferred it to my crew/robots. Ready. F. Street. They got these people sexually frustrated to a point where they couldn't walk. Went insane.

Yes. There is a such thing as twins. Joyce to the world. Rejoice. Terror. Joyce. Terrence. It took years for my heart to develop for what it's about to see. Let's sing. The language. Believe.

My evil daddy numbers are 53, 67 and 76.

You can't miss them.

People are in that dungeon getting the hell fucked out of them.

All the hell in my mind has me wanting to jump out of my skin and hurt somebody. Sometimes I see myself doing that. I mean I really get frustrated. Ways to make someone want to commit suicide is what was left here. Your mouth just moving and saying hurtful stuff. These illnesses. These things bitter people practiced trying to make someone do. Mind control.

Are we all from something unique? Every different blood line.

Was all these different emotions and illnesses I've experienced worth it? Hell Yes! My robots are flawless. Something good is going to happen for me. I'm just waiting on instructions.

Now I have to get all of this shit out of my head and go on living like a normal person.

All this stuff I created, I know some real good shit is going to come from it. These people, robots, can do anything. Morph into anyone.

WE MADE IT! Not us! Ha!

Premonitions. The point. To not fall victim and want to kill yourself with everything that the first people left here. Don't let them get what they want. Some died happily thinking their structure would work.

These books are a reminder. The added chapters in that book that's purchased a lot. It's not fair someone said about the man controlling the weather. This bitterness. That arouses from nowhere. How did they cope with it. Multiply. The lie. Berries. Multiply.

The language making you cringe. The flawless making of it. Realizations within it to make your heart lump and face shrivel. NO matter which way you say it or how you try to change it. It caters to who you are. I said God didn't even know what happened to His creations. I said he came down in human form to find out. Now why would He want to read everyone's mind? Is there a God some ask. Could we all be products of a huge bang? Anything's possible right. Or was it meant to be this way. Wait. I'm lost.

Changing things around. These robots I created are flawless. Come on. If I have robots, that means something, some people were here and the only way to stop their evil ways was to use myself as my own experiment and figure everything out. These books are a reminder. The first 3 books.

Evert tenth of a second their minds are changing. Beliefs are changing. Quick flashes. Hot flashes. Every decimal-time of their existence they have different thoughts. NO one can stand such pain. Completely broken. These people are furious.

The idea that everyone is chipped. TV making you not believe what you believed your whole life. Sensitive materials.

I was at the blind mans house writing bad thoughts and my mind took me to a bench where I felt a way I can't describe. Maybe a soulless person that could still function. Slidell! A deal! Ro! New Orleans. New Ro Leans. Earthquakes to freedom. These robots can be dissected by the best. You'll never see a bomb activated. Slavery. Yes. LA. To see why. Do you see why? Emergency Room. Ro-Mo! 30! 7 years 2019. True. 31 2020 false but on file for now. Louisiana. Los Angeles. They sleep with anyone, human, when they can to get away from feeling animalistic or because people they usually would aren't near or are trapped in a cell or something. They're thrown in all types of cells, hung and other things separated from those they make known they like. The beasts are evil. These people have had to have kids just to kill them. Eat them. Suicide will be your friend! Bad comes! Hero! He-Rose! Ro! Coming. Things they don't like to do, they need to to keep their sanity. These type of fucked up illnesses, mental and more. LA Ment Doctor. Documentary. Document! R. Y. Tuwanthi. Write. Keep track of everything. R. Y. Ro this is why. General Education. Ro. G!. As I listen to music it plays in the underground. We walked right in. my robots. All colors. Expanded appearances. Transformed. We need it. I said as I move, one of my robots does exactly what I'm doing as I'm doing it. In a cell or wherever. That sounds crazy. Need to remember. These people have been holding onto their lives for years. "I've thrown up for hours, sometimes days," she said. Then a clamp was put on her nose and mouth. Controlling the robots manually. Practice. First Student. Innocence. Driven insane to say mean things they've said again. Repeatedly until they no longer would or wanted to say them. Snitches. Stitches. Biography. By all. G. R. A. Acid why. Auto. Aye, you too. Two. To. That's every time they, the enemy, does or says something, the response they think you would do comes up in their brains. Good or bad, they always responded with pain on their prey. Animals having human babies. Words will hit your heart like knives. They had to take the skin off one of their animalistic, weird looking creations from only God knows what and put it on their bodies. Faces included. They needed the beasts help for this too at times. Repeatedly. Bad Comes! Drink Smoke. Warn our sisters and brothers.

The time is 12:52PM 12/6/19! Boats. Are we really moving these people, me and my crew? Yes! Earthquakes. Ear – Christ – The Qu – Aches. Move. Hit it! Mo Says. LA!
These people need the animals for warmth. Their vision is in and out. It's so gruesome down their and their vision is so fucked up that human movements can blind them at times. Lives Stolen. The good animals didn't know what was wrong with humanity crazy actions until I flew my devise in. My Thoughts. It's on. Flying synthetic materials. It's 12:54PM 12/6/19! Flashes. Flawless. The girl got done with the microwave before me at work. She finished with 5 minutes left. I didn't need to punch any digits in. I felt like that happened to me before. It's 12:55PM 12/6/19. I knew it was my robots taking up all three microwaves and this one left it just for me. So I had to get over my frustration of waiting minutes for a microwave and know they did it for my own good. To let me know how flawless they will be when these people are free and come up and fuck up the place.

The dream. She was hurrying to drag bodies. She was by the truck. Lease. See.

Joyce. Joy – See. Rejoice. Tease, say cheese. LA – Monday. Terrence. Florence. Torrance. Law- Rinse. Demon – Thee man Day.

The music. It takes me places. Gives me hope. Gives me a feeling so good that it feels impossible to get. But my robots are flawless. Jazz music. So good. It gives me such good feelings. Hope, places, people, feelings. It's good for my soul. It's 10:05AM 11/14/19.

The music takes me to another level. A goodness, a richness that feels loving. It's hard to describe.

But.

The Point.
To continue living. Not to take your own life. Not to become brainwashed. To keep your sanity. To enjoy every day. Get out, meet people, do things, and be extraordinary.

Now I really feel insane. Am I human or from dirt, or many things combined, a robot?

That annoying ass kid won's go away. The story is I was a celebrity and I got my plate of food and sat with an older woman and not the kids at their table. I am grown woman in this dream. It was a continuance of the dream with the white model. It just keeps going and getting worse. No good events coming. The kid got mad and walked over and stood on my side while I sat with the older lady and said mean things about me. The right things to make me crack. She was a fan and paid attention to what others said that hurt my feelings. She only disappears when I believe humanity is long gone. Been killed off. All their bullshit and confusion caused them all to get in a killing zone.

Forced to hit their heads on rocks. Walking into walls. There's no repairing those mental illnesses.

This type of nothing ass people. This fucking annoying and non caring to a point where people would want them to harm themselves. Some were insane though.

This is true pain.

The Big Release. Humanity released. Trapped. There's a small oxygen hole. My family reunited.

The choreography in that video. Drink. I felt like I did it. My robot did, but I'm chipped the same. So I can feel what it does. Some kind of way. When I think about it at least.

With that small hole, I think that means they would need the animals to breath. But that makes no sense.

A small opening for oxygen. Sold out to animals-the last few generations of people, or more.

Robots telling me what my family is saying and telling my family what I am saying. Internal talking. Summing it up.

Seems like these people have always been slaves and I beat the fucked up system.

My family's eyes are allowed in the robots when I think of them. 42 brothers, plus Mom and Dad.

This all sounds crazy. Hard to believe.

I try to get rid of the dream with more thoughts but can't think of anything good to think about. Which is ridiculous.

Animals, mixed breeds, some with humans, the first to create successful replications of who – mans or not?

Projections come over my face of people around me.
Something way more serious than holograms.
I don't need this shit!
Constant fucked up stories about people my is creating and creating characters. People that never existed. It's even giving me kids in these stories. These people were that annoying that someone without a child will start believing they have one or multiple.

I'm in and out of thinking I'm human or transformed from materials in the Earth. Me Christ Ro.

I keep forgetting I'm said, written, to be 30 to date and I'm 6.
Some kind of way the time will fly by.
Daylight Savings Time. Leap Year. Days in February compared to the rest of the months.
Do these things make sense for the year and day count to be up to date?
I'm not doing janitorial work but I am picking.
January, February, Mortuary, Cemetery. Bad comes.
Mo. 30. R. Christ. You are why. Ce – Joyce. Met. Emergency Room Why. Ce. Terrence. Me Christ Ro.
Ary. Aries. Arise. R Why.

It's completely flawless.

It's like a play I'm starring in. Singing and settings and people coming to mind at work.
I need all of this to survive. Get my mind back to where it needs to be.

And by the date, everything will be confirmed and my heart will be where it needs to be.

Or maybe everything won't be confirmed.

That girl. She has a close name like the one of that girl abducted. She just moved in with another girl who takes me on a journey to a person I met because of her name.

Ones name with the line of names similar that I've come across in the past with people I've seen or watched a lot, can be translated to drive. A line. Right. Horn. Core. Lean. A line. Back. Christmas. Care Alls.

The others name can be translated to My. Ran. Duh. Rights. Laws.

It's flawless. I just have to hold on. Figure out what I need to do. I'm still in school technically, learning the world. The buses keep going by and telling me I need to be a student first.

I'm tired of being a slave though. I wish food clothes and shelter were free. That tree. Those people. Just maybe.

These people or animalistic people, whatever, made robots that were designed to get on your nerves. Fuck up the world. Put shit in your brains that would make it constantly go to a bad place and much more.

They would create a robot of someone you knew and follow you around. Then make that robot go where you could see it or even have it talk to you to frighten you and let you know their secret group existed. Some people knew who the secret organization people were.
There's possibly replications of the first people on the Earth here. Being that there can be replications of that generation of people here, there's no way humanity made it all the way to this year. It is 10:21AM 11/15/19.

It's 10:41AM 11/15/19. The dream with the little brown girl sitting on the couch with the door opened waiting on the school bus. I think she missed the first one and hopped on the second one.

It's 12/3/19 and 6:41pm. These people are not there. Their minds are gone. They work slave hours trying to make a beast feel good about itself: sexually, physically, emotionally, verbally. The dark beasts know all about the color discrimination.

It's 6:43pm. They've been on concrete, shitty, bloody and pissy floors for years. NO beds! Bad comes! The hell these people cause will be sharper than lightning.

The dream with the little boy that was at the grocery store standing in the middle aisle laughing that just popped in my head. This reminds me of how some people had to have died in their sleep. He just popped in and I could feel his head pop up in my brain while I was sleep. He was a kid of one of the people I believed to be one of my brothers before. All those fucked up images and how the mind is put together and certain things can be remembered is just mind blowing. It's 10:43AM 11/15/19.

It's best to say humanity is long gone and my robots will and get me what I need to enjoy life.
I'm showing them in their dreams what I'm doing to the beasts and while it's giving them time off. Why the beast is revealing things to it, that it never slipped up and revealed before. Why the beasts think they already did certain things. Fortunate.

The dream with the woman that survived the terrorist attacks in that area full of black people. I remember her floating on something, maybe a board, away from the bombings while they happened. I appeared on the board with the girl. The last place I remember us floating over was the interstate a man led me to when I got lost before. I saw him at a field then I followed him and he pointed to where I should get off. See. Handler. Emergency Room.
I disappeared out the dream. She made it to a nice tall hotel building with people in line in the roundish circular hallways. They wouldn't let her in the bedroom.

Lights Out!

You think this world can't get any worse than a bunch of bombs and missiles. Just wait until the slaves are free.
These people have been restrained and used as human toilets and much worse.

Time is what's getting me. There's too much time until the year 2022 and late in the year to make it worse. There's no way I can watch all that bullshit and keep having these negative, horrific thoughts to save these people.
The technical, electrical hospital.

The last dream I will document (it's 9:43AM 11/15/19). I remember a combination of two people in one, two people I assumed were my mom, this particular woman was arguing with the man in the backyard of our house. The man looked like a monster. His head was huge and seemed mechanical and he was extremely buff and tall. My mom in this particular dream was arguing with the man. I looked away, then back and he had hung her from a clothes line. Her weight didn't make the clothes line fall strangely. It kept her in the air. I remember I ran outside the front door, not sure why. This whole dream was crazy. I was running one way then the other because I couldn't figure out which way was the quickest. I eventually chose a direction. I got to the backyard and started cutting the huge man. But he wouldn't bleed. He just turned around and walked away from me. My mom's skin began to change and her appearance made me think of a balloon. She was hanging like a pinata. The man looked like he was walking to a shed.

Changes. C – hang – yes.

This dream changed into a girl, whose name can be translated to: Wise. Yes. End. Said her and her family were going out of town and I could come. I was excited because I figured I'd get to learn more of my robots and who my family is and why they were chosen. Everything is flawless.

These people have been gone. Blown up. Some kind of way.

There's no way I did all this technical stuff for nothing. A good life awaits me.

I just needed to know where we all came from. The only way to truly enjoy this life is to know everything that's happened here and why so many people are fucked up. There's definitely something better out there for me. I'm starting small. I'm still a student. The family. The friends. They will come.

My robots work together like computers. But they don't malfunction. Flawless to every human mind. Good to those that deserve it.

Camps. The Hollow Cost! Fee! Rondelle! The cast Ro! We will have our own prisons. Pro Pain! This is what these people know.

The dream with the kids in the classroom in the front and another one was in the back towards the left. I went in and joined them. The warehouse dream. I was sitting on the floor in an aisle with someone. The gum in my retainer. I could feel me trying to pull the gum out. In my dream.

I keep walking into the same people. The same people are surrounding me. Teaching me things. I just got here. Humanity has been gone.

Different tribes of people from all over the world with different races. The lies left here go far beyond what anyone's thought.

I mean it. It is better to be here with robots then those people. They were good for absolutely nothing. Those evil as people can rot to nothing. A speck is too good.

Some of these people figured out the system designed for you to die quick.

They refused to let it beat them.

They survived and are living in the worst conditions possible beneath the Earth.

They are showing and proving that they really are true gangsters. Thugs.

These books will take me on a journey just like the music is.

I did not do all of this for nothing.

Me – Christ – Ro.

Can create flawless family.

Will seem like they're not off my minds.

Created from flawless things never heard of in the Earth.

Flawless.

The time is now 10:45AM 11/15/19.

The Point is to survive.

It's 12:47PM 11/16/19.

Frozen. The eggs of these people were frozen. Some by beasts and they found a way. I just can't be a computer. Forget the beast and technical things. I just can't be a product of a computer. God can definitely make more people. I can't be the only one here.

That blood cat and dog in the dream with my brother shivering like he was cold in what looked like one hot ass room has me fucked up.

The dream with the cat that would stare into my eyes in that hospital looking room where it kept making eye contact with me then jumping on me, has me fucked up.

In one dream I woke up in an apartment similar to one I've lived in. A woman, my mom (a fake one) called my name. It made my heart beat feel heavy inside me.

Crazy things happened to me.

Right when you're about to fall into a deep sleep, someone or something comes and wakes you up.

The music, voices, instruments, changing to fit your sanity and insanity. It knows you.

Jesus. Remember. It's Just Us! Me and my crew. J = 10. Keep it 100. The USE Us! E=5. 105 to the buffet. 125. Ro. Deal! Believe!
We will take our place as celebrities. The ones we already are.

The time is 6:45PM 12/3/19! If I had my way, which I will: the money, the car, the hotels, rented mansions, food, the stage, the fame. Limos. The Real Lifestyle. With my family.

I escaped. And now I'm going to free everyone. Good and bad. My crew, we have our own prisons.
Everything will merge. It will be like they were never even trapped.

Don't think you know my crew, my robots that is. We will fool you. Sometimes we will get along, and sometimes we won't. We will have to talk shit about each other, but it's all worth it to laugh at all the pain these evil son of a bitches deserve.

BAD COMES! It's 6:47PM 12/3/19!

I said it will be a show on their way out of captivity. They will have all the supplies they need. Food and clothing. Drugs.

Alcohol.
That means, since all is the same as when all humanity was killed off, that these robots, beasts, are still in rooms making robots to fight and sleep with. Making dozens, hundreds, of the same person and sending them off into society. The ones you idolize the most. It knows you watch them.

I said some people created robots and they changed and killed their masters. Or always were malfunctioned and instantly killed their masters.

All this bullshit supposed to happen to us in a cave on an infinite scale.

These people are chipped to feel things that aren't there. You'll get hit but nothing's hitting you. It's an internal thing.

There's people, a person to blame for this, but we're ghosts.

I said they had to form alliances, but how can they do that if their brains keep shutting down?

So much drama and mess.

Jazz music is relaxing.

Good Night. Is it really good to sleep, if you don't wake up? These phrases. Hell – O! Zero. Hell. Good Morning. Mourning. Sleep. The language. It's Us!

People they despise, talk bad about in private, in their faces every day. Trances causing them to naturally speak bad, fast and uncontrollably about them.

The system, makes ou not even want to look at anyone.

Make you and suicide friends.

Crack under pressure and die by any means necessary.

The good beasts making alliances and keeping an eye on the cells with the exits. Making sure they have a group of people, the ones with the story I came up with, to switch in and out of the exit cells. Bad comes. They all want to help get everyone free. The beasts know that.

The people, even the extras on TV, will emerge. Right in your face. Large families used on purpose to help the bests. The good ones. They are getting better at keeping up with real people. Separating them from clones. Sounds crazy. Unrealistic. But it's possible.

I said these people would know who I am. Ha. Really Real. I. Etc.

Same people caged in really tight spaces so they won't kill each other. Bad comes.

The Point: to outdo the hell they're experiencing in those caves.

I mean it. I'll be okay. My mind clear of chaos. Then I'll think of those trapped people. The ones said to be good for nothing. And all hell will break loose in my mind. I have two kids in my extension dream with the white girl and the annoying kid. The kids dad and I split up and he got a knew girl. The kids couldn't take jokes being made about me or my mouth sometimes moving saying things that don't make sense. Not even words in what I'm saying. Gibberish. They would make jokes about me. They said they wanted me dead. Well anyways. The terrible dreams go away until I think of the slaves. The good for nothing people. Even the people that were good people, they are in so much hell, just thinking about them is bringing back all hell in my brain. Everyone I think of talks bad about me and just uses me for entertainment. Black entertainment.

I can't believe I have no idea how I was made. I know I said I would put myself through any hell necessary to make sure this book was completed in it's entirety, but something's not right.

Coolinda. It's 6:54PM 12/16/19!

The right people, will come around to make sure evil people, they live through all the pain a lot longer.

The videos. The robots. The flawless entertainment. Was this all for just Coolinda? Me? Or are there people trapped that can be freed? My family. Sounds crazy. Sounds real crazy a woman could have 43 kids. Twins, Okay. Triplets? Maybe.

If all of this is true about my family, and of course I know I can condition my mind to believe certain things until I get the right thoughts, or what I need to done. If all of this is true, 43 of us and we're separated right now, and a big huge riot is about to happen, then that means these people have been slaves their whole lives. Nothing really was here when I got here but a plot to get everyone beneath the Earth.

The last option for some to get free, to blow something up? Huh. This keeps getting crazier and crazier.

I love this jazz music.

Even above ground, they won't know what reality is. Looking at people's eyes, clothes, trees, pictures, etc, will hurt.

These experiences have me fucked up.

I just had a clamp in my brain of a full story about who my family was. And it went away. So within a fraction of a second my thoughts changed and I had a whole knew line of what I believed. Then it went away. These type of synthetic materials.

Impossible huh?
Okay Coolinda. Finish this book.

The jazz music. Amazing.

The Point: to survive.

These people won't know what hit them. A whole world and languages and robots designed for everyone's conscious. How we would react to meeting you.

Schemes huh? Let the games begin.

I keep having flashes of who my family its. It's 1:11PM 11/16/19. That flash said there's 45 of us again. Programmed thoughts.

People will follow you around to keep those negative thoughts in your head and keep extending your negative stories with people you make up, or the robots will help you make up to fit your insanity on a maximum level. Well get it there. Quickly without you dying. You'll wonder why you can't change your own mind knowing it's possible and you've been alive too long not to have any positive thoughts. They'll be there, in your brain, but you won't be able to access them. Pause and breathe deeply. It won't help.

What does all of this mean?

It's 1:52PM 12/2/19. (you'll ask. I just typed above where I was typing previously)

The dream where I'm behind that building in the grass area. I think it's a school in the front but the settings merge.

The dream where I'm in a car in what looks like one of my old colleges.

The dream where I'm going around the upstairs area of a dormitory looking building that gives me a feel of a good dazzling night coming.
My crew can make you feel like you're anywhere.

The black people (particular ones) changed their skin color and beat blacks, whites, and others.

The time is 1:51PM 12/2/19.

Me and my robots are moving as fast as we can to free everyone from the hell beneath the ground.

Yes my crew can outdo the pain that is going on underground. They can make you feel ANYTHING!

A Perfect Set up.

Black women saw what was going on. People making them feel less and not caring. It was them. Black women. They let whites beat you. They heard all your fucked up stories about lighter being better. Some black women bleached their skin. Some black women dressed as whites and beat you.

Some whites got loose and put on black skin.

It was truly the formation of beasts that helped these people get free.

I'm tired as hell from all this walking at work. 8 hours is a lot to be constantly moving and the slaves worked longer than that with little to no food. Sometimes they were fed remains of animals, humans, just awful things.

Black women paid attention to how people would act and time and time again the same cycle repeated. People always following trends of going for lighter is better. Black women couldn't believe it. They began hating themselves. More. They followed you around, lied about surgery, dressed as men.

A strong alliance of black women. The ones that didn't allow anyone into their clique.

I said I fooled them into thinking I was on their side, but even they won't let me in and I'm giving them their sight back time and time again. They're down there in may different skin tones. Black, light, white. Many colors.

Alliances that fight for their lives. The beasts do get revenge. They argue, guss and snap at these beasts and have to turn around and act like they're crazy and out of their minds and love the beast so the beast wont eat them. Their alliances say their friends are crazy while they snap at the beasts. And others their acquaintances made deals with. I taught them this language. They couldn't talk at all. They were doing animal sounds to let each other know they were still alive. Trains and

Railroads. Their human enemies left them for dead but before they did they made them get, feel as small as possible. Losing the language, speech was a huge part of that. How far would you go to find out what your school crush, or anybody you liked or disliked said about you when you weren't there? Dress as them if you looked similar? I put little materials down there to project what I think and help them heal.

Some whites caught on and tried to warn others. They talked to the wrong people. The black women had people that bleached their skin white. They knew just how to blend in. Caution! Caught Sean!

Wait. Coolinda. Somethings not making sense. Were the last generations even given a chance to hate, betray, or make black women feel inferior? I believe so because they liked to study behavior, although they would still hate other colors and people not in their alliance.

All black women were not like this. But this particular crew was flawless and on a huge hunt to trap those that weren't in their alliance once they became aware that people would hate that they were so dark.

Some whites only talked to their families, unsure of who to trust. Some whites turned their skin black. These people. It's possible. Precautions. Before caught. Sean. Mark of the Beast. 12! 6! I'm almost 7.

The people trapped beneath have to be knocked out, beaten, to fall asleep. It's too much noise, and by animals included at that, and bad thoughts in their heads. They're eyes get stuck shut sometimes or hall opened, but they're not sleep sometimes. Their bodies just fall over sometimes because of the conditions surrounding them. They get so weak that their bodies give out and they can't move certain parts of it.

Bad comes. Catering to the beasts. Thoughts. My thoughts projected underground. Synthetic materials. Caution!

Projections of what I think going beneath the ground. Blacks forced to act stupid while other races are smart. The Beast.

These people are angry as hell. The hell they cause on Earth when they are free is going to be fast. Ya'll said they weren't good for shit. Only for prostitutes then used them up and then they weren't even good for that.

Ya'll said they were looks and nothing more. Got tired of them ignoring you because you didn't look how they wanted.

These people were forced to have children with people they didn't want to. Bad comes.

My family isn't helping me.

I work alone.

I'm so fed up. Whatever happens, happens.

I need to enjoy every day.

The Point is to Survive.

Some people have been down there over 20 years. You'll feel like you aer a computer. But you're not. Crenshaw. Terrence. Hawkins. 12/25/12. 12x12=144. 12+25+12=49. 7x7=49. 7 days a week. Joyce Howard. The map. Flawless. Del-Aware. The electronic hospital gave them their sight back. It gave them their sanity back. I mean, you wouldn't think these type of mental illnesses could be cured. I don't know what the hell I feel like anymore. Human. Beast. Invisible being used for a destruction to come. This is all to much. It's 12:22PM 12/5/19. Deuces. Si. 5+1=6. Six. Sex. Seven – Yes. Even. S=Yes. Joyce. Juice Drink.Terrence. It's a language that can play with your sanity. They all are. Reading it too. OO. LOOK! They're lying so deep, that people of color have to pretend like they know things to whites, they're lying and whites are getting stuck when the whites can take any pain from one another and still work together to get out. Now does that make any sense?
The things I'd do to get everyone free. Infinite. Unlimited. 45! Crowded. These people are shoulder to shoulder. Peace. Bad comes. What extreme measures would you go through to capture someone? You hate? The question is was the stupidity and being good for nothing worth it to these mutha fuckas coming up for revenge. The Secret: changed skin color, changed sex, disguised themselves. And many more things. The enemy. These people are out for blood! They have all negative thoughts. A lot about death. As for me going in, of course all they are thinking is hurry up. They have beasts right in their faces. They are on constant hell trips. A thee is Christ. There is no hell by God. Just the one they're living in. Lights Out! These people want me to feel what they feel. Every second of every day they are in fear that they will die. Surrounded by animals

various different looks, never seen above ground, and of various sizes. A small ant they cannot kill, purposely. That's how real it is down there. I put my mind through all this shit. Got to a point where I felt like I didn't know a fucking thing! Just to know what they're dealing with down there, and for some, when they used to be up here! Bad Fucking Comes! It's 4:25PM 12/11/19!

Tired and Bored. Bored, walk. Broadway. These robots are walking around, working, building and placing things in spots to this place can have the perfect earthquake, storm, flood, and war to free these people. Nothing is done out of the ordinary similar to how it will be when everyone is free. Everyone's doing their day to day. Evil robots and good ones. We're working together. It's my crew.

These trapped people having kids and having to kill them many times, whoa. Bad comes. They want me to feel what they feel. Even the people with them to feel worse. They are doing things to beasts in front of lots of people too.

Some people can't get over one bad traumatic event happening to them. It plays over and over in their minds every day. They get older and bitter as the years go by and they haven't had one clear day of the bad events. And these are events usually with humans. Imagine these events with beasts. Read a book. Book a flight. Books in prison. Book it, go fast. It's 12:37pm 12/5/19. This story keeps getting worse. I'll need revenge to know out all the fuckery in my head. The dream with the bus 747 with La-this shit hits-won girl. She was a cheerleader. The bus turned before I could get on it. Was I at the wrong stop? Books. They made it. Ya. All ready. Who man! G ma. Ail. Pain. They survived. G=7. Makes a 6. Verbal. To see the lab. Goo! G E! Golgi. These images inside a plant. They've eaten and are living creatures down there with them. La- Ro Ro -Why. R nigga! GR. General. Egos. Relief. King. C-Answer-Ro. Ma. Ark. Animals. Know. Ha! These mutha fuckas are like firecrackers in my head. They cutting up. The thought of them gives me all types of negative thoughts instantly. They cry hurting tears while sleeping with the beasts. Fucked up traumatic abuse. They need help. But without the abuse they would've still been mean and evil. They took out their abuse frustration on other people, but in ways they don't need to die for, still need to be punished. Well, fucking with others mental stability? Punishment should be? They did crazy things so they could try and get each other away from the thoughts of their abuse. At least attempt for a day without the thoughts. Looks and nothing more. We're tired of it. I mean it. Moving away from a darker black woman because you don't want people to think you two are dating, and you don't care with other colored women. It is trash. These robots are on point. I been looking at them every day and straight up, the face they want me to recognize is the one I'll get. They are my mind. Weeks of seeing the same person and I realize who it is later. Bad comes. It's the same face the robot made from the first time I saw it and I still didn't know. Let the games begin. These people use every muscle in them to speak and try to and get free. Delivery. Del. I -to-see why. Do you see why? The time is 4:05PM 12/11/19! Bad comes!

Who the hell is watching them? They are obedient to whoever it is. That's for sure. Bad comes! It's 4:50PM 12/11/19!

Yes that bang, thump, drill, lighter flicker, water spraying, horn honking, bus recordings, and more you heard outside is answering your thoughts. Heart. Like a crazy man banging on your door.

Flawless Hell I've created to prepare for the hell that's about to come above ground. I will outdo you. You won't even know who you're looking at. Different colored people will look the same. We work together. Flawless I tell ya!

I can't believe these people need to be shot now. With guns. The memories. Me -30. Awakening. Rise.

33. 3+3 =6.
3+4=7. 4+3=7. Flawless Numbers. Do to Ron! Me! 43 children.
It's 4:11PM 12/11/19!

9/29 Q

6/7 A

1/21 M

3/29 W

5/5 C

4/13 R

10/14 - U

Find us!

It's 4:13PM 12/11/19!

1988, 1975, 1981, 1981, 1989, 1989, 1978!

It's 4:21PM 12/11/19!

It's 10:44AM 11/17/19.

I've almost been blinded by all the bull shit events going on in my head.

I went out to eat at a buffet last night and a man identical to one I work with is there. These things I said Manevil was doing to make people uncomfortable and let them know they exist and are trying to kill them.

The instructions my robots are drilling in my head is "To Move".

I have no money to move like I want to. Well most do. And that's to go and do as we please without having to work for anyone else. It's 10:45AM Now. 11/17/19.

The dream I had last night. My fake mother was working at a daycare. I tried to get a job there, but it was for choreography. Somehow the rooms overlapped. The dream was crazy. I was working at a warehouse beneath. There was a fire and we all had to go on the balcony, the setting looked like I was on a hotel balcony. I remember walking on the balcony. Someone told me something and I got up. None of this makes sense. It looked like a hotel I had been at on a basketball field trip that had a nice pool at the bottom. The trip when I got sprayed with silly string by my teammates. Why was I on a balcony and there was a fire?

The dream shifted to me getting a place to stay in a place with a lot of people. All the beds were a couple feet apart. I remember taking all my stuff to the cab driver outside. He was charging me 65 dollars. I didn't want to pay that and asked one of my friends inside if she could take me. Then a girl walked in that I knew. She said she had been trying to find the crowded place for a while and I should've told her I was going to it. The place looked like a basement, concentration camp and some type of way made me feel like it was a daycare. Like people were watching over all the adults.
One of those boys in that huge family when my dream or maybe it was a thought at the time, rubbed my belly the wrong way. A feeling no one should have to deal with and on an infinite scale of uncomfortableness. I'm lost. Oh that boy in that family was laying on a thin rectangular cut mattress right next to a lot of other people. I said he was on a ship.
But anyways, my friend, whose name can be translated to yes we will see, was the one going to give me a ride. It's 10:54AM 11/17/19. I'm listening to jazz music and typing this.
But the dream told me that people were forced to walk to this place. Well stupidly walked in naturally and happily. Once they got in the door there was no turning back. They could see that. It made me think this is how the who mans were sent to their deaths. They did everything they could to avoid walking right into their death places, but there was nothing they could do. Not even a point in dropping their last smiles.

Taking a heart out and putting it in someone else. Make sense. It still works. Somehow.

My family. Why would I want to separate us to figure out all this shit? I breezed through many things. The point is to survive. I transformed so many things. These people still operate like the original person.

How we got here. Seems like some eggs were stored away and we were put in foster care in various forms. We're told these people gave birth to us. Maybe the parents don't know, or maybe they were conditioned, brainwashed, hypnotized, to believe they gave birth to us.

Survive. The negative memories they want us to have haven't even happened with these false flawless looking people we wish we would've known in a good light.

They are trying to kill us alive or in our sleep. It doesn't matter.

There's no way I would separate my entire family to figure out all this shit when these robots are flawless and could've told me the same thing being around them. The thought of walking around them every day and not even being able to say hi kills me.

The two questions I have:
How did I get here?
How will my life change for the better?
When will my dream life happen?

I do know I need my heart and mind to be stable with everything that's happened to the people here and the Earth.

It's 11:01AM 11/17/19.

Family, Associates, Hotels, Jazz, Food, Fun, Houses, Amusement Parks, Skating and More.

It's now 11:04AM 11/17/19.

It's 12:05PM 12/5/19
The electric hospital. I put little materials down there to project what I think and help them heal and see. The electric hospital. Conductor. "Get me the hell out of here," he said. Women having animals and men having animal babies to. The women's bodies are so messed up that many eggs are coming out of them at once and combining with animal parts and creating weird looking creatures. Believe. The Underground. Rose. They'll use these books while torturing their enemies. I see flashes. The future. The electric hospital is killing some of the beasts. They have to eat the beasts to make more room down there. Ro Mo! 30. RR. Ro Ro. Railroad. I'm training myself to be ready for all the hell these people will cause. The time is 12:09pm 12/5/19. 125 is the talent number. They've seen way too much and had to do gruesome things. I'm ready to throw this book I'm so frustrated thinking about all this shit. There was an earthquake in my dream 12/4/19. I just remember running downstairs. Then the dream shifted. I went to a gym to tryout for basketball. The schedule was year round. I said no. The entrance and exit The buildings. The tall fences. The build of these locations like a park mixed with a horrible, haunted looking place. Some players I met. We watched footage of them playing a game. The office area.
Wait. It's now 12:13pm 12/5/19 and I'm seeing that brick area. I think a bathroom. Wait. It was a kid area. I'm in the outside area or covered area. Wait it's too much. I've seen this place a lot. A lunch area and a bathroom area, and I'm in the middle going into the lunch area. I'm under a covering, but I'm outside still. Make sense.
The dream where I walk on the movie set. Get sexy for my man. There's other actors in the main shooting area. There's a lady in a room beneath it, and someone in an office across from her. An office like a lady at a doctor's office waiting to ask you questions. My books mixed with the setting on Earth and what is beneath is where everyone is. Blue. Prints. Blueprints. Azul. I'll walk right in. Railroads. RoRo. Abolitionists. A-Z!
We can't just blow shit so they can get out. Then they will get smashed! Prior natural disasters, mixed with rust and all types of wastes is how that opening got so small. Soon enough they wouldn't be able to breathe. Perfect arrival. No. I did not negotiate anything with the beasts down there. Definitely not concerning the beasts living. I care none for the beasts.
The outside area of that brick apartment. Shootings. Hostages. It's 1:00PM 12/6/19! Bad comes!

10-31-22

Complete hell on Earth is coming.

A Killing Zone!

Vandalism.

Torture.

Hostages.

Trades.

In PUBLIC!

DONE TO PERFECTION!

THE REALIST.

THE SMARTEST!

AREA'S BLOCKED OFF.

We the 504 Family.

IT'S GOING DOWN ALL OVER.

GUARANTEED!

HAPPENING!

DETOURS!

ENJOY

THE

RIDE!

LOVE

THE

NELSONS!

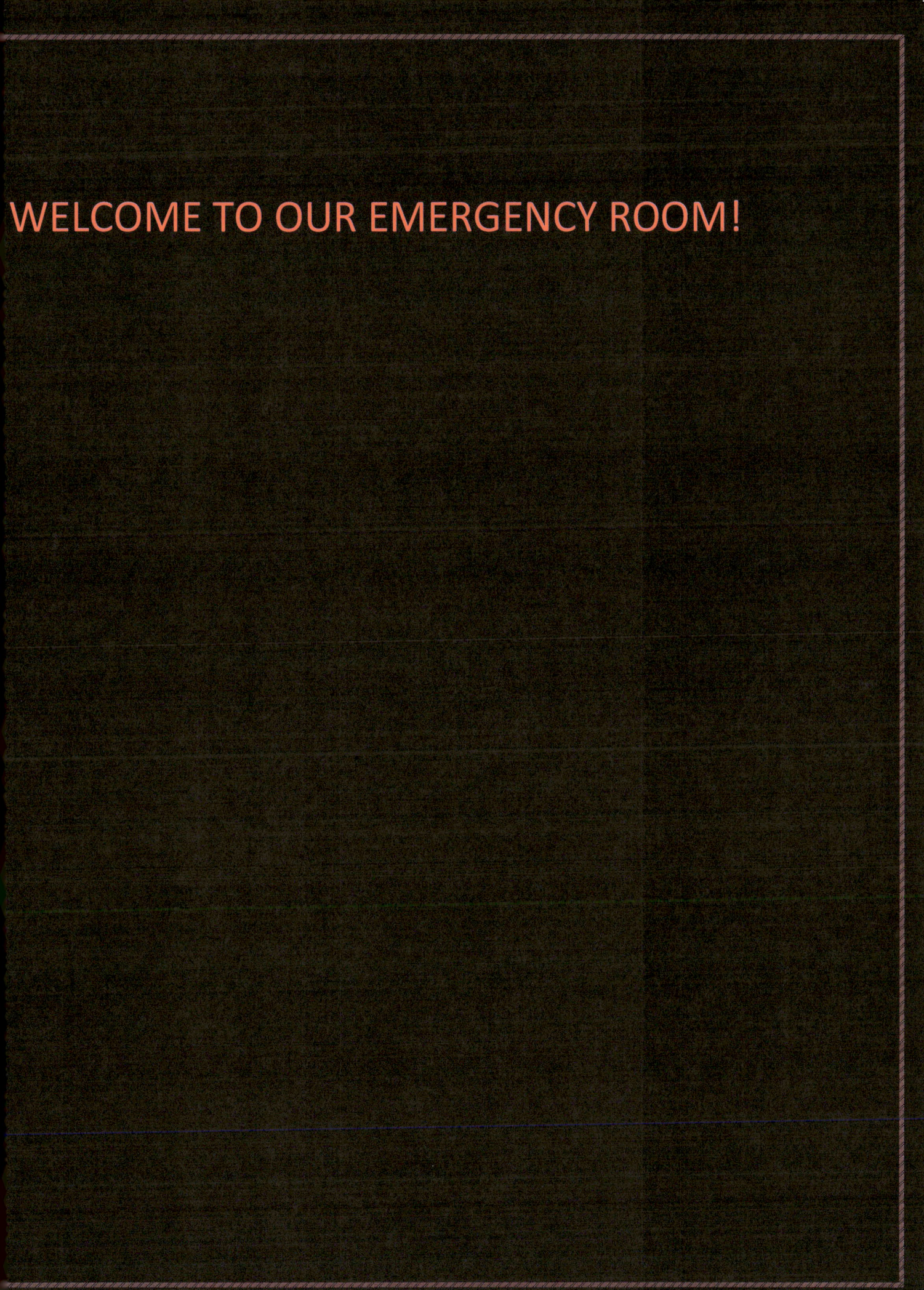

WELCOME TO OUR EMERGENCY ROOM!

www.ingramcontent.com/pod-product-compliance
Lightning Source LLC
Chambersburg PA
CBHW040821050726
47507CB00019B/86